Apart from enjoying an enviable reputation
as one of the best writers on the science
fiction scene, Harry Harrison is a man of
wide interests and accomplishments.
A first-class short story writer, an
experienced editor and anthologist, a
translator (from Danish and Italian),
a trained cartoonist, he has also been a commercial
illustrator, hydraulic press operator, truck
driver and is, of course, a first-rate novelist.

Also by Harry Harrison and available from Sphere Books

CAPTIVE UNIVERSE

THE JUPITER LEGACY

THE STAINLESS STEEL RAT

THE STAINLESS STEEL RAT'S REVENGE

THE STAINLESS STEEL RAT SAVES THE WORLD

DEATHWORLD Vols. 1–3

NOVA Vols. 1–2 (editor)

THE JOHN W. CAMPBELL MEMORIAL ANTHOLOGY (editor)

STONEHENGE (co-author with Leon Stover)

THE ASTOUNDING-ANALOG READER Vols. 1–2
(co-editor with Brian Aldiss)

THE YEAR'S BEST SCIENCE FICTION Vols. 4–7
(co-editor with Brian Aldiss)

Nova 3

EDITED BY HARRY HARRISON

SPHERE BOOKS LIMITED
30/32 Gray's Inn Road, London WC1X 8JL

First published in Great Britain by Sphere Books Ltd 1975
Copyright © Harry Harrison 1973

TRADE
MARK

Set in Intertype Plantin

Printed in Great Britain by
Hazell Watson & Viney Ltd
Aylesbury, Bucks

CONTENTS

INTRODUCTION

The winds of change continue to blow through science fiction, tearing at the flapping sails of a number of foundering ships while at the same time pushing forward new craft with novel cargoes. This is only fair. For many years apologists of SF have stated that this is the only fictional form aware of change in the world – and in addition is aware that change itself can be changed. We *can* shape our futures and our environment if we have the will. So science fiction itself must constantly change or it will die. But simple change for its own sake in literature is not a good thing; along that course lies self-indulgence and writing empty of all content or interest. But writers will continue to experiment and when the result is a good story it certainly must be published.

Of course these changes – as with most kinds of change – are not appreciated by everyone. Science fiction is now broad enough in scope to contain both highbrow and lowbrow; something for the seekers after cerebral stimulation as well as those who want only emotional titillation. It was Brian Aldiss who recently noticed on a blackboard the chalked message: GET SCIENCE FICTION OUT OF THE CLASSROOM AND BACK IN THE GUTTER WHERE IT BELONGS. The feelings can be understood. The devotee of star-smashing space opera is surely baffled by much that is labeled science fiction today and can seek relief only by reading his collection of E. E. Smith, Ph.D., yet one more time. Perhaps we ought to emulate the example of the organized Germans who classify things more exactly. I have four of my novels to hand that have been translated into that language, and I see that the first of them is simply a *Science Fiction Roman*. Clear enough. The next is a *Utopischer Roman*; clear though not exactly correct. Now the last two. One is labeled a *Utopisch-technische* collection of stories and the other a *Utopisch-technischer Kriminalroman*. Worse and worse. Not only are these categories not relevant to the American reader but the last one, the utopian-technical-criminal novel, is nothing of the sort.

7

No, I do not think that the Teutonic labeling system can be adapted for the American reader. Tried and true empirical experimentation is still the only way. Readers here must continue to read everything around in order to make up their own minds as to what they prefer. That this system works is evidenced by the jackets on most new SF books; the author's name is usually far larger than the title. This enables the faithful reader to seek out books by his favorite authors and rush them home for a good read.

Original anthologies of new science fiction can help these readers in their quest. Here in *Nova 3*, as in the other *Nova* anthologies, I have done my best to obtain the finest new writing by the most qualified writers around. This is not as easy as it might seem and it usually takes eight to ten months to assemble one of these volumes. The established writers, all busy and claiming they are overworked, must be cajoled and tempted and enticed. But they do deliver as can be seen in the Brian W. Aldiss, Philip José Farmer and Robert Sheckley stories here. These men, and others, are the secure artists who provide a continuity of excellence in science fiction – long may they write.

But, in addition to the golden glow engendered by reading a new story of an old master, there is the particular pleasure provided by a story written by someone who is completely unknown and who has never sold a word before. This was the condition of every writer at one time, a condition that is changed by a First Sale. It has been my pleasure to print a number of 'first' stories during my assorted editorial years. Some of the writers of these 'firsts' vanished back into the darkness from which they came, while others went on to become established writers. This present anthology is unique in that it contains the first stories of two writers, Dick Glass and Philip Shofner. May they march triumphantly onward to greater glories.

I have no favorites among these stories – or rather they are all my favorites for they are all quite different. I think that Norman Spinrad is out of his gourd and I have told him so. I found myself, for some reason, reading his manuscript for the first time at six o'clock in the morning. Reading and laughing so hard that tears filled my eyes. Philip José Farmer, on the other hand, is as sanely efficient as any man and continues as a writer of devastating strengths. Brian Aldiss is a true artist,

Robert Sheckley a cool pro, Naomi Mitchison goes from strength to strength. Let me simply say that I enjoyed greatly every one of the stories in this volume and hope that you may share that pleasure as well.

Harry Harrison

WELCOME TO
THE STANDARD
NIGHTMARE

Robert Sheckley

In Nova 2 *Robert Sheckley wrote a story that put paid to the classic space opera. At least he would have checked the further publication of more of this bombastic form of science fiction if the authors of these works read anything other than their own stories. Oh well. Perhaps he will have better luck in polishing off the 'war of the worlds' theme that began (and mostly ended) with the H. G. Wells book of the same title.*

Johnny Bezique was a spaceship driver for SBC Explorations, Inc. He was surveying a fringe of the Seergon Cluster, which at that time was terra incognita. The first four planets showed nothing interesting. Bezique went to the vicinity of the fifth. The standard nightmare began then.

His ship's loudspeaker came on, apparently activated by remote control. A deep voice said, 'You are approaching the planet Loris. We presume that you intend to put down here.'

'That's right,' Johnny said. 'How come you speak English?'

'One of our computers deduced the language from inferential evidence available during your approach to our planet.'

'That's pretty good going,' Johnny said.

'It was nothing,' the voice said. 'We will now speak directly to your ship's computer, feeding it landing orbit, speed and other pertinent data. Is that agreeable to you?'

'Sure, go ahead,' Johnny said. He had just made Earth's first contact with alien life. That was how the standard nightmare always began.

John Charles Bezique was a bandy-legged little man with ginger-colored hair and an irascible disposition. He was mechanically competent at his job. He was also conceited, disputatious, ignorant, fearless and profane. In short, he was perfectly suited for deep-space exploration. It takes a particular kind of man to endure the shattering immensities of space and the paranoid-inducing stresses of threats from the unknown. It takes a man with a large and impervious ego and a consistently high degree of aggressive self-confidence. It takes a kind of a nut. So exploring spaceships are piloted by men like Bezique, whose self-complacency is firmly based upon unconquerable self-conceit and supported by impenetrable ignorance. The Conquistadores had possessed that psychic makeup. Cortez and his handful of cutthroats conquered the Aztec empire by not realizing that the thing was impossible.

Johnny sat back and watched as the control panel registered an immediate change in course and velocity. The planet Loris appeared in his viewplate, blue and green and brown. Johnny Bezique was about to meet the folks next door.

It's nice to have intelligent neighbors, speaking intergalactically, but it's not nice if those neighbors are a great deal smarter than you are, and maybe quicker and stronger and more aggressive, too. Neighbors like that might want to do things for us or to us or about us. It wouldn't necessarily have to go that way, but let's face it, it's a tough universe, and the primordial question is always, who's on top?

Expeditions were sent out from Earth on the theory that, if there is anything out there, it would be better for us to find them, rather than to have them come dropping by on us some quiet Sunday morning. Earth's standard nightmare scenario always began with contact with a formidable alien civilization. After that, there were variations. Sometimes the aliens were mechanically advanced, sometimes they had incredible mental powers, sometimes they were stupid but nearly invincible – walking plant people, swarming insect people and the like. Usually they were ruthlessly amoral, unlike the good guys on Earth.

But those were minor details. The main sequence of the nightmare was always the same: *Earth contacts a powerful alien civilization, and they take us over.*

Bezique was about to learn the answer to the only question that seriously concerned Earth: Can they lick us or can we lick them?

So far, he wouldn't care to make a book on the outcome.

On Loris you could breathe the air and drink the water. And the people were humanoid. This, despite the fact that the Nobel-prizewinner Serge Von Blut had stated that the likeliness of this was contraindicated to the tune of 10^{93} to one.

The Lorians gave Bezique a hypnopaedic knowledge of their

language and a guided tour around their major city of Athisse, and the more Johnny saw the gloomier he got, because these people really had an impressive setup.

The Lorians were a pleasant, comely, stable, inventive and progressive people. They had had no wars, rebellions, insurrections or the like for the last five hundred years, and none seemed imminent. Birth and death-rates were nicely stabilized: there were plenty of people, but enough room and opportunity for everyone. There were several races, but no racial problems. The Lorians had a highly developed technology, but also maintained a beautiful ecological balance. All individual work was creative and freely chosen, since all brute labor had been given over to self-regulating machines.

The capital city of Athisse was a cyclopean place of enormous and fantastically beautiful buildings, castles, palaces and the like, all public of course, and all visually exciting in their bold asymmetry. And this city had everything – bazaars, restaurants, parks, majestic statues, houses, graveyards, funparks, hot-dog stands, playgrounds, even a limpid river – you name it, they had it. And everything was free, including all food, clothing, housing and entertainment. You took what you wanted and gave what you wanted, and it all balanced out somehow. Because of this there was no need for money on Loris, and without money you don't need banks, treasuries, vaults or safe-deposit boxes. In fact, you don't even need locks: on Loris all doors were opened and closed by simple mental command.

Politically, the government mirrored the near-unanimous collective mind of the Lorian people. And that collective mind was calm, thoughtful, *good*. Between public desire and government action there was no discernible distortion, gap or lag.

In fact, the more Johnny looked into it, the more it seemed that Loris had just about no government at all, and what little it did have governed mostly by not governing. The closest thing to a ruler was Veerhe, Chief of the Office of Future Projections. And Veerhe never gave any orders – he just issued economic, social and scientific forecasts from time to time.

Bezique learned all of this in a few days. He was helped along by a specially assigned guide named Helmis, a Lorian of Johnny's age whose wit, forbearance, sagacity, gentleness, irrepressible humor, keen insights and self-deprecatory manner caused Johnny to detest him immeasurably.

Thinking it all over in his beautifully appointed suite, Johnny realized that the Lorians came about as close to human ideals of perfection as you could expect to find. They seemed to be really fine people, and paragons of all the virtues. But that didn't change Earth's standard nightmare. Humans, in their perversity, simply do not want to be governed by aliens, not even wonderfully good aliens, not even if it is for Earth's own good.

Bezique could see that the Lorians were a pretty unaggressive stay-at-home people with no desire for territory, conquest, spreading their civilization, and other ego-trips. But on the other hand, they seemed smart enough to realize that unless they did something about Earth, Earth was sure as hell going to do something about them, or kick up a lot of dust trying.

Of course, maybe it would be no contest; maybe a people as wise and trusting and peaceful as the Lorians would have no armament to speak of. But he learned that that was an incorrect assumption on the following day, when Helmis took him to look at the Ancient Dynasty Spacefleet.

This was the last heavy armament ever built on Loris. The fleet was a thousand years old and all seventy ships worked as if they had been built yesterday.

'Tormish II, last ruler of the Ancient Dynasty, intended to conquer all civilized planets,' Helmis said. 'Luckily, our people matured before he could launch his project.'

'But you've still got the ships around,' Johnny said.

Helmis shrugged. 'They're a monument to our past irrationality. And practically speaking, if someone *did* try to invade us . . . we could perhaps cope.'

'You just might be able to at that,' Johnny said. He figured that one of those ships could handle anything Earth might put into space for the next two hundred years or so. No doubt about it, the Lorians had a lot going for them.

So that was life on Loris, just like the standard nightmare scenario said it would be. Too good to be true. Perfect, dismayingly, disgustingly perfect.

But was it really so perfect? Bezique had the Earthman's abiding belief in the doctrine that every virtue had its corresponding vice. This he usually expressed as: 'There's gotta be a loop-hole in this thing somewhere.' Not even God's own heaven could run that well.

He looked at everything with a critical eye. Loris *did* have policemen. They were referred to as monitors, and were excruciatingly polite. But they were cops. That implied the existence of criminals.

Helmis set him straight on that. 'We have occasional genetic deviants, of course, but no criminal class. The monitors represent a branch of education rather than of law enforcement. Any citizen may ask a monitor for the ruling on a pertinent question of personal conduct. Should he break a law inadvertently, the monitor will point this out.'

'And then arrest him?'

'Certainly not. The citizen will apologize, and the incident will be forgotten.'

'But what if a citizen breaks the law over and over again? What do the monitors do then?'

'Such a circumstance never arises.'

'But if it did?'

'The monitors are programmed to take care of such problems, if they should ever arise.'

'They don't look so tough to me,' Johnny said. Something didn't quite convince him. Maybe he couldn't afford to be convinced. Still . . . Loris worked. It worked damned well. The only thing in it that didn't work right was John Charles Bezique. This was because he was an Earthman – which is to say, an unbalanced primitive. Also, it was because Johnny was getting increasingly morose, depressed and savage.

The days went by, and everything went along beautifully. The monitors moved around like gentle maiden aunts. Traffic flowed evenly without the tie-ups or frayed nerves. The million automatic systems brought in vital products and took away wastes. The people strolled along, delighting in each other's company, and pursuing various art forms. Every last mother's son of them seemed to be an artist of some sort, and all of them seemed to be good at it.

No one worked at a paying job, no one felt guilty about it. Work was for machines, not people.

And they were all so reasonable about everything! And so accommodating! And so sweet-natured! And so highly intelligent and attractive.

Yes, it was paradise all right. Even Johnny Bezique had to admit that. And that made his increasingly bad mood even more difficult to understand, unless you happen to be an Earth person yourself.

Put a man like Johnny in a place like Loris and you have to get trouble. Johnny behaved himself for nearly two weeks. Then one day he was out for a drive. He had the car on manual control, and he made a left turn without signaling.

A car behind him and on his left had just moved up to pass. Johnny's abrupt turn almost beat the other vehicle's automatic reflexes. Not quite, but it was a near thing. The cars slewed around and ended up nose to nose. Johnny and the other driver both got out.

The other driver said mildly, 'Well, old man, it seems we have had a mix-up here.'

'Mix-up hell,' Johnny said, 'you cut me off.'

The other driver laughed a gentle laugh. 'I think not,' he said. 'Though, of course, I'm aware of the possibility that . . .'

'Look,' Johnny said, 'you cut me off and you could have killed us both.'

'But surely you can see that since you were ahead of me, and since you began to make an unauthorized left turn . . .'

Johnny put his face within an inch of the other driver's face. In a low, unpleasant snarl, he said, 'Look, mac, you were in the wrong. How many times I gotta tell you that?'

The other driver laughed again, a little shakily now. 'Suppose we leave the matter of guilt to the judgment of the witnesses,' he said. 'I'm sure that these good people standing here . . .'

Johnny shook his head. 'I don't need no witnesses,' he said. 'I *know* what happened. I *know* you were in the wrong.'

'You seem very sure about that.'

'Sure I'm sure,' Johnny said. 'I'm sure because I know.'

'Well, in that case, I . . .'

'Yeah?' Johnny said.

'Well,' the man said, 'in that case, I guess there's nothing for me to do but apologize.'

'I think it's the least you could do,' Johnny said, and stalked to his car and drove away at an illegal speed.

After that, Bezique felt a little better, but more stubborn and recalcitrant than ever. He was sick of the superiority of the Lorians, sick of their reasonableness, sick of their virtues.

He went back to his room with two bottles of Lorian medicinal brandy. He drank and brooded for several hours. A social

16

adjustment counselor came to call on him and pointed out that Johnny's behavior concerning the near-accident had been provocative, impolite, dominating and barbaric. The counselor said all of that in a very nice way.

Johnny told him to get lost. He was not being especially unreasonable – for a Terran. Left alone, he would probably have apologized in a few days.

The counselor continued to remonstrate. He advised social-adjustment therapy. In fact, he insisted upon it: Johnny was too subject to angry and aggressive moods, he was a risk to citizens at large.

Johnny told the counselor to leave. The counselor refused to leave with the situation still unresolved. Johnny resolved the situation by punching him out.

Violence offered to a citizen is serious; violence actually performed is grave indeed. The shocked counselor picked himself off the floor and told Johnny that he would have to accept restraint until the case was cleared.

'Nobody's going to restrain me,' Johnny said.

'Make it easy on yourself,' the counselor said. 'The restraint will not be unpleasant or of long duration. We are aware of the cultural discrepancies between your ways and ours. But we cannot permit unchecked and unmotivated violence.'

'If people don't bug me I won't pop off again,' Johnny said. 'In the meantime, make it easy on yourself and don't try to lock me up.'

'Our rules are clear on this,' the counselor said. 'A monitor will be here soon. I advise you to go along quietly with him.'

'You really do want trouble,' Johnny said. 'Okay, baby, you do what you have to do and I'll do what I have to do.'

The counselor left. Johnny brooded and drank. A monitor came. As an official of the law, the monitor expected Johnny to go along voluntarily, as requested. He was baffled when Johnny refused. No one refuses! He went away for new orders.

Johnny continued drinking. The monitor returned in an hour and said he was now empowered to take Johnny by force, if necessary.

'Is that a fact?' Johnny said.

'Yes, it is. So please don't force me to—' Johnny punched him out, thus sparing the monitor from being forced to do anything.

Bezique left his room a little unsteadily. He knew that

assault on a monitor was probably very bad stuff indeed. There was no easy way of getting out of this one. He thought he had better get to his ship and get out. True, they could prevent his take off, or blow him out of the sky. But perhaps, once he was actually aboard, they wouldn't bother. They'd probably be glad to get rid of him.

Bezique was able to reach his ship without incident. He found about twenty workmen swarming over it. He told their foreman that he wanted to take off at once. The foreman was desolated by his inability to oblige. The ship's main drive had been removed and was being cleaned and modernized – a gift of friendship from the Lorian people.

'Give us five more days and you'll have the fastest ship west of Orion,' the foreman told him.

'A hell of a lot of good that does me now,' Johnny snarled. 'Look, I'm in a hurry. What's the quickest you can give me some sort of propulsion?'

'Working around the clock and going without meals, we can have the job done in three and a half days.'

'That's just great,' Bezique snarled. 'Who told you to touch my ship, anyhow?'

The foreman apologized. That got Bezique even angrier. Another act of senseless violence was averted by the arrival of four monitors.

Bezique shook off the monitors in a maze of winding streets, got lost himself and came out in a covered arcade. The monitors appeared behind him. Bezique ran down narrow stone corridors and found his way blocked by a closed door.

He ordered it to open. The door remained closed – presumably ordered so by the monitors. In a fury, Bezique demanded again. His mental command was so strong that the door burst open, as did all doors in the immediate vicinity. Johnny outran the monitors, and finally stopped to catch his breath in a mossy piazza.

He couldn't keep on rushing around like this. He had to have some plan. But what plan could possibly work for one Earthman pursued by a planetful of Lorians? The odds were too high, even for a conquistador type like Johnny.

Then, all on his own, Johnny came up with an idea that Cortez had used, and that had saved Pizarro's bacon. He decided to find the ruler of this place and threaten to kill him unless people were willing to calm down and listen to reason.

There was only one flaw in the plan: these people didn't have any ruler. It was the most inhuman thing about them.

However, they did have one or two important officials. A man like Veerhe, Chief of the Future Projections Bureau, seemed to be the nearest thing the Lorians had to an important man. A big shot like that ought to be guarded, of course; but on a crazy place like Loris, they just might not have bothered.

A friendly native supplied him with the address. Johnny was able to get within four blocks of the Future Projections Bureau before he was stopped by a posse of twenty monitors.

They demanded that he give himself up. But they seemed unsure of themselves. It occurred to Bezique that even though arresting people was their job, this was probably the first time they had actually had to perform it. They were reasonable, peaceful citizens, and cops only secondarily.

'Who did you want to arrest?' he asked.

'An alien named Johnny Bezique,' the leading monitor said.

'I'm glad to hear it,' Johnny said. 'He's been causing me considerable embarrassment.'

'But aren't you—'

Johnny laughed. 'Aren't I the dangerous alien? Sorry to disappoint you, but I am not. The resemblance *is* close, I know.'

The monitors discussed the situation. Johnny said, 'Look, fellows, I was born in that house right over there. I can get twenty people to identify me, including my wife and four children. What more proof do you want?'

The monitors conferred again.

'Furthermore,' Johnny said, 'can you honestly believe that I really am this dangerous and uncontrolled alien? I mean, common sense ought to tell you—'

The monitor apologized. Johnny went on, got within a block of his destination and was stopped by another group of monitors. His former guide, Helmis, was with them.

They called on him to surrender.

'There's no time for that now,' Bezique said. 'Those orders have been countermanded. I am now authorized to reveal my true identity.'

'We know your true identity,' Helmis said.

'If you did, I wouldn't have to reveal it now, would I? Listen closely. I am a Lorian of Planner Classification. I received special aggression-training years ago to fit me for my mission. It is now accomplished. I returned – as planned – and performed a few simple tests to see if everything on Loris was as I had left it, psychologically. You know the results, which, from a galactic survival standpoint, are not good. I must now report on this and various other high matters to the Chief Planner at the Future Projections Bureau. I can tell you, informally, that our situation is grave and there is no time to spare.'

The monitors were confused. They asked for confirmation of Johnny's statements.

'I told you that the matter is urgent,' Bezique said. 'Nothing would please me better than to give you confirmation – if there were only time.'

Another conference. 'Sir, without orders, we can't let you go.'

'In that case, the probable destruction of our planet rests on your own heads.'

A high monitor officer asked, 'Sir, what rank do you hold?'

'It is higher than yours,' Johnny said promptly.

The officer reached a decision. 'In that case, what are your orders, sir?'

Johnny smiled. 'Keep the peace. Calm any worried citizens. More detailed orders will be forthcoming.'

Bezique went on confidently. He reached the door of the Planning Office and ordered it to open. It opened. He was about to walk through . . .

'Put up your hands and step away from that door!' a hard voice behind him said.

Bezique turned and saw a group of monitors. There were ten of them, they were dressed in black and they were holding weapons.

'We are empowered to shoot to kill if need be,' one of them said. 'You needn't try any of your lies on us. Our orders are to ignore anything you say and take you in.'

'No sense in my trying to reason with you, huh?'

'No chance at all. Come along.'

'Where?'

'We've put one of the ancient prisons into service just for you. You will be held there and given every amenity. A judge will hear your case. Your alienness and low level of civilization will be taken into consideration. Beyond doubt you will get off with a warning and a request to leave Loris.'

'That doesn't sound so bad. Do you really think it'll go like that?'

'I've been assured of it,' the monitor said. 'We are a reasonable and compassionate people. Your gallant resistance to us was, indeed, exemplary.'

'Thank you.'

'But it is all over now. Will you come along peacefully?'

'No,' Johnny said.

'I'm afraid I don't understand.'

'There's a lot you don't understand about me or about Terrans. I'm going through that door.'

'If you try, we will shoot.'

There is an infallible way of telling the true conquistador type, the genuine berserker, the pure and unadulterated kamikaze or crusader, from ordinary people. Ordinary people faced with an impossible situation tend to compromise, to wait for a better day to fight. But not your Pizarros or Godfreys of Bouillon or Harold Hardradas or Johnny Beziques. They are gifted with great stupidity, or great courage, or both.

'All right,' Bezique said. 'So shoot, and the hell with you.'

Johnny walked through the door. The special monitors did not shoot. He could hear them arguing as he went down the corridors of the Future Projections Bureau.

Soon he came face to face with Veerhe, the Chief Planner. Veerhe was a calm little man with an aging pixy face.

'Hello,' the Chief Planner said. 'Take a seat. I've completed the projection on Earth vis-a-vis Loris.'

'Save it,' Johnny said. 'I've got one or two simple requests to make, which I'm sure you won't mind doing. But if you do—'

'I think you'll be interested in this forecast,' Veerhe said. 'We've extrapolated your racial characteristics and matched them against ours. It looks like there's sure to be a conflict between our peoples over preeminence. Not on our part, but definitely on yours. You Earth people simply won't rest until you rule us or we rule you. The situation is inevitable, given your level of civilization.'

'I didn't need any office or fancy title to figure out that one,' Johnny said. 'Now look—'

'I'm not finished,' Veerhe said. 'Now, from a purely technological standpoint, you Terrans haven't got a chance. We could blow up anything you sent against us.'

'So you haven't anything to worry about.'

'Technology doesn't count for as much as psychology. You Terrans are advanced enough not to simply throw yourselves against us. There will be discussions, treaties, violations, more discussions, aggressions, explanations, encroachments, clashes and all of that. We can't act as if you don't exist, and we can't refuse to cooperate with you in a search for reasonable and even-handed solutions. That would be impossible for us, just as it would be impossible for you simply to leave us alone. We are a straightforward, stable, reasonable and trusting people. You are an aggressive, unbalanced race, and capable of amazing deviousness. You are unlikely to present us with clear-cut and sufficient reasons for us to destroy you. Failing that, and all factors remaining constant, you are sure to take us over, and we are sure to be psychologically unable to do anything about it. In your terms, it is what happens when an extreme Apollonian culture meets an extreme Dionysian culture.'

'Well, hell,' Johnny said. 'That's a hell of a thing to lay on me. I feel sort of stupid offering you advice – but look, if you know all that, why not adapt yourselves to the situation? Make yourselves become what you have to become?'

'As you did?' Veerhe asked.

'Well, okay, I didn't adapt. But I'm not as smart as you Lorians.'

'Intelligence has nothing to do with it,' the Chief Planner said. 'One doesn't change one's culture by an act of will. Besides, suppose we could change ourselves? We would have to become like you. Frankly, we wouldn't like that.'

'I don't blame you,' Johnny said truthfully.

'And even if we did bring off this miracle and made ourselves more aggressive, we could never reach in a few years the level you have reached after tens of thousands of years of aggressive development. Despite our advantages in armament, we would probably lose if we tried to play your game by your rules.'

Johnny blinked. He had been thinking along the same lines. The Lorians were simply too trusting, too gullible. It wouldn't be difficult to work up some kind of a peace parlay, and then take over one of their ships by surprise. Maybe two or three ships. Then . . .

'I see that you've reached the same conclusion,' Veerhe said.

'I'm afraid you're right,' Johnny said. 'The fact is, we want to win much harder than you do. When you get right down to it, you Lorians won't go all out. You're nice people and you play everything by rules, even life and death games. But we Terrans aren't very nice, and we'll stop at nothing to win.'

'That is our extrapolation,' Veerhe said. 'So we thought it would only be reasonable to save a lot of time and trouble and put you in charge of us now.'

'How was that?'

'We want you to rule us.'

'Me personally?'

'Yes. You personally.'

'You gotta be kidding,' Johnny said.

'There is nothing here to joke about,' Veerhe said. 'And we Lorians do not lie. I've told you my extrapolation of the situation. It is only reasonable that we should save ourselves a great deal of unnecessary pain and hardship by accepting the inevitable immediately. Will you rule us?'

'It's one hell of a nice offer,' Bezique said. 'I'm really not qualified . . . But what the hell, no one else is, either. Sure, I'll take over this planet. And I'll do a good job for you people because I really do like you.'

'Thank you,' Veerhe said. 'You will find us easy to manage, as long as your orders are within our psychological capabilities.'

'Don't worry about that,' Johnny said. 'Everything's going to continue just as before. Frankly, I can't improve on this set-up. I'm going to do a good job for you people, just as long as you cooperate.'

'We will cooperate,' Veerhe said. 'But your own people may not prove so amenable. They may not accept the situation.'

'That's the understatement of the century,' Johnny said. 'This'll give the governments of Earth the biggest psychic bellyache in recorded history. They'll do their damnedest to pull me down and put in one of their own boys. But you Lorians will back me, right?'

'You know what we are like. We will not fight for you, since we will not fight for ourselves. We will obey whoever actually has the power.'

'I guess I can't expect anything more,' said Bezique. 'But I see I'm going to have some problems bringing this off. I guess I'll bring in a few buddies to help me, set up an organization, do some lobbying, play off one group against the other . . .'

Johnny paused. Veerhe waited. After a while Johnny said,

'I'm leaving something out. I'm not being logical. There's more to this than I thought. I haven't gone all the way in my reasoning.'

'I cannot help you,' the Chief Planner said. 'Frankly, I am out of my depth.'

Johnny frowned and rubbed his eyes. He scratched his head. Then he said, 'Yeah. Well, it's clear enough what I gotta do. You see it, don't you?'

'I suppose there are many promising avenues of application.'

'There's only one,' Johnny said. 'Sooner or later, I gotta conquer Earth. Either that, or they're going to conquer me. Us, I mean. Can you see that?'

'It seems a highly probable hypothesis.'

'It's God's own truth. Me or them. There's room for just one Number One.'

The Planner didn't comment. Johnny said, 'I never dreamed of anything like this. From spaceship driver to emperor of an advanced alien planet in less than two weeks. And now I gotta take over Earth, and that's a weird feeling. Still, it'll be the best thing for them. We'll bring some civilization to those monkeys, teach them how things should really be done. Some day they'll thank us for it.'

'Do you have any orders for me?' Veerhe asked.

'I'll want to review all the data about the Ancient Dynasty fleet. But first I think a coronation would be in order. No, first a referendum electing me emperor, then a coronation. Can you arrange all that?'

'I shall begin at once,' the Chief Planner said.

For Earth, the standard nightmare had finally taken place. An advanced alien civilization was about to impose its culture upon Earth. For Loris, the situation was different. The Lorians, previously defenseless, had suddenly acquired an aggressive alien general, and soon would have a group of mercenaries to operate their spacefleet. All of which was not so good for Earth, but not bad at all for Loris.

It was inevitable, of course. For the Lorians were a really advanced and intelligent people. And what is the purpose of being really intelligent if not to have the substance of what you want without mistaking it for the shadow?

24

THE
EXPENSIVE
DELICATE SHIP

Brian W. Aldiss

*Literature would be the poorer without Brian Aldiss who is an
artist with a novel, a poet of the short story. The title of this
one is taken, fittingly, from a poem by W. H. Auden,* Musée
de Beaux Arts, *which ends with these lines:*

> *But for him it was not an important failure; the sun shone
> As it had on the white legs disappearing into the green
> Water; and the expensive delicate ship that must have seen
> Something amazing, a boy falling out of the sky,
> Had somewhere to get to and sailed calmly on.*

In the old days, there used to be a suspension bridge across
from Denmark to Sweden, between Helsingør and Halsingborg.
It's scrapped now. It became too dangerous. But it had a moving walkway, and my friend Göran Svenson and I often used
to use it. At one time, taking the walkway grew into a pleasant
afternoon habit.

We got on the bridge one day, complaining as everyone does
occasionally, about our jobs. 'We work so damned hard,' I
said. 'When do we have time to live?'

'I've got a theory,' he said, 'that it's the other way about.'
When Göran announces that he has a theory, you can be pretty
sure that something crazy is going to come out. 'I think we
work so hard, and do all the other things we do, because living
– just intense pure living – is far too painful to endure. Work is
a panacea which dilutes life.'

'Good old Göran, you mean life is worse than death, I suppose?'

'No, not worse certainly, but the next most severe thing to
death. Life is like light. All living creatures seek the light,
but a really hard intense white light can kill them. Pure life's
like that.'

'You're a fine one to talk about a pure life, you old lecher!'

He gave me a pained look and said, 'For that, I shall tell you a story.'

We climbed on to the accelerating rollers, and so on to the walkway proper. We were carried out over Helsingør docks, and at once the Oresund was beneath us, its gray waters looking placid from where we stood.

This is Göran's story, as near as I can recall to the way he told it, though I may have forgotten one or two of his weird jokes.

He was aware that he was on a boat in a fearful storm. He thought the boat was sailing up the Skagerrak toward Oslo Fjord but, if so, there must have been some sort of a power failure, because the interior of the ship was miserably lit by dim lanterns swinging here and there.

Maybe it was a cattle boat, to judge from the smell. He was making his way up the companionway when a small animal – possibly a wallaby – darted by. He nearly fell backward, but the ship pitched him forward at just the right moment, and he regained his balance.

When he got on deck – my God! What a sea! It couldn't be the Skagerrak; the Skagerrak was never that rough! Göran had spent several years at sea before the last vessels were completely automated, but he had never encountered an ocean like this. The air was almost as thick with water as the sea, so furiously was rain dashing down, blown savagely by high winds. There was no sign of coast, no glimpse of other vessels.

An old man made his way up to Göran, going hand-over-fist along the rails. His robes were dripping water. Something about his wild ancient look gave Göran a painful start. What sort of vessel was he aboard? He realized that the rails were made of wood, and the companionway, and the entire ship as far as he could see – roughly made, at that!

The old man clutched his arm and bellowed, 'Get up to the wheel as fast as you can! Shem needs a hand!'

Göran could smell strong liquor on the old man's breath.

'Where are we?' he asked.

The old man laughed drunkenly. 'In the world's pisspot, I should reckon! What a night! The windows of Heaven are open and the waters of Earth prevail exceedingly!'

As if to emphasize his words, a great mountain of water as big as an alp went bursting by, soaking them both completely as it went.

'How – how long's this storm likely to last?' Göran asked.

'Why, long as the good Lord pleases! What a night! I've got the chimps working the pumps. Even the crocodiles are seasick! Keep your weather-eye open for a rainbow, that's all I can say. Now get to the wheel, fast as you can! I'm going below to secure the rhinos.'

Göran had to fight his way first uphill and then downhill as the clumsy tub of a boat wallowed its way through the biggest storm since the world was created. He knew now that the Skagerrak would be a mere puddle compared to this all-encompassing ocean. They sailed on a planet without harbor or land to obstruct wind and wave. Small wonder the seas were so monstrous!

Forward, Shem was almost exhausted. Between them, the two men managed to lash the wheel to hold it. Every moment was a fight against elemental forces. The cries of animals and the groan of timbers were almost lost in the roaring wind, picked up and scattered contemptuously into the tempest.

Finally, between them, they had the ship heading into the storm, and clung to the wheel gasping for breath.

Göran thought himself beyond further fear when the ship was lifted high up a great sliding mountainside of water, up, up, to perch over a fearful gulf between waves. Just before they sliced down into the gulf, he saw a light ahead.

'Ship ahoy!' That was Shem, poor lad, pointing a finger in the direction Göran had been looking.

Ship? What ship? What possible ship could be sailing these seas at this time? What para-legendary voyage might it be on?

The two men stared at each other with pallid faces, and in one voice bellowed aloud for Noah. Then they turned to peer through the murk again.

At this point in his narrative, my friend Svenson broke off, to all appearances overcome by emotion. By now, the bridge had carried us halfway across to Sweden; beneath us sailed the maritime traffic of the tranquil Øresund. But Göran's inner eye was fixed on another rougher sea.

'Did you catch a second glimpse of the phantom ship?' I asked.

You've no idea what it was like to sail that sea! The water was not like sea water. It was black, a black shot through with streaks of white and yellow, as if it were a living organism

27

with veins and sinews. There were areas where fetid bubbles kept bursting to the surface, covering the waves with a vile foam. . . .

Yes, we saw that phantom vessel again. Indeed we did! As the ark struggled up the mile-long side of yet another mountain of water, the other vessel came rushing down the slope upon us.

It was as fleet, as beautiful, as our tub was heavy and crude, was that expensive delicate ship! And it was lit from stem to stern; whereas the ark – that old fool Noah had not thought to provide navigational lights, reckoning his would be the only boat braving those high waters.

We stared aghast, Shem and I, as that superb craft bore down on us, much as two children in an alpine valley might gaze at the avalanche plunging down to destroy them.

Japheth had fought his way through the gale to cling beside us. His arrival made no impression on my consciousness until I heard him scream and turned to see his face – so pale and wet it seemed luminescent – and it was only on seeing him that I could realize the extent of my own terror!

'Where's your father? Where is he?' I shouted, seizing him by the shoulders.

'He stubbed his foot down below!'

Stubbed his foot! In sudden wild anger, I flung Japheth from me and, turning, pulled out my sheath knife. With a few slashes, I had cut the wheel free and flung it over with all my might, fighting the great roar of tide under our keel with every fibre of my being.

Sluggishly, our old tub turned a few degrees – and that great beautiful ship went racing by us to port, slicing up foam high over our poop, missing us, as it seemed, by inches!

It went by, and, as it went by – towering over us, that incredible ship – I saw a human face peer out at me. For the briefest moment, our gaze met. I tell you, it was the gaze of doom. Well, such was my deep and ineradicable impression – the gaze of doom!

Then it was gone, and I saw other faces, faces of animals, all staring helplessly across the churning waters. Those animals – it was an instant's glimpse, no more, yet I know what I saw! Unicorns, gryphons, a centaur with lashing mane, and those superb beasts we have learned to call by Latin names – mega-

28

therium, stegosaurus, a tyrannosaur, triceratops with beaked mouth agape, diplodocus ...

Of course, they all sliced by in a flash as the miraculous ship – that doppelgänger ark! – sped down the waters. And then they were lost in the murk and spume. A flicker of light, and once more our ark was all alone in the hostile sea, with the windows of heaven open upon us.

And I was wrestling with the wheel, on and on – maybe forever ...

I burst out laughing.

'Great story, great performance! You are trying to persuade me that you sailed on the ark with Noah? Who were *you*? Ham, no doubt!'

He looked pained.

'You see, you are so coarse, old chap! Your scepticism does you no credit. Concentrate your attention on that fine ship which almost rammed us. What was it? Where was it sailing? Who built it? And what happened to it, what happened to all the creatures aboard?'

'An even bigger mystery – did poor old Noah's toe get better?'

He made a gesture of disgust. 'You refuse to take me seriously. Just consider the tragedy, the poetry, the mystery, of that apocalyptic encounter. I sometimes ask myself if the wrong vessel survived that gigantic storm. You know that God was very angry with that drunken old sot, Noah. Did the wrong set of men and animals survive to repopulate the Earth?'

'I can't imagine a pterodactyl bringing a sprig of olive back into the ark.'

'Laugh if you will! Sometimes I wonder what alternate possibilities and possible world flashed past my eyes in that moment of crisis. You haven't my fine imaginative mind – such speculations would mean nothing to you.'

'You began this sermon by talking about just pure intense living – I suppose in contrast with all the muddled stuff we get through. Are you saying that this moment when you saw this – "doppelgänger ark", as you call it, was a moment of intense living?'

He glanced down at the docks of Halsingborg, now rolling under our feet. The new art museum loomed ahead. We had almost arrived on the Swedish shore.

'No, not at all. Being so imaginative, my moment of intense living was to invent this little mysterious anecdote for you. I live in imagination? Too bad you are too much of a slob to appreciate it!'

Then he dropped his solemn expression and began to laugh. Roaring with laughter, we moved down the escalator to terra firma.

Next day, we saw in the newscasts that two small children, a boy and a girl, had been drowned in the Øresund just outside Halsingborg harbor, and at about the time we were passing overhead.

DREAMING AND CONVERSIONS: TWO RULES BY WHICH TO LIVE

Barry N. Malzberg

If science fiction, and science, and perhaps the world, has a conscience, the name of that conscience is Barry N. Malzberg.

THE DESTRUCTION AND EXCULPATION OF EARTH

Subject was persuaded to no longer refer to himself in the egomaniacal first-person quite recently. Sometimes I forget but am trying to control myself. It is a matter of self-discipline. God help me. Someone must. I cannot take the responsibility any more.

Subject was encouraged to this 'sense of depersonalization' by two aliens who visited him at quarters in the early evening hours some days ago. Visitors convinced subject that they were 'aliens' through the use of persuasive devices too strong and distasteful to be recorded in these notes. Initial doubt gave way to unquestioning acceptance. These boys do not fool around. They are serious. They mean to accomplish their purposes and they will because they are beyond us. We are one of the least intelligent of all the intelligent races in the galaxy as we have had cause to be reminded over and again.

Subject said, 'Yes, you are aliens. Even though you seem to look like humans, I believe that you are aliens. I believe. No more, no more; how can I help you?' I have never been able to bear physical pain. My specialty is moral anguish.

The aliens responded – that is, just one of them spoke, the other being 'unequipped with vocal devices' – that subject could be of great help in accomplishing the reform of his planet so that said planet could, its corrupt elements removed, join the 'galactic federation of peaceful, peace-loving, peace-oriented civilizations.' Subject, whose record on the war has been clear for many years, said that he was interested and more than willing to help but did not quite grasp what role he could play toward this end, no matter how willing he was to cooperate.

Alien spokesman gave detailed instructions, too livid and technical by turns to find a place in this memoir which must be kept brief. Ego-removal was broached. 'The trouble with you creates,' stated the spokesman, 'is that you are selfish and limited. You are so involved in filtering reality through your narrow, superficial personality-referent that you miss the span of it. The first thing for you to do is to stop taking yourself personally. Think of yourself instead as a machine, a device, a means of enactment through which important messages and activities will pass. The exculpation of Earth. Eliminate once and for all the curse of ego.'

Subject eagerly agreed to try this. He had always wanted to be a machine, finding emotions more burdensome than otherwise because of an unfortunate personal life, which I will not discuss. I will not discuss my personal life in these notes, even under threat of torture. I agreed to cooperate with the aliens in any way possible in order to bring about the exculpation of earth, an era of galactic progress and their hasty exit from his rooms.

'That is good,' said the alien with a wondrous and sparkling grin, which quite moved me since I am rarely the recipient of smiles. 'We know that we picked the proper contact.' Aliens then left with subject: one detailed pamphlet summarizing the overall plan, one list detailing subject's duties and necessary supplies, and one threat. The threat had to do with what would happen if I crossed them; I will say no more. The list and plan I memorized and then incinerated as per instruction, so that no evidence would be left.

Aliens were assured that subject would serve them. Aliens said that he had better and that there would be no further contact of any sort. They will not return but merely observe and report for further action from their headquarters. *Despite the fact that there is, then, no physical evidence of this meeting, I swear that I am telling the truth.*

In accordance with earlier plans, subject then attended a 'postgraduate and nurses' mixer' at a local hotel. Nothing was supposed to happen until the next day. Outfitted in his good suit and with a photostat of his college degree in case credentials were actually checked, subject paid three dollars to a deaf mute at the door and with some trepidation joined the postgraduates and nurses within. Never had I had any luck with girls, godammit.

But still I push on; smiling for the world, hopeful, honest, and doomed. Subject decided to put into effect the process of ego-removal urged by the alien and to act like a machine. To think of himself as a machine. Much to his surprise, aided by a mild drink, subject found himself deep in conversation with Beverly M— (out of delicacy for who knows to what uses this memoir will be put I am concealing specific identities), a psychiatric social worker from the Bronx who, like he, was there alone. Beverly, in her midthirties and unmarried appeared to be delighted with the machine. We left at an early hour and returned to this very apartment. I have never been so surprised in my life.

Subject and the psychiatric social worker engaged in the act or acts of generation three times between midnight and seven A.M. of the day of the First Exculpation. His chiseled features, so alert and fine, congealed with lust! His heart overflowed with secrets devious and terrible he wished to tell his first love but cunningly the machine fed the secrets into binary code, concentrating only upon the detailed and mechanical intricacies of performance. I was superb, gentlemen. You would not have thought I had it in me.

As a result of this, Beverly left the subject quite reluctantly to return to her job, promising that she would return to the apartment that very evening and 'really go at it for once and for all.' Subject smiled ironically, thinking of many things and permitted his webbing and tentacles to drift over Beverly's dress during a passionate kiss.

He then phoned his employer and told the employer to 'go and shove it,' carefully omitting any details of the exculpation however. The aliens had told me to concentrate upon the tasks fulltime and to live on savings which fortunately I had. When employer became abusive, subject told him to 'fuck himself up a tree' and hung up rather blithely. I then dressed and took the subway uptown to purchase the weaponry on the list.

Subject bought: two reconverted M-1 rifles, one hand grenade, one hand-grenade launcher, one fatigue jacket, one duffel bag and three captain's bars, infantry, USA. The captain's insignia were not on the list but I always wanted to be an officer and felt that in the New Era it would be a harmless indulgence.

I then, per instructions, raced downtown and located myself on the abandoned thirty-first floor of a building adjoining the square, awaiting the visit of the campaigning senator scheduled for two hours hence. The senator, promptness and efficiency being those qualities that made him so dangerous to the aliens, was there exactly on time and, equipment at ready, I used the rifle to kill him. I then used the hand grenade to incinerate personnel and property in the ensuing confusion.

It would have been exciting to stay and watch developing events but as the aliens had suggested I left immediately, made an incisive withdrawal through the service entrance, and arrived home with the duffel bag a half hour later. No one looked at me in the subway nor did I regard any of them. Machinery in machinery, I ground toward my destination unmolested.

Subject then took to his bed for several hours, preparing himself for the great tasks that lay ahead and also trying to forget how the senator's head had looked as it exploded to the shot like a flower. Strange, strange, the guilt I felt although the aliens had warned that guilt would be an inevitable part of the exculpation and could be controlled by concentrating upon being a machine. I am a machine. I am a machine. Subject reviewed the events one last time, then thought about the coming assignment. I was only sweating a little by now and heartbeat was in the normal range: seventy-eight strokes per minute at rest. Horrible: it was horrible! The coming glory of the planet through union with the galactic overlords justifies the minor upheavals that must occur.

Promptly at six, Beverly returned. I had completely forgotten her and left the stuff all over the room. She noted my complexion and asked what was wrong and precisely 'what the hell was the meaning' of the weaponry which I had thoughtlessly unloaded and scattered over the room to admire while sitting in my captain's bars. She asked questions of subject which he elected not to answer. How could I answer? She asked more questions. She would not stop. She began to scream. What could I say? She came upon me with threats that would have aborted the exculpation before it was properly begun. The bitch would not keep quiet. I begged her but she would not stop. She threatened to go to the 'authorities' and then she threatened again. She went toward the door as if she were leaving to see the 'authorities' immediately.

Subject did the oh God the necessary. Subject performed his tasks and well.

Tomorrow. Tomorrow at noon it will be the mayor. Now I sit here and wait. Subject remains in quarters pending his next assignment. He thinks of this and he thinks of that, running his hands over the grenade. He considers how good it would be to have another visit from the aliens if only to confirm that he was really doing the job he was appointed to do and that it is not his fault if there were complications. The aliens would reassure me and do something about the body: they could not leave me alone to confront the logistics.

The aliens have not come. After a time subject realized that they were never going to come and that he was on his own to accomplish the mission as he could. How did I ever get into this? Why does everything always fall upon me? I must not think of this; it is a singular and moving thing to be charged as I have with the responsibility of the destiny of the earth. Of the universe for all I know.

Of all recorded time for that matter. Why not? Aliens returned at 7:00 P.M.; greeted subject in his rooms, took expressionless note of corpse which had been placed in a subtle but decorative position of removal beyond the skylight. 'What is this?' the alien equipped with vocal device stated, 'what is going on?'

Subject told them what was going on. 'I told you what was going on,' I concluded to the alien, having spoken with many flourishes but at intense brevity since the alien warned me not to fool around. 'Why have you come back? You said that you would not return.'

'We said that we would not return,' alien grumbled, 'but had no awareness that things. Would come to this pass. The girl an unintended victim. A scattering of fire.' Transcription is breaking down or perhaps the alien's transmission was breaking down. His voice had lost that soaring evenness of pitch and assurance, which is the way I will always remember him, no matter what. 'Business is business,' the alien said, 'but this is not business. You were not supposed to become emotionally involved. You were warned. Warned of the dangers. Dangers of emotional involvement.'

Subject explained with all the control left available to him that he had done the best he could. A novice at this great task

35

he would certainly get better. 'Then why . . .' alien stated, pointing to Beverly or what remained of Miss M——, '*why* . . .' and added something to the effect that this was a victim outside of the plan. Am not sure of this. Recollection faults. What do you want of me?

Subject explained or tried to explain that victim had stumbled into information about plan and had had to be eliminated for its continuing safety. Alien became abusive and said that subject was totally incompetent in his assigned task and would have to be dealt with. He said I would have to be dealt with. At this point, the nonspeaking alien made threatening gestures which could not be misinterpreted within the context of the day. The corpse glinted. The skylight seemed to emit virtual streams of light, pure radiance which my fevered skull converted into reason. I dashed for the M-1 rifle (cheerfully reloaded only hours before for the next assignment) and killed the nonspeaking alien. Apparently he had vocal devices after all. After all he had vocal devices. He perished in a glaze of green beneath me.

'Now wait,' the speaking alien said, 'you are becoming overcharged. This understanding never was. To be broached. Business is business. Involvement is one thing but this enthusiasm. Stop,' he said, 'stop,' it said, 'stop,' the monster said, 'stop,' the fiend stated and I shot this alien too in its voicebox and it died more horribly, gentlemen, than I care to describe in this vital and essentially aseptic set of notes. It was necessary; he would have interfered with the execution of the great task. That was what *he* called it. The great task. I cleaned up the rooms but necessarily this took some time and I missed the schedule of the assignment by a full day and a half for personal reasons.

Nevertheless, I caught up. I shall always catch up. Subject will catch up on everything. Alone: on my own, unwavering, committed; I knew that it would always be this way. At the end it would have to be on my own. Aliens or no aliens, Beverly or no, depersonalization or not . . . I shall clean up the world.

INTRODUCTION TO THE SECOND EDITION

This is the third time that I will murder my mother. The first two times were not entirely satisfactory but brought me, regardless, toward the more central material: one of these go-rounds I will surely get it. 'You lousy bitch,' I say, raising the knife, 'you ruined everything. My whole attitudes toward sex were entirely warped for thirty-eight years by your pointless moralizing. Also you insisted that I get a fifty-cent allowance when my three best friends were all taking more than a dollar. I'll never forgive you for that. Never!' I say and in the midst of her protests and shrieks, drive the knife straight toward her heart and part her like a fish, watch with some limited satisfaction while she collapses to the floor. 'Grrll,' she says, dwindles, and vanishes. They have made great progress with the simulacrums but still have difficulty in mimicking human speech.

'So much for that,' I say, sheathing the knife and placing it back in its proper place on the table, turning away from her and toward the exit before my time-span is ended and the lights collapse on me. (I find this very embarrassing.) Behind me I hear the sound of the Sweepers; before me I hear the sound of the machinery taking coins but my business is done for the day, I push straight ahead, past the crowds and there on the street I merge with the others and am gone. Still damaged, still cursed, the taint of my mother lying crosswise against my heart until I realize again, gasping in the open air, how they have always cheated me and how yet I will be back tomorrow.

For the fourteenth time I allow my father to kill me. I have killed him only eight times myself; there is some vague imbalance here but it is not to be corrected and only barely understood. 'This is for you,' he says, standing before me terrific and powerful, the man that I have not seen thus for thirty-three years, stripped to the waist, the prematurely gray hairs of his chest winking at me in the dangerous light, 'this is for ruining your mother's figure, turning that gay, small girl into gloom and disaster, sowing the seeds of disunion in our marriage, locking me into my miserable job, ruining my life. I don't have to take this any more,' he says almost conversationally and raises the gun; he fires the gun, I feel the bullet in my intestine and with a grateful moan fall to the floor dying for him as I have always wanted. Spaces contract, sounds diffuse and I come to myself in the Recovery Room where an old attendant who looks strangely like an uncle leans over and asks me in a whisper if I want to go again. 'A bargain rate,' he says, 'another death for half-price or you can take a kill for only three-quarters. Wouldn't you like to kill?' he says with a horrid wink and I tear the helmet from my head and stumble from the table, leaving quite rapidly although some tug of responsibility makes me turn at the door and say politely, 'No, I don't want to get hooked on this; I'll take it within limits.' Infinitely compassionate, infinitely tender, the old attendant nods and I push my way into the street, gasping in the open air, knowing how they have always cheated me and how yet I will be back tomorrow.

For kicks I elect to kill an old girl friend. I have not seen her for fifteen years; now, as I last remember her she stands before me, naked to the waist, pathos and lust intertwined in her features, her delicate hands cupping her breasts as last she did. 'You can if you want to,' she says with great sadness, 'but I'll never have any respect for you as long as I live if you think I'm so cheap,' and I administer poison: shovel the vial between her lips and administer it in choking draughts. She falls with a gasp, her limbs coming open and I am seized by need, a mad necessity comes over me and I collapse on the floor to mount her but before I can do anything her body retracts, retracts very quickly and attendants seize me by the shoulders. 'Not here,' they say, 'you know perfectly well that that isn't part of your contract,' and with great speed and force they usher me through the hallways and toss me past bystanders into the street; gasping in the open air I know that they have cheated me again and yet I will be back tomorrow.

I am told that my contract has expired and am offered a new series of treatments at a higher rate. 'That's impossible,' I say, 'you're extorting money from me and besides I don't need the process at all; I'm perfectly free,' and they say to me, 'If that's so don't renew, go into the street,' and suddenly I realize that I am not free and I do not want to go into the street so I renew for twenty-five more treatments at three times the per-treatment cost which it was when I began and they thank me and dismiss me and I say, 'When will I be free? It doesn't seem to *work;* when will I be purged of these needs as you promised?' and they rub their hands and shake their heads, say vaguely that there is no way of telling but the rate of purgation in the long run is very favorable and besides the treatments of

38

themselves are cathartic and I go gasping into the street feeling that they have cheated me again and yet I will be back tomorrow.

I allow my mother to kill me. It is the culmination of an old grudge; it has to do with my poor eating habits and sloppy table mannerisms. 'I'm sorry, sorry, but this is necessary,' she says and cuts me ear to ear with a knife and I fall dying and yet ascending, moving toward consciousness and my mother leans toward me: her face has the calmness and certainty of a very young girl and 'Yes,' she says, 'yes, yes, yes,' and falls toward me; I touch her, feel a well of excitement, realize that she is as fully at my mercy as once I was at hers and this fills me with perverse excitement, excitement is not the word for it, it is more a feeling of latent *gathering* of profound forces and drawing her against me I perform upon her an unspeakable act, which even within the context of this important and highly confidential series of case notes I dare not repeat; perform upon her this act again and again and it is satisfying, more than I had bargained for in the beginning of course but less than that which I now know may await me at the end. Unquestionably I have reached a new level. All of the time I thought that things were heading toward repetition and it turns out that the Institute was merely holding out on me. Ah the cunning, the cunning! as I leap upon her and ride my mother down all the halls of forever, sensing behind me approving chuckles, the rubbing of energetic palms and the contract for permanent treatment which I always knew, someday, they would offer me.

BREAKOUT
IN ECOL 2

David R. Bunch

Of course we must have some kind of international population controls or we will out-populate our food supplies and starve — or worse. We are all vaguely and uncomfortably aware of this, but only mildly, so that very little is being done about it. Wryly, David R. Bunch gives us a glimpse of one of our possible futures if we don't shape up now.

We counted our blessings, knowing how lucky we were, we marshals in Ecol 2, that the juices were thin in our old-man veins now; and we laughed just thinking of those youngsters being whammed silly all the time by the chemistry of their healthy young bods. And we watched The Board. For Sign. It was our job!

I remember especially a night. Although, naturally, by the very nature of our job, we had many and many a night and many and many a day to remember and many many 'very interesting situations' to mentally tally up. Old Bronk and I — Old Bronk, my ride partner! How can I ever forget Old Bronk!? We each raced for our scoots this night that The Board went wild with Sign. Like some superfast firemen going for the pole we were in our great speed, and we were soon streetborne. There was no doubt that we were two who were dedicated to Mission, and when that signal came in for trouble we were on it like a cat on a tuna can, full-fresh-and-open tuna can. We were ready to go, sail, ride, speed, get there. Those smart youngass hardons weren't about to put anything over on Old Bronk and me. Not in our Area of Responsibility. Which was, in a way, the world, the whole Ecol-drawered spread. Yes! In a way . . .

The discrepancy this time was in a corner of a southern-western district of Ecol 2, and we floorboarded our scoots, as the saying is; we raced the wind. The leatherglass thongs on our handlebars' gleamy reach lay out along the air made solid by our swift passage, and the long leatherglass cowboy fringe on our big-stud cowboy saddlebags rippled with the speed of our charge. We were minions of the law – streetborne on scout scoots and, in our own ways, the saviors of the entire people-plagued universe, the whole Ecol-drawered package.

The night came apart with bedlam as we rode. All the districts that bordered Ecol 2 threw up warnings and each one offered standby, if it transpired there should be the need. (Which standby meant, per district, two or three old juicy-noodle duffers such as Bronk and I, far past capability of any erection or lewd desire, would be alerted and, in their fine purity, kept awake all night hard by the seats of their scoots.) And there were the standard and standing plans of mobilization for General Outbreak. For who knows, when the Wall chips even a little the whole big wide sturdy standing may soon tumble away.

'Some young smartass hardon, I'll betcha,' I yelled at Old Bronk through my road mike, 'couldn't stand the gaff of this spring weather.'

'More'n likely may be it's just this overcrowdin',' Old Bronk yelled back. 'Worse'n the full times of the moon, really, to send people all giddy nuts. I still say what they should do is give all them young smartass hardons either castration or aging shots. Aging shots, properly applied would solve the troubles of the whole world. All of them. Even wars. Hee haw huck! Believe me!'

'Yeah?' I said hard against the wind tearing at me and my scoot. 'You may be right, Old Bronk. And then again, you may be wrong, Old Bronk.' I was just making noises, really. Small talk, you know, as we rode. I knew Old Bronk was right, ultimately and finally, although I didn't for a minute think he had meant it that way, ultimately and finally. Aging shots properly applied would solve it all; no doubt about it. We'd all, each and everyone, be dead! No need for Ecol drawers, or anything else, then. . . .

'Look at us,' Old Bronk Bronked on, 'we'd never in the world kick up a fuss like this on The Board. Even if we could, now would we? Or even want to?'

'Speak for your own, Old Bronk. Who says we wouldn't if we could, or even want to? But no one has to worry about mine now. Limp as a juicy noodle forevermore, now, and I've accepted the facts. And God knows, that's really the reason we've qualified for our jobs, you and I. A proddy rammer young smartass hardon could never do it, and you know it, now could he?'

'Nope, a proddy rammer young smartass hardon could never be a law marshal in this proud service of the drawers where that we serve, and that's the truth. His sympathies 'uld be all otherwise. He'd screw it up!'

We found him cowering in a tiny cluster of plastic weeds, a little old downspread guy all drooped, not much bigger than a simple dwarf. 'Why man,' I said, 'what's your act? You're probably about as capable nowadays as a bent soda straw. And that's not much, man! Hee haw hee.'

'Come out wit' yehre hands up flaggin', and no nonsense wit' the law!' Old Bronk shouted, all business and all bustly fully the law marshal now, from his white white hair inside his clear helmet to the very toes of his scoot boots black proud gleam. He'd dismounted, had Old Bronk, had kicked his scoot stand down in a very businesslike way with one of his high blacks and was now ready for come-what-would. I had to admire him, because that's the way to do it in law enforcement. Always be stance ready and keep your zap hand clear-out-free, ready to fill it fast if need there should arise. I was a little more casual most times myself, sometimes seeing the comedy in a situation, the freakiness of it all more than the lawman's law enforcement pose. I sometimes thought I'd probably get it because of this, and die laughing.

What a way to go!

The little man came out smiling. 'I knew I'd be captured,' he said, 'Everything's *so* organized! But it was worth it just to give it a try and get away for a while from that pod. I didn't have any idea of doing anything to upset anything, like, say, a population status quo. Just wanted to get away. For my own special reasons. Besides, "doing anything" still takes two, doesn't it? Hee hee hee.'

'Man, it must be really bad in your pod of detainees or your stick of potential population disrupters, as it were,' I allowed, trying to strike contact with the skimpy one and ease him a little across Old Bronk's icy pose. Maybe the runt man really was a pretty decent sort, and something in conditions had just for the nonce got him, had become intolerable for him and had set him off for a sinner's and a criminal's show. Guess that could happen to anyone, anyone at all. Some time. He just stared for now, his mouth seeming not able to do it, break out for words, I mean. 'What do you guys do?' I went ahead. 'Stamp and fuss and bellow around a lot, like hard-up old mount-on cattle bulls inside a tightass fence?'

'Nah,' he said, finally unlocking his jaws for speech let loose in a flood, 'not at all in my pod or stick of detention, we don't do that, and it's not what you think over there, it's not. Not really at all. Sure, we're in the drawers, as everyone else is in the drawers, of a certain age now, but we don't register much on the Tote Boards, not much at all ordinarily, we don't, I'm sure of that. Just pretty stable in my pod mostly, and we all know we're doing this bit just because of the law and the times and we suffer it out, or not really suffer, I mean, but do it because most of us over in my slab were old marrieds on the outside, anyway, and very very used to nothing much most of the time and pretty generally all along and steadily. *For years and years and years!* Except for outside noises, I could—'

'What *is* it then?' Old Bronk cut in curtly. 'Why are you out here wastin' the government's time, money and patience this-a-way by causin' a chase? Do you realize what each break like this costs your government in wear and tear on scoot tires, scoots, fuel, general mobilization for standby, extra marshals' time for those alerted from off-time to draw overtime, not to mention the intangibles, such as potential danger to life and limb of the personnel of the scoot troops, both active and on-call; not to add the price for the Service Riders' service time, both man and vehicular, when and if we apprehend? *Do you?*'

He shook his head, entirely dumbfounded and struck giddy by Old Bronk's intensity, I could tell. 'Besides, you know you can be shot for somethin' like this, breakin' the law,' Old Bronk brayed on. 'Yeh're not only technically, but actually and actively a lapsed pant, man! Yeh're Ecol drawers are showin', boy. Like statutory rape in the old days, man, it's open and a shut case. Yeh're in a *heap* of trouble, plenty, and you know it, fellah. Yeh're guilty for all that anyone could say.'

'I'm guilty,' he said, 'sure. But not like you think. Hell, I've still got on my drawers.' And he pulled up the inmate's loose-fitted striped gown to show us his undies, and it was so! Even the plug-ins were still on them, flapping and dangling.

'But – but—' Old Bronk sputtered now, coming loose from his starched shiny pose, 'what in the thunderin' hell—'

'Just my kind of luck,' the small one rambled on. 'When

our district got the orders, down from Central Birth Freeze, and we were all Ecoled in for those control pants, my wife, old fridgy-fridge herself, was billeted in the women's control compound right on the other side of my little cubicle in the pod. Just my kind of rotten luck that this one-in-an-umpteen-thousand-chance kind of rotten thing would happen to me. Well, she'd keep screechin', see, just as she will when I go back, and she learns I'm there. Screechin' and screechin' through the walls.'

'Wanted you over there, huh?' says Old Bronk, a hell of a lawman, but very short sometimes on practicals, I have to say. 'Wanted you to tear right through them walls to get to her, huh, so you two could go to town? Go to bed, I mean! Haw haw hee.'

'Nah nah nah, not at all at all. And I can sure tell you've never been hitched, not for any length. She just kept screechin', "Ha, ha, ha, you horny old goat meat. *Ha, ha, ha!* They gotcha now! They gotcha! And that'll show ya how to quit bein' a pig." Twice a year – on the good years! – was piggy?'

So we put the Ecol handcuffs on him and led him over to a bright orange talk-in pole nearby where he would call for a wagon that would take him on down. The wagon Service Riders, more infirm and less glamorous than the scoot patrol troops such as Bronk and I, some even old ladies, would take him back to his compound and hook him into his circuit where his Ecol undies would start registering all of his erotic urges, on the big Tote Boards in Ecol 2. And this is S.O.P. now for every breed-capable male and female on the whole Ecol-threatened earth, all over the world! They are somewhere in their compounds, in Ecol drawers, registering their erotic urges, and none, for all the risks involved, is allowed to do anything about it until someone dies in the district of responsibility. Then the couple, male and female, next in line . . . married, of course . . . or a service performed on the spot before they do it to keep everything decent . . . for those who care . . .

'I still say it was worth it. For a while . . . just to get away . . .' This I heard him muttering as the Service Riders, two perky old gun-swung ladies so it chanced, about seventy-five years young, loaded him in to whisk him back to that control cubicle just a thin wall away from old fridgy-fridge, his wife. Under the circumstances this time all other punishment for breakout was waived!

THE
COLD WAR ...
CONTINUED

Mack Reynolds

Mack Reynolds is science fiction's political prodder, one of the few authors who is capable of visualizing something more than feudalistic capitalism or intergalactic empires in the future. His stories actually project present political situations into the years ahead to see how they might develop in a realistic and logical fashion. That he can do this as entertainment, not lecture, is a blessing we should be thankful for.

Happily, it was a grim night. It was cloudy and there was a fine drizzle. Paul Kosloff didn't know whether or not the grounds of the mansion were patrolled, either by men or by dogs, but, if they were, either man or beast was going to be shelter-conscious.

Most likely, the grounds were so patrolled. The one he was seeking out was known to be security-conscious almost to the point of phobia.

The iron picket fence surrounding the estate was his first hurdle. There were no trees near it and it was too high to easily climb. Besides, undoubtely it was gimmick-wired at the top in such manner as to tip off the guards – either that or electrocute him. He was going to have to go through it.

The main gate was out of the question. He had seen the two men stationed there, one to each side in armored booths and undoubtedly armed to the molars. He continued to stroll along, on the other side of the street, following the fence. And, yes, behind the house was a smaller gate and unattended.

Paul Kosloff crossed over to it. It had a heavy lock. He brought a scrambler from his pocket and activated it, then an electronic lock pick which he had gotten from the boys in the Rube Goldberg department. Its magnets sucked up to the lock, over the keyhole, and he slowly rotated it. When the lock reluctantly gave up its secrets, he pushed the gate open and slipped through. He relocked it, then deactivated the scrambler.

Thus far things were going better than he had hoped. Bending almost double, he scurried toward the rear of the mansion.

Luckily, this part of the estate was in gardens, complete with trees, complete with shrubs. He had a good chance of going undetected, certainly until he got reasonably near the house.

The dog, running hard, a brown streak with distended, slavering jaws, was almost upon him before he spotted it. A Doberman pinscher, recognizable even in this light by its long forelegs and wide hindquarters.

Paul Kosloff had worked out with war dogs while taking commando training long years before. He had just time to fling himself into position before the dog jumped. He spun sideward to the left and his right hand shot out and grasped the right paw of the large smooth-coated terrier. He continued to swing mightily. The dog had time for only one loud yelp of confusion, before he smashed it into the trunk of a tree.

It fell to the ground, momentarily, at least, stunned. Paul Kosloff, to make sure, kicked it twice in the side of the head, immediately behind the clipped ears.

He wiped the back of his left hand over his forehead, finding a beading of cold sweat there. He shook his head and continued on his way toward the house.

A chink of light began to manifest itself, and a door was opening. He dodged behind the bole of a large tree, and flattened himself against it.

A voice called, 'Roger! Is that you, boy?'

Paul Kosloff held his breath.

'Roger! What have you got, boy?'

A few moments later, there was a curse and Paul Kosloff could hear someone approaching.

The voice was closer this time. 'Here boy, here boy. Damn it, what were you yelping about?'

As the footsteps came closer, Paul Kosloff slithered around the tree trunk, keeping it between himself and the other.

Completely on the other side, he bent double once again and headed for the house and the open door. It was all in the laps of the gods, now. Was there anyone else on the inside? Behind him, he could hear the guard, still calling the Doberman. The fat was going to be in the fire if he discovered the unconscious watchdog.

46

Paul Kosloff hurried into the interior of the large house and found himself in a small guard room, furnished only with a single table and two chairs. On the walls were flak rifles, shotguns and laser beam pistols.

There was another door at the far end of the room. He got through it in a hurry and closed it behind him before speeding down the dimly lit hall beyond. Given luck, he wouldn't run into any servants. Not at this time of night. It was past two o'clock.

He came to a small elevator and looked at it for a moment, but then shook his head. The man he was seeking was noted as a nut on burglar alarms and related devices. He might have even something like an elevator rigged.

He found a flight of narrow circling stairs slightly beyond. A servant stairway by the looks of it. He started up. His destination was on the third floor, he knew. He wondered if there were more guards.

At the third floor, he peered cautiously down the ornate hallway. And, yes, there was a guard before the door that was his goal.

The other's back was turned. Paul Kosloff took a desperate chance and sped across the heavily carpeted hall to the room opposite. The chance paid off. The door was unlocked. He entered the room beyond quickly, closed the door behind him.

He fumbled at the wall for a light switch and found it. The plans of the mansion he had studied had been correct. It was a billiards room, the table in the exact center. He strode over to it, took up the eight ball and then returned to the door and flicked off the light.

He had to gamble now that the guard's back was still turned. If it wasn't, he'd had it. He opened the door a narrow crack and rolled the ball toward the circular staircase. It began to bounce down the stairs, at first slowly, then faster. It didn't sound much like footsteps to him, but it would have to do.

He kept the door open, the slightest crack, and watched as the guard came hurrying up and hesitated, looking down the stairwell. The pool ball was well along by now and going faster. At this distance, it sounded more like a person descending as fast as possible.

The guard suddenly flicked his hand inside his coat to emerge with a laser pistol, and began hurrying down.

Paul Kosloff gave him a few moments, then left his hiding place and hustled along the hall. He gently tried the doorknob of the room that was his destination. It wasn't locked. He opened it and walked through, nonchalantly.

The man reclining in the bed, reading, looked up at him.

'Paul Kosloff?' he said.

'Well, I'm not the ghost of Spiro Agnew,' Paul Kosloff said, closing the door behind him. 'What in the hell is this all about?'

'How did you get in without detection?'

'I didn't completely. You've either got a dead dog or one with a whale of a headache out in your garden. Once again, what's this all about?'

'A double motive,' the man in the bed said. 'First, I wanted to find out whether you're as good as you're supposed to be as an espionage-counter-espionage agent. And, second, I wanted to give you an assignment without anyone, anyone at all, even knowing we've ever met. Do you know who I am?'

'You're the head of what some of us field men call The Commission of Dirty Tricks of the State Department. Few people in this country realize that the Soviet Complex isn't the only power that has tough and unscrupulous people operating.' Paul Kosloff pulled up a chair and sat and crossed his legs.

The other looked at him. 'Very few people know of me. In my section, we need publicity like a broken leg.'

Paul Kosloff said evenly, 'Yes, I know. I was just a child when the Bay of Pigs took place, but there have been other farces since. Publicity doesn't help.'

The man in the bed was obviously not pleased at that. He said, 'Kosloff, do you consider yourself a patriotic American?'

The other said reasonably, 'How could I be? When a special bill was brought before Congress to grant me citizenship, it was decided my odor was too high and it was turned down. Let's face reality. I'm persona non grata everywhere, including the country of my birth – Russia – where they took a dim view of my 'defecting' even though I was a child in arms at the time and all the rest of my family had been liquidated in the purges. Relatives smuggled me out over the Finnish border and finally got me here to America.'

The commissioner said, 'What I should have said was, "Are you basically pro-American or anti-Communist?" '

The international troubleshooter looked at him. 'I thought they meant the same thing.'

The man who worked directly under the president on

48

matters so shielded that not even the most avid of muckraking columnists were aware of them, shook his head. 'Not necessarily.'

Paul Kosloff was getting tired of the routine. He said, 'All right. I've been ordered to contact you secretly. What do you want me to do?'

'Stop a revolution.'

'That's my specialty. That's what you people have been having me do for . . . as long as I can remember. Why the build up? Do I have to assassinate some present-day Trotsky or Mao, or what?'

'The revolution is about to take place in Maghrib.'

Paul Kosloff stared at him. 'They've already got a Marxian government there.'

'That's what I've been building up to. The revolution we're talking about is against the communist-socialist-anarchist government there. A certain Colonel Abou Inan wishes to overthrow the Marxists.'

'Why not let him?' Paul Kosloff growled.

'Because if we do, it's one more nail in the coffin of our economy.'

Paul Kosloff waited in silence.

The other said impatiently, 'I assume you haven't read a book published back in the 1950s by Vance Packard called *The Waste Makers.* In it he pointed out that although the American population was a small fraction of the world's, the United States economy was using up some fifty percent of Earth's resources. He also pointed out that ten years before the United States had been the largest exporter of copper in the world, but was now the largest importer. His book was largely ignored and all efforts were continued to raise the gross national product year after year. One by one we lost self-sufficiency in almost every raw material we needed for our industry.'

'What's all this got to do with it?' Kosloff said.

'We need Maghrib's oil, her nickel, copper and chromium. We need them badly. We reached accommodation with Moulay Ismail's Marxist regime and purchase almost everything they produce.'

'Well, why couldn't you do the same with this Colonel Abou Inan?'

'Because that's the strongest plank in his revolutionary platform. He contends the nondeveloped countries with raw materials, such as Maghrib, are being robbed by the industrialized nations such as the United States, Common Europe and Japan. He wishes to shove prices for raw materials sky high.'

'Can he do it?'

'Probably, and, if he does, so will the other nondeveloped countries. Eventually, it could mean collapse of the economies of the developed nations.'

'So where do I come in?'

'We want Colonel Inan stopped by fair means or foul.'

Paul Kosloff looked at him cynically. 'So who are you going to send in to try the fair means?'

He took the supersonic to London and from there a jet to Gibraltar and from there a ferry plane to Tingis, capital of Maghrib. The faint scars from the plastic surgery he had gone through were all healed. He had spent the time that took poring over material on Maghrib and Moulay Ismail and his government, in the State Department files.

He hadn't liked what he found about Moulay Ismail. The North African, although self-labeled a Marxist, evidently had no intention of becoming a part of the Soviet Complex but was going it alone, in the tradition of Tito of Yugoslavia. He hadn't come to power the easy way. The commies seldom do, as Paul Kosloff well knew, but the Maghrib revolution had been particularly ruthless and bloody.

He found that his was a one-man expedition. So hush-hush was it that only the commissioner who had given him his instructions knew that Kosloff was on his way to forestall Colonel Abou Inan. It was absolutely imperative that the world never learn that the United States was involved in frustrating a counter-revolution against a Marxist régime.

He was far from happy about the assignment. From what he had read of Moulay Ismail, the other was exactly the type of man Paul Kosloff had spent his adult life fighting, and from what he knew of Abou Inan, the man had all of his sympathies. However, Paul Kosloff was a dedicated member of the Western team and it wasn't up to him to formulate policy. He fully realized that on occasion the freest of governments must resort to devious ways, to compromise, to outright Machiavellianism, if it wished to survive. He didn't like it, but Paul Kosloff wasn't starry eyed.

There wasn't a great deal of traffic between Gibraltar and Tingis. There were only two other passengers, both of them, by their looks, North Africans. In fact, one wore the djellabah, that traditional hooded robe of heavy camel wool of the desert African.

At the Tingis airport, he followed the other two to the administration buildings. He'd never been in this city before and they seemingly knew their way around. They entered through a metal detection booth. Paul Kosloff wasn't worried. The only metal he carried was a wristwatch, a small pocketknife and some coins. They passed him through and he went on to the customs counters.

His bags were already there and the raggedly uniformed officials going through them with minute care. They found nothing that mattered. Paul Kosloff wasn't silly enough to pass over a Marxist state's border carrying anything suspicious.

Next was the immigration desk and the unshaven official there looked at the passport Paul Kosloff presented, then up into the other's face.

'Why do you come to Maghrib, Mr. Smithson?'

Paul Kosloff, alias Kenneth Smithson, said easily, 'Vacation. I'm an amateur historian and I want to check out the theory that the Carthaginians first settled Tingis. I'll do other sightseeing too, but that's my big interest.'

The other grunted, stared at him some more, but then took up a rubber stamp and stamped the document and handed it over. 'Welcome to the Democratic People's Republic of Maghrib,' he said.

There were a couple of battered-looking mini-hover-cabs in front of the airport. Carrying his own bags – there didn't seem to be any porters – Paul Kosloff approached one. He put his luggage in the back and sat up next to the driver.

He said, in French, 'Take me to the best hotel in town.'

The driver said, *'Oui,'* dropped the lift lever of the hover-cab and they took off.

He had been in North African and Near Eastern towns before and thus was neither surprised nor impressed by the appearance of Tingis. If anything, the city was a bit shabbier than usual. Some decades past, it had been in the hands of France and what semimodern architecture existed obviously went back to that time. Most of this seemed concentrated in the town's center, along with governmental office buildings.

Otherwise, there were mosques, what had undoubtedly once been the palaces of sultans and other high Moslem officials, occasional fountains and wells and huge horseshoe-shaped gates.

Vehicular traffic was at a minimum, pedestrian, swarming. The sidewalks were jammed and the crowds overflowing into the streets. Some rode or led burdened donkeys and he even spotted two or three camels in the *souk* area on the outskirts. He reminded himself not to bother going into the *souk*. He had seen North African markets before and they stank.

About half of the pedestrians wore European type dress, the other half were in djellabahs for men, haiks for women, those white, sheetlike abominations that so completely swathes the wearer that only one eye shows. The prevailing hat on the men was the fez, though occasional turbans were to be seen. Footwear, even on those with European clothing, usually was the *babouche*, the backless slippers of a desert people.

All in all, Paul Kosloff decided, a pretty crummy-looking bunch. At least the commies had gotten far beyond this point in the Soviet Complex.

They pulled up before a large hotel that had undoubtedly once been luxurious. It was on the weather-beaten side now. There was a large black in front in what was probably meant to be the costume of the sultan's guard, back when they'd had a sultan in Maghrib. He had a monstrous but phony-looking scimitar in his sash.

There didn't seem to be any bellhops. Paul Kosloff got out of the cab and brought his bags from the rear. He had picked up the legal amount of dirhams that he was allowed to bring into the country in Gibraltar so was now able to pay the driver, who didn't refuse the proffered tip as was supposedly the custom in Marxist lands.

He took the luggage and approached the door. The black opened it for him but didn't make any motions toward the bags.

Paul Kosloff approached the reception desk and asked for a small suite. His cover was that he was an American businessman on vacation. He would be expected to be in ample funds.

He handed over his passport and the clerk said, 'We will have to keep this for twenty-four hours for police registration,' peering at it suspiciously.

His suite, he found, was as run-down as the Hotel El Mebruk's lobby. However, there was hot water, somewhat to his surprise. He took his time cleaning up and then brought from one of his bags a tourist guide. The guide went back to the days before Moulay Ismail's revolution, but the map of Tingis was undoubtedly still valid, though possibly they had changed some of the street names. He looked up the boulevard the hotel was on, then traced with his finger to another location.

Well, there was no use putting it off. He slipped the guide into his pocket, reached down into the bag again to emerge with an impressive-looking, king-size camera. He hung it around his neck, tourist fashion, and headed for the door.

The boulevard outside was named in both French and Arabic, *Boulevard of the July Revolution*. According to the guide book, it had once been *Boulevard Pasteur*.

This was evidently the best part of town, if any part of Tingis could be thought of as best. At least the average pedestrian was a bit less shoddily dressed. Paul Kosloff stuck his hands in his pockets and sauntered along, once again, tourist fashion. He peered into shop windows, took occasional snapshots. He was obviously in no hurry whatsoever, and obviously had no particular destination.

He took a full hour to assure himself that he wasn't being followed. He hadn't expected to be, but you never knew in a Marxist country.

He drifted down a narrow street that seemed largely devoted to small shops of a type tourists would frequent looking for souvenirs of North Africa, or bargains in the various products manufactured in the Soviet Complex that were sometimes cheaper than in the West, including art objects from China.

He took the time to gawk into various windows, and sometimes entered a shop to inspect the wares. Marxist or not, this part of Tingis looked like every other North African town he had ever been in. It would seem the regime hadn't gotten around as yet to nationalizing small enterprises.

He entered one establishment, somewhat larger than most of the others, and stared at the display of camel saddles, leather dolls, copperware and yellow *babouche* slippers. There was one other customer present and the proprietor was showing her about. She didn't seem to be any more avid than Paul Kosloff to actually buy something. Finally, she left.

Paul Kosloff went over to the shop owner and said, 'Battista?'

53

The other was seemingly a late middle-aged Arab, on the fat side, djellabah-clad and sporting a bedraggled, gray-streaked beard.

He frowned and said, 'My name is Mohammed-ben-Abdallah.'

'Your name is Joseph Battista and you're an American Italian. I was instructed to contact you. I'm Paul Kosloff.'

'Of course. The commissioner informed me you were on your way by tight-beam. Shall we go into the back room?' He turned his head and called out something in Arabic.

A young man of possibly twenty-five entered from a back door. He looked at Paul Kosloff questioningly. The older man spoke to him again in Arabic and he answered and went over and stood at the door to the street, as though awaiting customers.

Paul Kosloff followed Joseph Battista into a back room. As soon as the door was closed behind them, he made a motion with his head. 'Who's that?'

'Supposedly my son, actually another of our men.'

There was a very low Arabic-type table in the small room's center, with hassocks about it. The two men seated themselves.

Paul Kosloff said, 'How good is your cover here?'

'Excellent. I've been a small shopkeeper in Tingis for nearly twenty years.'

'Good. Did the commissioner tell you what my assignment is?'

'No, but I can guess.'

'Oh, you can, eh? Well, what do you guess?'

'You've come to help Colonel Abou Inan. Who else would they send but the famous Cold War's Lawrence of Arabia to overthrow this corrupt government of Moulay Ismail?'

Inwardly, Paul Kosloff winced, but he said, 'I'm going to need a .38 Recoilless and a shoulder harness holster, a Tracy, an electronic mop and a scrambler. You can provide them?'

'Yes, of course. I have already been instructed.'

He got up and went over to a cabinet and brought forth the articles Paul Kosloff had called for. The troubleshooter came to his feet, shrugged out of his jacket and put on the shoulder holster, under his left arm. He put the Recoilless, noiseless gun in it, and drew it twice to see if it was riding correctly. Then he got back into his coat. The electronic mop looked like a pen. He clipped it into his breast pocket. He took off his watch and handed it to Battista and took up the Tracy and put it on his wrist. It looked identical to the other watch but wasn't. It was a watch, true enough, but also had other qualities.

Battista said, 'Why in the world do they call it a Tracy?' He seated himself again.

Kosloff said, adjusting the metal straps, 'I understand that in the old days they had a comic strip detective who used a two-way radio that was strapped to the wrist like a watch. This, of course, is more than that. It operates on a tight-beam and can't be tapped.' He picked up the scrambler, which looked something like a cigarette case and dropped it into a side pocket.

He sat down again too. 'Now then, brief me a bit on Colonel Inan. They don't have much on him in Greater Washington.!!'

'I don't have much on him either. He keeps on the move, usually accompanied by his two top lieutenants, Colonel Harun Idriss and Major Abd ibn-Tashfin.'

'Where is he now?'

'The last report I had, near Ksar-es-Souk, in the mountains near the edge of the desert on the southern border. If he's pressed too hard, he can slip across into Algeria.'

'If he's on the run all the time, how can he recruit? How can he spread his message?'

'He goes from town to town, bedouin encampment to bedouin encampment. In each, he has followers. He holds secret meetings, addressing new converts, giving speeches. Before Moulay Ismail's men can locate him, he's off and away again. You must realize he has supporters everywhere including practically every eman and muezzin in the country. As a Marxist, Moulay Ismail is largely rejected by the Islamic church. Inan also has the support of much of the army, and thus is only half-heartedly sought by them.'

'So,' Paul Kosloff mused. 'There are three of them and always on the move. How could I get in touch?'

'Abou Inan has various followers here in Tingis. I can get in contact with them and arrange a meeting for you. They'll be overjoyed to know that a top operative from Greater Washington is coming to Colonel Inan's assistance. Undoubtedly, you are in a position to promise financial aid. Any revolutionary organization can use money.'

'Okay,' Paul Kosloff said grimly. 'Locate Abou Inan for me. Now one thing. You say just he and his two closest lieutenants are usually together. What would happen to this revolution if all three were ... eliminated?'

'The revolution would collapse,' Battista said definitely. 'They are its heart and soul and brains. Abou Inan is a sharif, a direct descendant of Hasan, grandson of the Prophet through his daughter Fatima. Many of the simpler people of Maghrib think Inan a saint.'

'I see,' Paul Kosloff said.

'Which brings to mind something I must warn you about,' the other said. 'Serge Sverdlov is in Tingis. From what I understand, if you're the Cold War's Lawrence of Arabia, he's sort of a Tito, Castro and Che Guevara rolled into one.'

Paul Kosloff's eyes narrowed. 'Serge, eh? Yes, I've run into Serge on occasion. I thought he was in Indonesia on some commie cloak and dagger assignment or other.'

'Possibly the Kremlin is of the opinion that Maghrib takes precedence with this threat of counter-revolution by Colonel Inan. Most of Moulay Ismail's police are inexperienced clods. But Serge Sverdlov would have lots of know-how if he devoted himself to getting Abou Inan's team.'

'Yes,' Paul Kosloff mused. 'If he had to liquidate half of the male population of southern Maghrib, Serge would get them. Where is he located?'

'At the Soviet Complex embassy.'

Kosloff stood and said, 'Okay. You'd better wrap up a couple of souvenirs for me to leave with, so that it'll look as though I bought something here. Contact me at the Hotel El Mebruk, under the name Smithson, as soon as you've set up arrangements for me to meet Colonel Abou Inan and his lieutenants.'

Back at the hotel, he unwrapped the souvenirs Battista had given him and put them on a table in the suite's living room. They'd help give him authenticity as a tourist. The shop-keeper had included a pair of leather slippers and two leather dolls, both in local costume. One was a camel driver and the other a water boy, complete with goatskin water bag over his shoulder and several tiny copper cups.

Paul Kosloff brought the electronic mop from his breast pocket and activated it and began going about the room, pointing it here, there, everywhere, and especially at any electric fixtures. Shortly, it began to beep, beep, beep and he located what he was looking for. The bug was in the base of the telephone.

56

He took the mop into the bedroom and then the bath and searched them as well. Neither was bugged. He went back into the living room and to the stand where the phone was. The fact that there was a bug in his suite didn't mean that it was being monitored, of course. They probably had a bug in every room in the Hotel El Mebruk, but surely not enough men to monitor them all at once. And from what he had seen thus far of the Maghrib economy he doubted that the bugs would be computerized.

However, he couldn't take the chance. He brought the scrambler the shopkeeper had given him from his pocket, set it on the stand next to the phone and flicked its stud.

He had to work fast now. There was always the chance that the scrambler would be detected and someone on the other end of the bug become suspicious. Then the fat would be in the fire. What American tourist would be equipped with such sophisticated cloak and dagger devices?

He took his Tracy from his wrist and propped it up on the room's desk and sat before it. He pressed the tiny stud and said, 'Paul calling. Paul calling.'

A thin voice came back. It was the commissioner's. He had arranged for Kosloff's Tracy to be tuned into his alone. They were *really* going ape about security on this assignment.

Paul Kosloff said, 'I've arrived in Tingis and made contact with Battista. The subject is in the south. Battista thinks he can find out where. He also thinks I'm here to help the subject and evidently approves of that.'

The thin voice said, 'It is not important what Battista thinks.'

'The subject has contacts here in Tingis. Battista believes he can make arrangements for a meeting.'

'What's your excuse for such a meeting?'

'It will have to be that I'm an agent from the United States coming to offer him assistance. He'll take that bait and reveal where he is.'

'Fine. Get in there and do the job. Make sure on this one. We'll never get another chance if you fail. He'll be leary of our government from then on. Do this right, and there's a hefty bonus in it for you.'

'I don't want a bonus,' Paul Kosloff growled. 'I didn't sign up with the Western team for money. And, listen, there's a complication. Serge Sverdlov is here in Tingis.'

There was a momentary silence. Then, 'Sverdlov is in Indonesia.'

'Battista says he's here in Tingis. This guy's the sharpest counter-espionage man in KGB.'

The thin voice said, 'I know who he is. Well, for once you and he are on the same side.'

'Yes, but he'll never know we're on the same side. And he's got all of the resources of Maghrib behind him, plus those of the Soviet Complex. If anything happens to my cover, he'll be on me like a ton of uranium. Can't you at least send me a couple of heavies from Paris, or wherever, to run interference?'

'Absolutely out of the question. They might stumble onto your real mission. Nobody must know about this but you and me. You're on your own.'

'All right,' Paul Kosloff said in resignation.

'Good luck,' the thin voice said, before fading. 'And reconsider that bonus.'

Paul Kosloff said bitterly, after deactivating the Tracy, 'Does he think I'd take on a job like this for the sake of a bonus?'

He went over hurriedly to the scrambler and flicked off its stud.

So he was up against Serge again. And this time not backed by limitless resources, manpower, and equipment. This time all on his own. He wondered if the Russians were onto the fact that Paul Kosloff was in Maghrib. Had Serge Sverdlov been especially sent to counter him? Not knowing, of course, Kosloff's real mission.

For the next week, Paul Kosloff spent most of his time in the hotel, taking all of his meals there. He trusted the plastic surgery he'd had in Greater Washington but he was taking no chances. Altered facial features alone are insufficient to disguise a man. He suspected that Serge Sverdlov had spent many an hour before a film screen studying shots of Paul Kosloff leaving and entering buildings, walking along streets, getting in and out of vehicles. The KGB would undoubtedly have many of these. He, himself, had spent similar hours looking at films of Serge Sverdlov and was of the opinion that he could have picked the Russian out even though masked. The set of shoulders, the way the head was held, the stride, the shape of hands, and all the rest of it.

No, he had no desire to have Serge Sverdlov spot him on the streets of Tingis.

On the third morning, he found an envelope that had been

slipped under his door during the night. He slit it open with his pocketknife. The note inside was typed and unsigned.

It read: *Tokugawa is in town. His cover is that he is a member of a Japanese trade mission here. He is staying at the Japanese embassy.*

'It sounds like a convention,' Paul Kosloff muttered. 'Serge Sverdlov, Tokugawa and myself.' He grunted. Joseph Battista was a more efficient operative than Paul Kosloff had originally given him credit for being. He wondered what system the American agent used for detecting the other underground operatives.

There was nothing for it, he was going to have to check out the newcomer. He knew where Sverdlov stood, but not the Japanese. He couldn't afford to begin operations and run into the risk of coming up against him. Possibly, it was something entirely divorced from his own mission. Possibly, but he doubted it.

The approach might as well be a direct one. That evening he left the hotel by a side door and got into a cab as soon as possible, still conscious of being spotted on the streets. He ordered the driver to take him to the Japanese embassy. There was no way he could think of to avoid being seen entering the building, if the place was being observed. And what excuse would a vacationing American have for entering the Japanese embassy? Could he claim that he planned to return to the States by traveling East, completely around the world, and wanted a Japanese visa? The trouble was, an American didn't need a visa to visit Japan.

He left the cab half a block from the embassy and walked the rest of the way, wanting the opportunity to case the place before entering, to check whether or not it was being watched. He couldn't make out any obvious plants, however. There wasn't even a local police guard at the entrance.

He entered and approached the petite Japanese girl at the reception desk. She was in western garb and the room was furnished western style.

Her French was perfect. 'Good evening, sir.'

Paul Kosloff said, 'I wish to see Colonel Tokugawa.'

Her almond eyes turned wary. 'There is no Colonel Tokugawa here, sir.'

'Tokugawa Hidetada. Supposedly he's here on a trade mission. Tell him Paul Kosloff wishes to see him.'

'I assure you, sir ...'

Paul Kosloff simply looked at her.

She flicked on a desk communicator and spoke into it in Japanese, then listened. Her eyes widened slightly in surprise. She deactivated the device and looked up at him.

'Yes, sir,' she said.

A door behind her opened and the top Japanese counter-espionage operative entered. By his appearance, he couldn't have been less offensive. He even wore thick-lensed glasses.

'Paul,' he said, his hand outstretched. 'I didn't at first recognize you. Plastic surgery, of course.'

Paul Kosloff said, 'Hidetada,' and they shook.

'Please come in here, Paul,' the slightly built Japanese said, leading the way back through the door he had just entered from.

Beyond was an office, simply furnished. On the desk were several piles of what were obviously reports, all of them of course in Japanese.

'Sit down, Paul. It seems a long time since last we met during the Asian war.'

Paul Kosloff took a chair and said, 'Yeah. And thanks all over again for taking those two commies off my back. I spent three months in the hospital afterward.'

The Japanese bowed his head agreeably in response and said, 'It was my duty, Paul. We were on the same side . . . then.'

Paul Kosloff looked at him.

Tokugawa Hidetada said gently, 'Paul, I am afraid we are not on the same side now.'

'Go on.'

'Paul, Japan desperately needs the raw materials of Maghrib, resources that are largely going to the United States today. It is in our interest that Colonel Inan not come to power.'

'Granting that I know what you're talking about, and I'm not admitting that, *why*?'

'He is a fanatic. We prefer his lieutenant, Colonel Harun Idriss. Although Idriss largely supports Inan, he is at the same time the leader of a group in their organization that has differences. Colonel Idriss is anti-American. You know, the American imperialism thing. If he came to power, he would switch trade to Japan. However, he is faithful to Inan and on his own would never attempt to replace him. But if something happened to Colonel Inan, then it would be Idriss who came to power.'

'I see. And you think the American State Department wishes to see Colonel Abou Inan win his revolution?'

The Japanese said gently, 'Yes.'

Paul Kosloff thought about it. He said finally, 'To sum it up, then, you wish this anti-Marxist revolution to take place but you want Colonel Idriss to come to power rather than Colonel Inan.'

'Yes, Paul. And, believe me, in spite of past associations, I cannot let you stand in my way. Japan cannot. We must have the oil, copper and nickel of Maghrib or industrially we die.'

Paul Kosloff came to his feet.

'I'll be seeing you, Hidetada.'

'Paul, I am warning you.'

'Yes, I know. I'll be seeing you, Hidetada. The next time you write, give my regards to your wife. I'll never forget that *tempura* she cooked for us.'

By the time he left the embassy, night was well along. The Hotel El Mebruk wasn't as far as all that. He decided to walk and try to sort things out. It was unlikely he would be spotted by Serge Sverdlov or any of his men with it this dark.

Things were piling up. The governments of the Soviet Complex and Japan, not to speak of the United States, wouldn't have their top espionage men in the country unless the revolution some of them wanted, and some didn't, was imminent. For that matter, he wondered if Common Europe also had some of their cloak and dagger aces around, and, if so, where they stood. Would they want Moulay Ismail to remain in power, or be overthrown? From what he had read in Greater Washington, this Colonel Inan made a lot of sounds about uniting North Africa, to present a united front to the developed countries, including Common Europe. Did Common Europe want a unified Arab world? He doubted it.

Paul Kosloff was going to have to get moving. He was going to have to get to this Colonel Inan before Tokugawa Hidetada did. Not that his long-time friend and colleague wasn't also interested in eliminating the colonel, but he wanted to replace him with Haran Idriss, an anti-American, pro-Japanese. Which would be just as disastrous for the United States as a successful Inan revolution.

There was another element. Both Serge Sverdlov and Tokugawa were as devoted to their own governments as Paul Kosloff was to the United States. They were dedicated. Serge, of course, would shoot down Paul Kosloff between yawns, but even with Tokugawa friendship would not be enough if he felt Kosloff to be obstructing the Japanese cause. Paul Kosloff hated to think about it, but it worked both ways. If absolutely necessary, he would not hesitate to take whatever measures were called for. It was not a pretty world, this one of international intrigue and cold war.

All of which was brought rudely home to him as he passed an alley.

Something there is in the man of action that must be an instinct, possibly one come down from the caves, from the time of the saber-tooth, from the time of the cave bear. An instinct for danger. Had Paul Kosloff not had it, he would have been dead long years since. You are walking across a battlefield, supposedly cleared of the enemy. Suddenly, seemingly without cause, you throw yourself to the ground. A burst of machine gun fire goes over your head, or a mortar shell explodes a few yards from you. Had you not flopped down upon your face, you would now be a mangled corpse. Why did you do it? You haven't the vaguest idea.

Suddenly, unconsciously, he dropped to one knee and his right hand blurred for his holstered .38 Recoilless. A pencil-thin hiss of light cut a foot above his head. A laser!

The other was only the vaguest of shapes, back a few feet in the alleyway. His six silent bullets ripped the man through from the crotch almost to the neck line.

Paul Kosloff shot his eyes up and down the street. He could see no one close enough to have observed the split seconds of action. He moved in quickly, bent over the fallen would-be assassin.

To his relief, the man was a complete stranger. Seemingly, he was an Arab. That, of course, meant little. He could have been a hired killer in the pay of Sverdlov, Tokugawa or, for all he knew, of some other element on the scene with whom Paul Kosloff was not as yet acquainted. Possibly even an adherent of either Moulay Ismail or Colonel Inan, although he doubted the first. The Marxist's government would not have to cut him down on the street. At their will, they could arrest him and put him to the question before dispatching him. And he doubted that the killer would have been sent by Sverdlov. The Russian, too, would be in position to eliminate him more efficiently than this demi-buttocked attempt. He doubted that Serge Sverdlov knew he was in the country.

But that cut down the possibilities drastically. Who else could possibly know he was here and would want to eliminate him? Battista? Could he be a double agent? Twenty years as an American agent in Maghrib – but that didn't mean a goddamned thing in this field. A double agent for whom?

He frisked the dead man quickly, efficiently, but, as he had suspected, the other bore no identity papers, nor anything else that would give a clue to who he was, who had sent him on his mission of death.

Paul Kosloff had to get out of the vicinity. The other might have an accomplice around, possibly a driver of a get-away car, possibly a back-up man. And, above that, a supposed American tourist should not be found bent over a corpse and in possession of a .38 Recoilless.

He hurried to the street, double-checked for anyone in the vicinity, then hurried along back to the hotel, his right hand ready to dart in for the gun again at the slightest indication of additional hostility.

Back at the hotel, he made no further effort to contact Battista but kept even closer to his rooms than he had before. In spite of the supposed ultra-security involved in this operation, he was already known by too many to be present in Tingis. The American agent knew where Paul Kosloff was and the only reason for their getting together again was when the plans had been completed for his meeting with Colonel Abou Inan.

At the end of the week, there was a discreet knock at the door. It was the boy who had been at Battista's shop, the agent's supposed son and also in the employ of the American government. When Paul Kosloff opened the door, the other side-stepped in. The international troubleshooter led him into the living room and looked at him.

The other was sharp. He pointed at his ear and then around the room, his face questioning. Paul Kosloff took him to the phone stand and pointed at it. He brought his electronic scrambler from his pocket and activated it momentarily.

He said, 'I'm afraid to keep this on for any length of time. Don't say anything you don't want heard.' He flicked the device off again.

The younger man nodded and said, 'Mr. Smithson, sir, I have made the arrangements for your drive into the countryside. I have rented a car.'

'Excellent,' Paul Kosloff said enthusiastically. 'When can we leave?'

'Immediately, sir. The car is outside the hotel. I am to be your chauffeur and guide.'

'Wait just a moment. I'll pack a small bag and get my camera.'

Paul Kosloff waited until they had got into the countryside on the outskirts of Tingis before saying anything of importance. American agents were now equipped with listening devices that could reach right into a car and take in a conversation. He assumed that the Soviet Complex operatives had similar advanced gear.

He said finally, 'All right. What's your name?'

'Nafi-ben-Mohammed.'

'What's your real name? You're an American, aren't you?'

'No. I am a national of Maghrib. I was educated in the American school of Tingis, before it was closed by Moulay Ismail. However, as you know, I am employed by the American government through Mohammed-ben-Abdallah, supposedly my father.'

Kosloff nodded. He said, 'Where are we going?'

'Colonel Abou Inan is still in the vicinity of Ksar-es-Souk, in a small town named Goulmimi. He is anxious for the meeting with you.'

'How far is it?'

'Perhaps five hundred kilometers.'

'About three hundred miles, eh? Can we make it in one day?'

'The roads are quite good. Built by the French in the old days. We should be able to.'

'Good. I'd just as well not have to stop for the night. No stops except for gas and food. Then there won't be any record of the trip.'

'Yes, sir.'

Paul Kosloff looked at the younger man from the side of his eyes. He said, 'What do you think of Colonel Inan?'

The other's voice took on a different tone. 'He is the sole hope of Maghrib.'

Paul Kosloff thought about that. He said, 'Are you armed?'

'Yes. The same as you. With a .38 Recoilless.'

'Ever had to use it?'

'Yes, sir. I've been in this service ever since the take-over of Moulay Ismail.'

'Dedicated, I see.'

The Moslem boy was embarrassed. He said, finally, 'My two older brothers were killed by the Marxists.' Then he added, 'They aren't really Marxists, of course.'

'They aren't? How do you mean?'

'A good many so-called Marxists in all parts of the world, including the Soviet Complex, pay lip service to his name and work but their governments have no similarity to what he was talking about. He wanted the State to wither away, they strengthen it and keep it in their own hands and to their own profit.'

Paul Kosloff looked at him from the side of his eyes again. 'Did you pick that up in the American school?'

The younger man was embarrassed again. 'No, sir. I used to study political economy on my own. That is why I support Colonel Inan. He wishes to bring both capitalism and democracy to Maghrib. He realizes that the country is not sufficiently developed to achieve to a more advanced society.'

'How do you mean, both capitalism and democracy? And how do you mean, a more advanced society?'

'The words are not synonymous, of course. You can have one without the other, in spite of our western propaganda to the contrary. For instance, we have had democratic societies down through the ages. In your own country, the American Indians were democratic before the coming of the white man, but they were certainly not capitalistic. Nor were the Greeks of the Golden Age. The economic system then was based on slaves. The government, though, was democratic. Hitler's regime was certainly not democratic, but it was capitalistic. Capitalism is an economic system, democracy a governmental one. Undoubtedly, one day capitalism will become antiquated, as both slavery and feudalism were in their time, but that does not mean that the next socio-economic system will not be democratic.'

The international troubleshooter said, 'Do you have a map of Maghrib here in the car?'

'Yes, sir. In the dash compartment there.'

Paul Kosloff got it and opened it up. 'Okay. Tell me the route you're taking, town by town. I want to know where we're going and how we're going to get back.'

'Oh, that won't be necessary. I'll drive both ways, and I know the route quite well.'

Paul Kosloff said coldly, 'I want to know in case something happens to you and I have to drive back myself.'

Damn it. Was he going to have to kill this one too? Thus far, he had liked the boy.

The town of Goulmimi was located in the High Atlas mountains about sixty-two kilometers from the desert city of Ksares-Souk. It was small and built of mud and reminded Paul Kosloff somewhat of the adobe pueblos of the American southwest. There were swarms of children, swarms of flies, a sufficiency of mangy dogs too listless to bark even at strangers.

Nafi seemed to know where he was going. He pulled down a narrow, dirty alley and came to a halt before a one-room mud brick house.

'We will wait here until summoned,' he said.

It was already evening and the light beginning to fade. Paul Kosloff took up his bag and they went inside. He looked around. There was a sole window in the rear of the hut. He went over to it and stared out, checking a possible means of emergency exit. It was just large enough for him to be able to wedge through, in case of need. It opened on another mud street, identical to the one they had just driven down.

There was no furniture in the hut. In fact, nothing at all save a pallet of straw covered with some dirty rags. Nafi, evidently perfectly at home in this atmosphere, squatted on his heels and looked patient. Paul Kosloff sat down with his back to the wall, his eyes on the door.

The knock came quicker than he had expected. He assumed that when they had entered Goulmimi they had been immediately spotted and that eyes had been on them ever since, though they had seen few adults in the streets.

He had his hand ready for a quick draw and motioned for Nafi to answer. There was a filthy-looking Arab there, djellabah-clad and barefooted. H spoke to Nafi in Arabic.

The young agent turned back to Paul Kosloff. 'You are to go alone. The colonel and his men await you.'

'All right.' He came to his feet, took off his coat and worked out of his shoulder holster. He handed gun and harness to Nafi. 'Take care of this for me.'

He followed his guide a few houses down the street to another mud house. The Arab opened the aged wooden door and held it as though in invitation for Paul Kosloff to enter. He did. The guide didn't follow.

Inside, it was already dim but Kosloff could make out the forms of three men seated cross-legged on a rug. They were dressed in brown wool djellabahs, the hoods over their heads so that their features could not be made out very well. However, the one in the center had a certain air of command, even through the clothing. The one on his right had a pistol in his hand and it was directed at Paul Kosloff's stomach.

The one in the center said softly, 'Harun,' and the one to his left came to his feet and approached the newcomer, taking care not to get between Paul Kosloff and the gun. He ran his hands over the international troubleshooter's body in a practiced frisk, then turned and spoke in Arabic and resumed his seat on the rug.

Paul Kosloff said, 'Colonel Inan? I am Kenneth Smithson, of the American State Department, assigned to open preliminary negotiations with you.'

'So we have been informed. This is Colonel Harun Idriss, my Chief of Staff, and this is Major Abd ibn-Tashfin, the leading theoretician of our movement. Please be seated, Mr. Smithson.'

Paul Kosloff also assumed the cross-legged position on a rug opposite them. He had to play this right. It couldn't be too obvious, or he'd never get his opening. He had to look authentic.

He said, 'Frankly, Colonel Inan, my superiors have doubts about some elements of your program and would like them resolved before they grant you the all-out support the State Department will possibly provide.'

The colonel pushed back the hood of his djellabah to reveal a dark, handsome face in the Semitic tradition. His nose was large and hooked, his eyes bright and piercing and intelligent.

He said, in his excellent English, 'Of course, Mr. Smithson. Proceed.'

Paul Kosloff said earnestly, 'Of prime importance is your proposal to double or more the price of the raw materials we are at present buying from Maghrib. Can we assume that this is but a campaign promise, as our politicians call them in the States? That is, that you don't really plan to go through with it?'

The colonel shook his head. 'No. It is no empty promise, Mr. Smithson.'

'If the other underdeveloped nations go along with you, it could eventually mean the collapse of the economies of the West.'

Abou Inan nodded his head this time. 'Yes, the collapse of the economies of the West, as we know them today.'

Paul Kosloff stared at him.

Major Abd ibn-Tashfin spoke up. 'You see, Mr. Smithson, the economies of the West are destroying our world with their ever-expanding production. Within decades, there will literally be no more raw materials. Our oil, our minerals, our forests, will have disappeared. The economies of the West, including your United States, must be forced to face reality and readjust. Yours is a waste economy! Let me use a few examples of planned obsolesence in your country. You build automobiles that will break down within three years or so, when it is quite possible to build them to last fifty years. You make lead batteries for your cars that are deliberately designed to wear out after a year and a half, where it is possible to build them to last the life of the car. You make electric light bulbs that burn out in one thousand hours, when they could be manufactured to last for practically the life of the house. The houses you build are slum houses in less than twenty years, while your grandparents could build them to last a century or more. All this, of course, to increase sales, to increase profits. Your socioeconomic system is one based on production for profit, not for use. It is a mad system and we of the more backward countries must do something to force you to change, or when you go down to economic chaos, you will drag us with you.'

Paul Kosloff was taken aback. He said, 'But we've got to have your raw materials if we're to keep going. We no longer have our own. And you've got to have the money we pay you for them, if you're ever to become a developed country.'

The colonel said softly, 'That is the point, Mr. Smithson. We are never going to become a developed country. Nor are any of the other underdeveloped nations. For one thing, there isn't enough copper, lead, zinc and other basic necessities of industry to allow the backward countries to ever catch up with you. You've totally wasted these irreplacable gifts of nature in your mad scramble for increased gross national product.'

'There are some other elements too, admittedly,' his Chief of Staff said. 'The population of the underdeveloped countries is growing far faster than the small industrial and agricultural growth they have achieved. And there seems to be no end. India, for instance, has a smaller per capita product today than she had when Ghandi and Nehru took over from England. How

68

this problem can be solved, we do not know. Perhaps through all-out collaboration of all countries. Thus far, there is no such thing. The advanced nations do not really care about our problems. We must force them to care.'

Paul Kosloff said, 'Then you are deliberately planning to wreck the economies of the West?'

'Not wreck them. Force them to change. If you are made to pay triple for your copper, I doubt if you will continue to make such items as ladies' lipstick containers out of it. If you pay triple for your chrome, I doubt if you will continue to make your cars garish with it. Somehow, we of the backward countries and you of the advanced, must amalgamate in such a way that we can improve our living standards without industrialization, but only by judicious exploitation of our raw materials and agriculture.'

Paul Kosloff pretended to think about it. He came to his feet and said, 'Just a moment. I wish to return to the hut in which you quartered me and get a device there with which I can communicate by tight-beam to Greater Washington. What you have said is most interesting. We weren't aware of your motivations.'

'Of course,' the colonel nodded.

Paul Kosloff left and returned to the hut where Nafi was still waiting.

He said to the young agent, 'Give me a gun.'

The other frowned at him.

Kosloff said impatiently, 'They want to see an example of the type of weapons we can supply for the revolution.'

The other handed the gun over and Paul Kosloff put it into his belt, under his coat. He turned and left the hut again and headed back toward the one occupied by Colonel Inan and his two top men. It was dark now and the streets were empty. He supposed that the colonel had deliberately kept his followers away from the secret conference, knowing that any spies might have reported the contact with an American emissary.

He squared his shoulders as he walked. It was simplicity itself. All he had to do was walk in and start firing. They would never suspect him of having a gun, since he had already been searched. He doubted if they were very old hands at intrigue. They were obviously too idealistic, too honest.

A slightly accented voice from behind him said, 'Very well,

Paul Kosloff. Put your hands behind your neck.'

He did as he was told and a hand came around from behind him and plucked the .38 Recoilless from his belt.

The voice said, 'Turn now.'

Paul Kosloff turned and said, 'Hello, Sverdlov. You're making a mistake, this time.'

The Russian KGB man was slightly smaller than Paul Kosloff but perhaps more lithe. His teeth were white and his smile good, but there was something about his eyes. It was said in international espionage circles that he had killed more men than the plague.

'Ah?' he said. 'Please elucidate, Kosloff.'

'This time, I have the same assignment you have. We're on the same side.'

'I doubt it.'

'I've been sent here to eliminate Colonel Inan and his two lieutenants. My government wants to see the regime of Moulay Ismail continue.'

'Ah, but mine doesn't,' the other said softly.

Paul Kosloff bug-eyed him.

The Russian agent chuckled. 'You see, Kosloff, in spite of the fact that we of the Soviet Complex and you of America have reached détente, the battle for men's minds goes on and will not end until one of our sides or the other prevails. We wish to see Colonel Inan's revolution succeed. If it does, his regime will be the first major element to collapse your economy. We have not been able to control Moulay Ismail, in spite of the fact that he calls himself a Marxist, but we won't have to control the colonel. He wants to do exactly what we would like him to do. We of the Soviet Complex have within our borders all the raw materials we need. You don't.'

Paul Kosloff looked at him for a long empty moment. He said, 'You mean that I, an agent of the West, have been sent to rescue a Marxist regime, and you, an agent of the Soviet Complex, have been sent to ensure a capitalist take-over?'

Serge Sverdlov chuckled again. 'Quite a contradiction, eh?' His finger began to tighten on the trigger of the large military revolver he carried.

A voice clipped from the darkness of a narrow alleyway between two mud huts, 'That will be all.'

Serge Sverdlov spun and, simultaneously, from the doorway of another hut a laser beam hissed out. Paul Kosloff took no time to discover who was the target of the deadly ray gun. He fell to the ground and rolled desperately.

Somebody had screamed in agony.

The Russian was also on the ground but seemingly not out of action. Footsteps came pounding down the street from the direction of the car.

Paul Kosloff had recognized the voice that had interrupted Serge Sverdlov as that of Colonel Inan. Evidently, the three revolutionists hadn't been as naïve as he had thought. They had followed him to check what he was doing.

Two djellabah-robed, hooded figures emerged from the narrow alley and spread out, seeking shadows. They both carried guns. Serge Sverdlov, from his prone position, began to bring up his revolver.

Nafi-ben-Mohammed, his own gun at the ready, came dashing up. He took in the figures on the ground. Paul Kosloff was still trying to roll to some sort of cover.

The Russian's pistol barked, at the same time that the laser beam hissed from the doorway across the street again. Tokugawa Hidetada stumbled forth from the mud hut, reeling, his pistol dropping from his hand.

Nafi's gun came up, the .38 Recoilless went ping, ping, ping, and two of the three slugs thunked into the prone Russian agent.

From the shadows into which the two figures from the narrow alley had faded came the colonel's voice again. 'Drop that gun, or you die, Nafi-ben-Mohammed!'

Nafi obeyed orders, then quickly leaned down over Paul Kosloff. 'You are unhurt?'

Paul Kosloff, in disgust, came to his feet. Now he could make out the fallen body in the narrow alleyway from which the colonel had first called.

'What is this, a damn massacre?' he growled.

He went over to Tokugawa Hidetada. His once Japanese colleague was going out fast. Paul Kosloff knelt beside him. 'Is there anything I can do?'

The small man attempted a rueful chuckle. 'In the crisis, I attempted to come to your succor, friend Paul. I am not very clear on what has happened. Whom did I shoot?'

Paul Kosloff took a deep breath. 'One of the Colonel's men, Hidetada.'

'It would be my fate for it to be Colonel Idriss,' the Japanese groaned. He closed his eyes in pain and never opened them again.

Paul Kosloff stood and looked back at Sverdlov. The Russian was also dead.

Colonel Abou Inan and Major Abd ibn-Tashfin emerged from the shadows, their guns still at the ready. The colonel's eyes took in the two fallen secret agents, then went back to his own valued follower.

He turned to Paul Kosloff and said, indicating the Japanese, 'Who is this man?'

'Tokugama Hidetada. His government wished to see Moulay Ismail overthrown, but Colonel Idriss come to power rather than you.'

'I see. And this one?' He indicated the Russian.

'Serge Sverdlov, of the KGB. His government wanted to see your revolution a success, so that the United States would be embarrassed.'

'I see.' The colonel looked at Paul Kosloff and Nafi for a long thoughtful moment. He said, 'I heard enough of your conversation with the Russian to realize that you are not truly interested in supporting my cause. Perhaps I should kill you, Mr. Smithson, but I am not one who kills unarmed men. Please leave. And so far as your nations are concerned, the United States, the Soviet Complex, Japan, all I can do is paraphrase the English poet. A curse on all your houses.'

Nafi blurted, 'But Colonel, we came to assist you.'

'It seems unlikely, boy. Now leave.'

Paul Kosloff and the Maghrib youth returned to their car. In silence, they got into it and started back for Tingis.

After a time, Paul Kosloff put his Tracy to his mouth and said, 'Paul calling. Paul calling.'

The commissioner's thin voice came through shortly. 'Yes, I receive you. What is happening?'

Paul said flatly, 'Everything and its cousin has gone to pot. Sverdlov's dead. Tokugawa Hidetada, of Japan, is dead. I'm not, but probably should be. Your strategy laid an egg. Colonel Inan will undoubtedly take over here.'

'You fouled this up, Kosloff!'

'It's according to how you look at it. It was foul before it started,' Paul Kosloff said wearily. 'Oh, yes, and one more thing. I'm tired of being the Cold War's Lawrence of Arabia. It's getting too complicated for me. I'm resigning.'

THE
FACTORY

Naomi Mitchison

*Lady Mitchison will be seventy-five this year and has been
publishing about a book a year since 1923. She spends at least
three months of each year in Botswana where she is the
adopted mother of the chief of the Bakgatla tribe, and still
more time in Scotland where she runs a three-hundred-acre
farm, as well as working as a member of the Highlands and
Islands Development Council. When describing her and her
manifold activities superlatives come easy – so suffice to say
that this piece of fiction is a tight, grim and near perfect story
about our environment.*

The factory people have been ever so nice, really they have.
They needn't have; they'd kept all the regulations, strictly
kept them. We couldn't have had the law on them in spite of
what Ted and the newspaperman said. But it's been a bit of a
shock, I won't deny that. Above forty years I've been on the
farm and my husband he'd been born there. You get to belong
with a place and know every brick, you do. Not that I wouldn't
sometimes say to him, 'Wouldn't you like a nice job in town
and not the cows every blessed morning and evening of the
year?' But that was what he wanted. You know, he wants it
yet. He misses it.

   It was a calf died first and the vet, well he didn't know
what to make of it: ever such a nice man, Mr. Thompson the
vet, but I haven't seen him now, not for a year, and he used to
drop in most every week and eat a slice of my cake. Kind of
fits they had, the poor little dears, heifer calves they was. And
then the cows began to take sick but they didn't die, not at
first, only the milk went off. You know, I wonder sometimes if
anything ever ailed any of the folk that drank the milk. But
then, I'll never know. The next to go were my ducks. I found
them dead in the long grass. Thought it was a stoat, I did, but
there wasn't a mark on them.

   It was then the gentleman that used to have the trout fish-ing began to notice there was sick fish floating belly up. That got round to Mr. Thompson and he took samples of the water and sent 'em to London. Clear water it was, all along the river; many a nice bunch of watercress I picked off the edges in the old days and looked down at it bubbling away over pebbles.

We'd all been ever so pleased when the factory came on the old mill site. It was giving a bit of extra work and men stayed at home that would have needed to go and get work in the towns in the old days. I remember me saying to my husband, why wasn't that there when our boys went off? Once they go, you see, there's nothing to tell of them, they wander off. One of them's in Australia now, a terrible long way, and then there's our Ted. He had a job up in Yorkshire. Yes, I used to think, if the factory had only come sooner! And they could have given their Dad a hand with the Sunday milking so he could have lain in bed once in a while. Well, he can do that now.

It was before the samples came back that poor Rover took his first fit. Oh, he was ever such a good dog, he could bring the cows in on his own. We put him on the rug in front of the fire and gave him milk. But he died. Mr. Thompson, the vet, was there and he couldn't understand it. There was my poor husband with Rover in his arms and Mr. Thompson standing there ever so upset. Mopped his eyes, he did. We were that worried about the cows too.

I found one of the kittens dead the next day, the black and white one. That settled me. I sent off a wire to our Ted saying as how there was trouble. I didn't tell my poor husband but I got Ted's room in the attic all ready. He came the same day and we heard about the sample. Well, they found there was a trace of something, a long name it had and must have come from the factory. Mr. Thompson was ever so puzzled. He couldn't see how so little could have done so much harm. But he rung up the factory and there was a man from London, a government man, who come down to see about it. That was the day my hens began to go, but they went quick, one big flutter and then dead.

And there was our Ted in a proper rage. Talked about suing the factory. There was nowhere else could be blamed. Two of the cows had died by then, the rest were poorly. Mr. Thompson said we must stop selling the milk. Not that there was

74

much to sell. I gave it to the kittens that were left and wondered if I should have. You know, I kept on catching myself putting out scraps for Rover.

Ted went off up the road to the factory; his Dad tried to stop him, said it wouldn't do any good. But Ted went steaming off and his poor Dad went back to the cows. There was another one going. One of the neighbors was giving a hand to bury them.

Ted was a long time gone. I put the kettle on to boil and then took it off. There was a dead rat outside the door. I never thought I'd grieve to see a dead rat. It was late when Ted got back and he seemed terrible downhearted. 'They showed me the regulations,' he said. 'It appears they kept to them. Took me all over they did. Safeguards. Checks. Warnings. The government man, he saw them too. Nothing wrong with any of the chaps working there; special gloves and all they wore.' There wasn't anything I could say. He went on, 'You don't know, Mum. Regulations. Stacks of them. So then this is an act of God. Where's Dad?'

But I didn't hardly like to tell him that his Dad was down at the cow shed, cleaning, cleaning, cleaning where the dead cows had been. Taking down the board with their names – Daisy, Cowslip, Elsie. Burning them.

Mr. Thompson came in. He had been up at the far end of the wood. There was a young fellow there with a pair of golden retriever pedigree dogs. The bitch was due to pup in a few days time. It was the same story. Mr. Thompson was worried because old Mr. Hugget at Rose Cottage always had a pig at the back and it seemed the pig began to sicken, so Mr. Hugget took it off to the slaughterhouse; they didn't see anything wrong with it. Then he started smoking the sides and ham the way he had always done. But what was going to come of it when he started eating the bacon? Mr. Thompson was ever so upset over this. But I couldn't somehow seem to care.

It was after that the newspapermen began to come and we had our photos in the papers. It made a break like, for we were feeling that low, all of us. The cows were all going or gone. The rest of the kittens were dead. Every blessed one of my ducks and hens. Ted and the newspapermen they began totting it all up in money, what we had lost. But we couldn't think of it that way, not at first. It was just that we had always had these living things round us, we were used to the little noises,

75

gabble and scratch, lowing, rustling, barking. A quiet farm isn't a farm at all somehow.

A gentleman came down from the factory. He explained how it wasn't their fault, they had kept strict regulations and what they were making was ever so useful, a poison spray to deal with some kind of insect that had come from abroad. He kept using long words we couldn't make out. He offered us a check for £800 and a paper for us to sign. It seemed a lot of money to me. Most years we didn't make the half of £800. But there was the milk and eggs that we kept for ourselves. I didn't know.

Dad was for taking it, saying as it wasn't their fault and nothing in law that they was bound to do. But Ted came in and he had one of the newspapermen with him. Ted took the check out of his Dad's hands and tore it right across. All that money! It was vexing.

And the newspaperman he said to Dad, 'Are you aware, sir, that you will have to leave your farm? It will be unsafe for stock for many years.'

'Who says?' Dad asked dazed like.

'That's the verdict,' said the newspaperman. 'Ask your vet.'

'Of course if that were to turn out to be the case,' said the gentleman from the factory and he looked kind of annoyed, 'we would see that compensation was on a generous basis.' All those long words and Dad and me struck all of a heap. We hadn't thought. Not of that one. Neither of having to leave the place.

But it was true. Mr. Thompson said so too. I've been to the farm since. We try and keep the glass in the windows and the tiles on the roof. But the weeds! You've no idea the way a decent field grows up. Nettles and dockens. And coming through in the yard everywhere. Why couldn't this stuff kill the weeds instead of killing our beasts? You hardly see even a sparrow now.

But they gave Dad this job, cleaning and caretaking. Maybe you would say it wasn't a man's job. And his heart's not in it right enough. And they put us in a little house with roses and all in the garden, oh ever so nice they've been, I don't know what we would have done but for the factory.

THE
DEFENSIVE
BOMBER

Hank Dempsey

When this story was written United States airplanes had been bombing Vietnam for years too bitter to count. While this anthology was being edited and published the bombing continued, though still without cause or reason. May it have stopped forever by the time you read these words.

Like all Tokyo hotels the Okura was an ant nest of industry, a crush of hurrying people, rushing porters, harried clientele; a flux of movement everywhere, from the varied restaurants on the lower floors up to the bars in the tower above that looked out upon the romantic sea of illuminated smog below. The three men in dark suits were Oriental and invisible, moving through the crowd so easily that none remarked their passing. They came by different ways and met on the nineteenth floor, casually as though by chance, then walked slowly to the door of room 1913 where the largest of them waited, then knocked softly as soon as the hallway was clear. In a moment the door opened and a young man looked out at them, glancing from face to face.

'Iran Tuan Nham?' the large man asked. The youth in the doorway nodded.

As though this were a signal the three of them pushed forward, crowding close to Iran Tuan Nham who was startled and opened his mouth to speak. But before he could say anything there was a muffled thud, not unlike the sound of two books being clapped together, and he shuddered and died as the bullet from the silenced revolver penetrated his heart. He could not fall because the three men held him up and rushed him backward through the door which closed behind them. Just a few seconds later a bellboy trundled a laden trolley by, completely unaware that anything unusual had taken place.

Iran Tuan Nham looked passively out of the window as they

left the sun-glittering blue of the Pacific Ocean behind. The Boeing 707 of Air Japan crossed the beach-fringed, freeway-slashed California coastline, throttling back to begin a long slow turn. Lower it fell as its landing gear thudded into place, dropping down toward the white towers of San Diego, swooping even lower until it was beneath these towers and setting down upon the runway of Lindbergh Field. Flight 398, Tokyo-San Diego had arrived. Unhurriedly, Iran Tuan Nham gathered together his belongings, took his raincoat from the rack above and joined the line of exiting travelers.

John Patrick Hanrahan had been a United States customs officer for twenty-three years and he was used to the job. He neither liked it nor disliked it: he did it. Everything was routine including a routine alertness so that in his time he had apprehended jewel smugglers, heroin runners, hemp-heads and many others, because of their nervousness, or a beading of sweat upon the brow, something out of the ordinary. Of course it was hard with Orientals. They all looked alike for one thing. Like this guy. The picture on the passport could have been any one of them. Black hair. Sallow skin. Those eyes. Not smiling, not giving anything away. Young, twenty-three the passport said. Could have been thirteen or thirty-three for all he could tell. Occupation: student.

'Is this your first visit to the United States, Mr. Nham?'

'It is. I am here to attend your university. It is upon the invitation of your State Department. A scholarship.'

'That's very good,' Hanrahan said as his rubber stamp came down, the student already forgotten as out of the corner of his eye he sized up the next woman in line. Mink stole, sweating. Nervous or just hot? The rich ones were the amateur smugglers, that was for sure. He beckoned her forward while looking her up and down with his coldest face.

'Will you open them up, please?' Miguel Rodriguez, United States customs officer, said. All luggage on the flights from the Orient were looked through. There were too many things out there that made a very good profit for smugglers, part-time or professional. Drugs, pearls, ivory, gems, all small, all easy to hide. With practiced skill he flipped through the neatly packed clothing, then ran his fingers lightly around the lining of the two suitcases. Nothing there, nothing of suspicion among the toilet items. A soft plastic bag in the pocket of the second case. He withdrew it carefully and held it up. Military-looking buttons, pins, insignia of some kind – marked very prominently with a red star. Holding out the bag to its owner he allowed his eyebrows to rise more than slightly.

'These are from the uniform of a North Vietnamese flying officer,' Iran Tuan Nham said expressionlessly. 'I have brought them as souvenirs to American friends who have so graciously invited me to your country where I shall study at your university.'

'Well, now how about that!' Miguel was impressed. 'Those dark spots there might even be blood. Shot down.' But their owner showed no desire for conversation and merely stood and watched quietly, impassively. Miguel put them back in the pocket, closed the cases and scrawled a cabalistic symbol in chalk upon each of them, then turned to the next man down the counter.

Without haste Iran Tuan Nham smoothed out the clothing and relocked the cases, then, taking one in each hand, walked past the porters to the exit to the street. There was a row of waiting taxicabs here, great yellow swollen things, big as were all of the American cars that were parked row upon row in the lot beyond. This was obviously a very rich country.

'Mr. Nham?' a voice asked. He turned about and said, 'That is my name.'

The gaily dressed youth was very nervous. He chewed at the ragged moustache that drooped over his mouth, his eyes moving from side to side constantly, looking at everyone that passed. Suddenly he leaned forward, so close he breathed in Nham's face, his breath smelling unpleasantly of meat, and whispered.

'*In proportion as the antagonism between the classes vanishes...*'

'. . . the hostility of one nation to another will come to an end,' Nham responded. 'Is there any reason why such a long countersign was needed?'

'It's from Karl Marx.'

'Ahh, yes, that explains it. A very long-winded writer.'

The young man seemed annoyed at this. 'Come on, here's the car.'

A very unlikely vehicle shuddered to a stop just before them. The body, which was shaped like a stepped-on bathtub, was purple in color and glistened with stars. The back wheels appeared to be twice as big as the front so that the car leaned forward as though ready to spring. The rear engine was exposed and the exhaust pipe rose high into the air like a snake. The driver, also young, wore a fringed buckskin outfit and a hat of red, white and blue stripes and stars. He jerked his thumb to the seat beside him as the first man took Nham's bag and climbed into the back. No sooner were they seated than the car leaped forward and rushed toward the exit from the airport.

'You can call me Dick,' the driver said. 'And he's Spiro. Not our real names, you know, a precaution for later. How was the flight?'

'A wise precaution. Very smooth, thank you.'

'No trouble with customs or immigration or anything?'

'None that I noticed. Of course we might be under surveillance.'

'We ain't being tailed,' Spiro said, watching the road behind them.

'I'll make sure of that.'

The car sped up a ramp and onto a great highway where countless rows of cars hurtled by at tremendous speeds. With practiced skill the driver inserted their vehicle into the stream, cutting in and out to change lanes. The stench of burned gasoline was unbelievable, the entire scene a surrealistic one to Nham. He held hard to a handle on the dash before him as they suddenly shot across the lanes and out an exit, turning quickly into a side street between high buildings in apparent indifference to a large red sign that read STOP. The car shuddered to a halt at the curb and the driver pulled on the handbrake and jumped out.

'I'll wipe it down,' he said, taking a rag from his pocket and scrubbing at the steering wheel. 'You two get to the other car and wait.'

'Come on.' Spiro grabbed up the bags again and Nham hurried after him.

'What is he doing?'

'Fingerprints. That rig is hot. He hot-wired it at Cal West about an hour ago. The dude who owns it is still in class so he hasn't called the fuzz. And if they're trying to follow us they'll be looking for that Baja buggy and not this Detroit iron.'

He put the bags into a battered and very dirty sedan and got behind the wheel. A number of the terms he used were obscure but Nham understood the plan well enough.

'Very well done.'

Dick hurried up a few moments later. 'No cars, no one watching. We're clean.'

They continued through back streets to a residential part of the city, elegant homes set among green lawns and palm trees.

'Look, this may sound funny,' Spiro said, chewing at his moustache again. 'But could you, like, close your eyes? Just for a bit. The street names, you know . . .'

'I understand.' It was a wise precaution. He kept his eyes resolutely shut until the car stopped. They were in the driveway of a one-story house, very much like the others, and he knew that he could lead no one here no matter what forms of coercion were used. The side door opened as they approached, then was quickly closed and locked behind them.

'This is the rest of us,' Dick said. 'Pat, Martin-Luther, meet the man.'

He first shook hands with Pat, a slim girl with very sincere eyes, long, straight blond hair and surprisingly large breasts inside a white sweater. Vietnamese girls were slight and usually very small on top. Martin-Luther was a very dark Negro with long stiff hair that had been combed out into a great sphere around his head. His grip was hard and he did not smile.

'Listen, let's go into the living room,' Pat said, eagerly. 'Drinks there, a toast, you know, this is a historical moment.'

'You better believe it,' Dick said, then led the way.

'Bourbon, scotch, tequila, you name it, my dad has it,' Pat said. 'He's at work now, Mom's playing bridge, we're okay.'

'Thank you, but I do not drink alcoholic beverages.'

'Sure, well, there's always coke. Or would you like a cup of tea?'

'The coke will be fine. But if you have tea . . .'

'I'll make some. But, you know, we could toast first.'

They stood in a circle, no longer smiling, their glasses raised. 'How about you, Spiro,' Pat said. 'It was your idea, the whole thing.'

He straightened up and stopped chewing his moustache.

'All right. Here's to it then. Success.'

'Success.'

They spoke the word together, emotionally. There was no turning back now, not with him here.

'Is it all right?' Spiro said. 'I mean to know what your name is, really is?'

'Of course. That is no secret now. I am Lieutenant Tran

81

Hung Dao. Iran Tuan Nham was a student from Saigon who was on his way here. I used his passport and identity merely to enter the country.'

'You say *was* . . .' Pat spoke from the doorway where she stood, holding a steaming cup. 'Is he dead?'

'I assume so. I do not know. I was not involved in that part of the operation. I was sent to Tokyo where his things were given to me.'

'He's dead,' Martin-Luther said it flatly. 'Have you forgot there's a war on? He's not the first one to die.'

'Nor will he be the last,' Lieutenant Dao said. The girl still stood with the cup before her, eyes wide with the reality of death coming that close. Dao had been a lot closer, very often. 'If that is my tea I would appreciate it.'

'Yes, sure, I'm sorry.' She hurried over with the cup of hot water, a white packet in the saucer beside it.

'Tea?' he asked, unsure.

'In the bag, just put it in the water, that's right. Milk and sugar?'

'Sugar, please, if it is not too much trouble.'

'Everything is ready for today,' Spiro said, 'if you want to do it today.'

'I am perfectly agreeable as long as it can be done before nightfall. Everything has been arranged?'

'All set. The stuff is back in the hills, a ranch, burned out in the fires last year so no one's there. But it has a landing strip. We put down a deposit to rent a plane, this afternoon. I have a pilot's license, you have to have it to rent a plane.'

'You are a flyer then?'

'No. I took a couple of lessons so I could talk right, sound like I knew what it was all about. But I have a fake license. It's just a photocopy but we touched it up so it looks like the real thing. Look good to you?' He held it out and Dao bent over it.

'I have no way of telling. It appears to be very official.'

'We rolled a guy for it,' Dick said, smiling happily. 'My department. You might say I worked my way through school that way. Rolling guys I mean. We hung around the airport until we spotted a guy parking a private plane that looked a lot like Spiro here.'

'The man in this photo has no moustache.'

'I'll shave mine off before we go.'

'See, all worked out. I mugged the guy in the parking lot, out cold, got his wallet. Then we used the Xerox machine in the library to copy the license. Cleaned the money out, he was heeled, over two hundred bucks, put the license back in the wallet with all his credit cards then dumped it in a mailbox. That way he doesn't cry to the pigs about it being missing and people notified.'

'Very good. If the license will stand up to examination.'

'They don't look close. I hung around and watched them rent out a couple of planes. It'll work.'

'How is the tea?' Pat asked.

He took a sip of the bold, bitter, badly. brewed mixture.

'Very good. My kindest thanks. Do you have my uniform?'

'Rented it from a costume place in Hollywood yesterday, took all the buttons and crap off,' Dick said. 'We got a French Air Force one like you said.'

'Ours is modeled after it. If you would please bring it in I have my buttons and insignia here.'

'I'll sew them on,' Pat said, hurrying out.

Dao took the plastic bag from the suitcase and sealed it again.

'I need nothing else from these cases. Would you kindly dispose of them so they cannot be found? And this passport as well.'

Dick took it from him. 'Burn this. Bury them in the country. No sweat.'

'The wings go here,' Dao said, touching the left breast of the uniform above the pocket. 'The buttons of course you know. These are my lieutenant's insignia.'

'You speak great English,' Pat said, threading her needle.

'That is why I was chosen. It is my field, I have my degree in English literature, Shakespeare is my specialty. Before I became a pilot of course.'

'Fly MIGs?' Martin-Luther asked.

'I did. But transports from China the last few years.'

'Christ, I need a drink,' Spiro said, pouring a good two inches of bourbon and raising it to his lips. Martin-Luther took him suddenly by the wrist.

'Don't get drunk, man. Can't do nothing with you wiped out.'

'Listen to him,' Dick said. 'Put it down.'

Spiro looked from one to the other, chewing at the straggling hairs on his lips. 'Shit. I got to shave this thing off. I just wanted a little one.'

'A little one,' Martin-Luther said. 'Later. Before we leave.'

He took the glass and put it on the table. Spiro's neck was red as he stamped from the room.

'He's a good kid,' Dick said. 'But got too much imagination. He'll be all right.'

'I have no doubt about that. I think you are all all right. I think you are very brave and fine people to do what you are doing. What you are doing is harder to do than to surrender and fight in the army or the navy. I have been asked to tell you officially that the People's Republic of Vietnam considers you heroes—'

'I don't want to be no fuckin' slope hero,' Martin-Luther burst in. 'I want to be an American who wants us out of this goddam war before we tear ourself and the world in two. I want some of the goddamn megabucks we been spending on bombs spent in the black ghettos so my people can get away from the rats and the dirt and have what every honky bastard has, just some kind of decent life. That's what I want. And you people can stay over there and do exactly what you want to each other.'

'I agree completely.' Dao's voice was just as coldly angry. 'We will stay in our country and you will stay in yours. That is just the way I would like it.'

The tension slowly eased away. Martin-Luther made himself a drink and sipped it, scowling at nothing. Pat finished her sewing on the uniform and showed Dao a room where he could change. When he returned wearing it they were aware of a difference, as though he were bigger, stronger.

'I can put the cap in my pocket, and I will wear my raincoat which will conceal the uniform. But I will need a scarf of some kind around my neck.'

'My dad has one,' Pat said. 'As long as you give it back.'

An hour later they left in two cars. Spiro drove Dao, his breath still strong with the last small drink that had been poured for him.

'We're going to Brown Field. You know where it is?'

'I have studied the maps you supplied with great care. It is south of San Diego, approximately fourteen miles, perhaps two miles inland from the ocean, the same distance north of the Mexican border.'

'Right on. There's a rental place there. They're holding a four-place plane like you said. I left a deposit. We're supposed to be going to San Francisco, that's the flight plan I filed. Everything will be okay.' The last was more a question than a statement and his knuckles were white where he gripped the steering wheel too hard.

'Everything will go fine,' Dao said, in what he hoped was a relaxed tone. 'Once I have the plane your part will be done. You will not be connected with what happens.'

'We have plans for that. Dave – I mean Dick – look, forget that name will you please? Dick and I are supposed to be camping in Arizona. We really are, we have the camp site receipts. But we drove back last night, then we'll leave again as soon as you take off. They'll never tie us into this.'

They turned into a narrow road that wound up through low, sun-scorched hills to the airport. Brown Field, a naval training station during the Second World War, now a little-used civilian field. Past a silent, faded mess hall, rows of sealed barracks a drab setting for the colorful rows of light planes. Spiro parked the car where it could not be seen from the flight line and they walked slowly toward the office with the large RENTALS sign over it. A middle-aged man chewing an unlit cigar looked up from behind the desk when they came in.

'My name's Morgan, I phoned about a rental, mailed a deposit . . .'

'Yeah, right here.' He flipped through the file folders on the desk. 'License.'

Spiro handed it over, attempting to be nonchalant and realizing that his hands were shaking. Dao was silent and calm beside him and it helped a bit. The man at the desk squinted at the license, then wrote in the forms before him. He started to hand the license back – then halted and looked at it closely. Spiro felt as though he were going to die.

'You know you got less than three weeks before this thing expires?' the man said.

'I know.' His voice sounded strange in his own ears; would the other notice? 'But I'm just going away for two days. I'll renew it when I come back.'

The license was returned, the papers passed across the counter. Cramping the pen in his fingers he forged the signature he had practiced so often.

'The red Comanche,' the man said. 'Third down the line

there, tank full, altimeter zeroed for this field. Here's the keys.'

Spiro nodded, unable to speak again, and left with Dao close behind him, forcing himself to walk slowly.

'You get in the pilot's side,' Dao said. 'Pretend to work the controls. I will do everything with the dual controls.'

The climbed in and Dao tested the controls with slow precision, moving the rudder back and forth and flapping the ailerons up and down while Spiro beat his fist into his palm with silent agony. Dao was priming the engine when there was the quick sound of running feet and a man's voice calling to them loudly. They sat in numb silence as the man from the office hurried up.

'Listen, you forgot your copy of the agreement. You don't want to do that.'

'No, of course, sorry,' Spiro said, aware that his face was damp with sweat and hoping the other would not notice it. He opened the door and took the paper. The man looked at him and frowned. Then shrugged slightly and turned back to the office.

Dao did indeed know how to fly. He started the engine, revved it until it was running smoothly, then released the brakes and taxied out to the runway. The tower gave them clearance, then they were rushing down the ancient, patched concrete and into the air.

'I thought I was going to die,' Spiro shouted above the roar of the engine.

'It went quite smoothly. What is my heading?'

'What? Oh, east I guess, follow the roads. It shouldn't take us long.'

'Would it not be wise to go north until we are out of sight of this field? Toward San Francisco.'

'Right, good idea, I'll tell you when to turn.'

The ranch was beyond the coastal plain and rolling hills, almost at the foot of the Sierra Nevada mountains. A handful of blackened buildings and a dusty landing strip with a car parked at the end, three people standing beside it. Dao flew low the length of the strip, then pulled up in a tight turn. It seemed in good repair. Throttling back he headed back into the wind and did a neat three-point landing in the middle of the strip, then taxied to the waiting car and killed the engine.

'Was it okay, go all right?' Pat asked, white-faced now that planning had become reality.

'They here, that's enough to know,' Martin-Luther said abruptly. 'We dug the stuff up and got it in the car.'

They climbed down from the plane and looked in the open rear door of the sedan.

'Five pounds of black powder each,' Dick said. 'Packed into old gallon paint cans. Plaster of Paris on top to fill the cans.'

'And the fuses?' Dao asked. Dick grinned, but not happily.

'Well, that was kind of hard to do. The kind they wanted, I mean. So I used regular fuse cord cut for fifteen seconds like they said . . .'

His voice ran down into silence at the cold anger in Dao's face, his finger shaking with rage as he pointed at the cans.

'You mean you did this thing without consulting us? Did not put on the friction fuses as you were instructed? Jeopardized everything with your stupidity. Do you think I have three arms? I can fly the plane with one hand, yes, while at the same time pulling the ring to actuate a friction fuse. That I can do. But how can I fly, light a match, ignite a fuse, put out the match, pick up the can—'

He choked into impotent silence and they were silent as well, Dick looking at the ground with his fists clenched. Dao looked into face after face and they did not answer him.

'The answer is that I cannot. So what do we do? Too much has been done to abandon this project now. I will fly the plane. One of you must come with me to light the fuses.'

They were ashamed of themselves even as they found excuses. It was no longer a game. Lieutenant Tran Hung Dao, the professional, listened in angry silence while they talked. He had nothing more to say. But he did notice that Martin-Luther had not joined the others so was not surprised when he spoke now.

'Bunch of cheap honky copouts.' He spat meaningfully into the dust before their feet. 'Been having a good time? Playing at war? Well the war's come home now and you want no part of it. What about it, Lieutenant, can you set me down someplace after the fun is over?'

'I see no reason why not. If you will show me where.'

'I'll just do that.' He jerked his thumb at the plane. 'C'mon you ofay bastards, load up for the man.'

Little more was said as they stowed the cans in the two rear seats. Pat had three disposable cigarette lighters in her

87

purse and she gave them to Martin-Luther. 'Good luck,' she said.

'We'll need it, kid. Now split, whitey, because the inferior races are now going to carry the ball.'

Dao took off the raincoat and scarf and handed them to Pat, then pulled on his uniform cap. The engine started easily and they taxied to the end of the strip and turned around. Before they took off the car was already bouncing back down the rutted road and Martin-Luther snorted with contempt. 'What's the plan?' he asked as they became airborne.

'Ream Field first. Come in from the sea, very low, make a pass. Turn, make a second pass and back to sea again.'

'That's all?'

'That's the beginning.'

The plane climbed to five thousand feet and hummed back toward the Pacific Ocean, just inside the border. Dao examined Ream Field with great interest as they passed just south of it. The Helicopter Capital of the World, a major training base. Copters lifted and landed, stood in long neat rows. Then they were over the water and starting a long turn, dropping lower. The waves were sharp and clear just below them as they headed back toward shore. Dao rammed the throttle as far forward as it would go and the engine roared loudly in their ears.

'Get ready!' he shouted. Martin-Luther, his lap full of cans, flicked the lighter on and off and smiled crookedly. 'I sure am,' he said.

The beach appeared suddenly ahead with the low dunes behind it. The plane zoomed up over them and there was the airfield just beyond.

'Windows open – ready – light the first when I say *now* and keep lighting them. Pass them to me. *Now!*'

The light plane rushed at the row of parked helicopters and Dao felt the wire handle slapped hard into his palm. He heaved the can up and out of the window and was ready for another one. Two more went after the first before they reached the buildings beyond. He waved his hand at Martin-Luther who snuffed out the fuse he had just lit.

'Lemme drop one this time?' he shouted.

'Yes. But no casualties if they can be avoided. Matériel, machines and trucks, they are our targets.'

The light plane screamed up and around in a gut-wrenching

88

turn, then they were headed back in the direction they had come. The scene had changed drastically in the few seconds since they passed. Smoke was billowing up from the row of copters, men were running; the airfield a beehive disturbed. Faces stared up at them, then the sailors and marines dived for cover as the plane appeared again.

'That's mine!' Martin-Luther shouted as he lit the fuses again. Passing two of the homemade bombs to Dao he lit another and dropped it in the direction of a parked gasoline truck. It must have hit right on it because the black explosion was followed instantly by a billowing column of flame. He shouted wordlessly with excitement and banged his fist against the window edge. 'What now?' he asked as they hedgehopped the beach and were back over the sea.

'Anything following us?'

'A 'copter I think – no, it's just turning. They don't know what happened, just don't know what hit them.'

'I hope that is true. The element of surprise is all we have. North Island is our next target.'

'You got to be kidding! They got fighter planes there, guns, Christ, flattops with AA batteries, cruisers . . .'

'All with their weapons unloaded I am sure. We will find out soon.'

'I give you that, Tran, you got guts. Take on a whole goddam big navy base.'

'The bigger the statement we make, the better it will be heard. A single pass there will suffice—'

'I'll buy that, baby!'

'Then we will go straight on, very low, to the Naval Air Station at Miramar, north of San Diego. It is no more than two minutes flying time. A single pass there, and then I land and surrender. I am in uniform, a prisoner of war, I will be treated just as we treat your fliers that bomb our country. As I said, a statement. But what about you?'

'Me, Miramar is perfect. Look, they got runways a couple of miles long, they end way out in the shrub. Go to the end, go off into the dirt when you turn, throw up a big cloud of dust. I'll bail out in the dust, lie quiet, get away while they're grabbing you. I can do it.'

'I sincerely hope that you do. Now get ready, there is the base ahead.'

Buildings, hangars rose before them, the gray forms of looming warships beyond. There seemed to have been no warning. Dao reached for the first bomb and waggled the wings in a sudden turn.

'There, F-4 fighter bombers, the kind that have ravaged my country.'

The bombs sent up black columns of smoke and hurtling chunks of metal. One after another fell; then they were past the flight line and turning toward the harbor beyond. The aircraft carrier was dead ahead, the island rising up like a tall building, faces peering at them from it. As they zoomed close they had an instant glimpse of a marine on the bridge with his automatic clutched in both hands, pointing at them, firing. It was the only sign of resistance they were aware of. Then the can was dropping toward the deck, bouncing and falling over the side to explode harmlessly in the water.

'Stay low, follow the freeway,' Martin-Luther called out.

Dao started to answer him -- then grabbed at the controls as the engine spluttered and died.

'What is it?' Martin-Luther screeched in the sudden silence.

'Don't know. Something hit the engine. All the oil is gone.'

'A bullet? They shot us?'

'Maybe. Piece of metal. Where can I land?'

'Nothing here, all roads and houses. In the water?'

'No! I might be drowned, not be found. They must understand who did this and why. Lindbergh Field the other side of the harbor. I think we can make it.' He touched the controls delicately to lengthen their glide.

'What about me?'

'I'm sorry. You will have to come with me. Perhaps you can get out of the plane.'

Martin-Luther cursed wordlessly, slamming his fist against the seat as they came in low, their landing gear just above the tuna boats at the dock, over the street and clearing the fence about the field, setting down neatly at the end of the runway, still going too fast for Martin-Luther to jump free.

A low service truck darted out of the terminal ahead, pulling into the runway before them, braking to a stop, the driver diving out the far side and running.

Dao stood on the brakes so the plane skidded and slewed, crashing sideways into the truck. They were dazed, pained and numb with the impact, the bombs rolling about their feet. Before they could recover, react, the doors of the terminal burst

90

open and passengers, mechanics, airline personnel, pilots, stewardesses, everyone ran toward the wrecked plane.

'They know,' Martin-Luther said. 'The radio, they heard.'

'We will surrender, just as your pilots do. They bomb our hospitals and schools, three-quarters of my home town, Nam Dinh, has been destroyed. Thousands killed. Yet we only imprison your pilots.'

Martin-Luther did not answer, could not, just stared at the screaming mob with wide eyes, unable to move, filled with a sudden presentiment of what was happening.

'Lock your door!' he shouted suddenly. 'Jam it shut, don't open it, wait until the cops come, the military, we gotta hold on.'

Lieutenant Tran Hung Dao now understood as well, looking at the screaming mouths, the clawed hands, the upraised tools. He clutched at the door handle as a wrench crashed into the window by his face.

'Prisoner of war! I am in uniform. For ten years you have done this to my country. Five billion dollars in bombs a year. Killed, maimed, women, children . . .'

The door was pulled from his clutch and fingers tore at him.

'Policeman! There, you, help me . . .' The policeman's fist hit him square on the face, destroying one eye.

Many hands pulled him from the plane, tore open the other door and wrenched a screaming Martin-Luther to the ground.

Fists, heels, shoes, ground and tore the life from them, battering them into blindness, maiming them before they killed them, tearing the clothes from their bodies to get at the softer flesh beneath.

The Marines, from the Marine Corps Depot beside the field, had to climb a high fence, so by the time they arrived there was little left. But they did stamp at the bloodied remains with their hard boots.

The crime these two had committed was unforgivable. They goddamn well got what they deserved.

ENDORSEMENT,
PERSONAL

Dean McLaughlin

Despite great evidence to the contrary, scientists are human beings.

Dr. Norbert Denhouter
Director: Midwest Institute for Advanced Studies
Iowa City, Iowa 52240

Dear Norbert:
I have your letter asking my estimate of Dr. Todd Macomber. From your tone, I infer you have her academic and professional record in hand, and that what you want from me is a more personal evaluation. I presume also that my reply will not be circulated, but will go into your private files. You ask for candor. I am delighted to reply.

Before I proceed, I should point out that although she was once a student of mine, there has been no direct contact between us for many years; that it was from Pasadena, not here in Bloomington, that she received her degree. I am led to suspect – perhaps incorrectly – your request was motivated by the fact that she left Bloomington after only one year.

I can assure you, her work was most satisfactory. Vividly, though it was all of seventeen years ago, I remember her quick intelligence, her clear understanding of everything I taught, and her firm independence. Advice she would accept, and judgments she would listen to, but she would make her own conclusions, and decisions were her own.

It was I who suggested that she apply to Pasadena. I also endorsed her application and helped to arrange the financial assistance which made it possible for her. In all these things, I was persuaded by the superior quality of instruction available there, and the prestige which a degree from that school would bestow. I believed, and still believe, it would further her career. I was proud of her, though I had little enough reason to feel pride.

About her private life I know practically nothing. Now she would be in her late thirties. She is a member of the Physics Department in Evanston, where she has been ever since her return from two years of postdoctoral study abroad. I am not sure, but according to my most recent information she holds the rank of Associate Professor. I am also informed that, although she is not presently married, she has a daughter who would now be in her midteens. Discretion has always prevented me from inquiring more deeply, though inevitably gossip has circulated. I have not myself seen the child. I would suggest you ignore the matter.

I have sometimes suspected that because of such extraneous factors, plus the fact that she is a woman in a profession dominated by men – many of whom, I regret to say, seem jealous of their positions – she has sometimes been passed over for promotion, and that for the same reasons she has been omitted from consideration for positions at more prestigious institutions such as your own. I am not otherwise able to explain why she has remained in Evanston – forced by lack of modern equipment to devote almost all her efforts to theoretical studies. Nevertheless, among those of us familiar with her work, she is widely respected. Frequently, she is invited to take part in discussions at neighboring universities.

However, you have asked for my personal judgment. I shall give you something better than that, for her ability can be comprehended most effectively by thinking upon an event from one of the few occasions since her days in Bloomington when I and Dr. Macomber have been in the same room. It was much talked about by those of us who are active in research, though even now Dr. Macomber's role is not widely known. Usually, it is spoken of as the time Morris Fabricant threw his chalk on the floor.

Even isolated by the administrative demands of your Institute, you may have heard mention of it. You may even remember the circumstances, although I'm not sure how well you keep up with the literature these days. It was the summer before last. That spring, Dr. Fabricant had reported in *Physical Review Letters* his series of experiments with Californium 247, and his startling conclusion that nuclei of this isotope could be divided into two distinct types, and that these types displayed separate and different rates of decay. He believed that he had developed techniques by which it was possible to differentiate between them, although they seemed otherwise identical.

You may remember, also, that he toured the country, visiting all the important departments to talk about his discovery. I believe he even went to Copenhagen. He did this as a challenge. He was that confident his work was free of error.

Of course, we were all anxious to subject his findings to ruthless and exhaustive criticism, for – had he been correct – it would have meant a fantastic breakthrough in our understanding of the process of nuclear decay. We wanted him to be right, of course, but – even more – we wanted to be absolutely sure he was right. That is the way scientific work is done. Had he been right, he would almost certainly have been in line to receive the Nobel Prize.

When he came to Chicago, I was among those asked up from Bloomington, and Dr. Macomber was invited down from Evanston. I did not know it when the meeting began, or I might have spoken to her. There were a lot of us there. The auditorium was crowded, and I did not see her. At the conclusion of Dr. Fabricant's presentation, every objection and argument we could imagine was thrown at him. Dr. Fabricant filled the blackboard with his equations and formulae and theoretical models, and he demolished every point that was raised. He is, as you know, a brilliant man. He made us seem like fools.

Dr. Macomber's contribution is not credited in the transcript. However, having been there, I know it was she who asked what became, as it turned out, the final question. Nor were her exact words recorded. According to the published transcript, the tape at this point was indistinct. I consider these omissions unfortunate. I sometimes suspect they were not accidental.

Dr. Fabricant replied at some length and . . . I must say it was very strange. No one said a word. It was something all of us realized at the same moment.

This much is clear in my recollection. Together, Dr. Macomber's question and the reply Dr. Fabricant gave, made it instantly evident that what Dr. Fabricant had thought was a characteristic by which his two types of nuclei could be identified was actually nothing more than the presence or absence of a previously unsuspected aspect of the excited state of a nucleus in the transitionary period immediately before emission of a decay particle. It was natural, of course, that the excited nuclei would decay more quickly. Once Dr. Macomber brought our attention to the matter, it was obvious. It had not been obvious before.

That was the moment when Dr. Fabricant threw his chalk on the floor. It shattered. He walked out of the room. I presume he went directly back to Berkeley, but that is something I do not know.

I cannot emphasize adequately that nothing about this incident should reflect to Dr. Fabricant's discredit. His ability is universally recognized, nor do I call it into question now. We have all made similar mistakes at one time or another, and in this case we were all equally deceived. All of us, that is, but Dr. Macomber. It is a measure of her own competence that she perceived the error that had slipped past even the best of us.

Dr. Macomber is a brilliant woman. I recommend her to you highly and without reservation. She would be an excellent addition to the staff of your Institute.

Annemarie joins me in wishing you all of the best. Please remember me to the beautiful Janis, and to your wonderful children. Four, is it now? How I envy you.

Most Cordially yours,
Charles Latourette

PS: Nobby – a personal favor please. As I say, I've had no direct contact with Dr. Macomber for many years. I'm hoping you will find it possible to offer the opportunities your Institute can provide, and which she has long deserved. If that can be done, it is likely you will encounter her daughter at some time or another. I would be grateful – call it an old man's whim – if you could let me know should you notice any perceptible resemblance to me, however slight. A photograph, if possible, would be most welcome. Please give Dr. Macomber my warmest personal regards.

C. L.

THE
NATIONAL
PASTIME

Norman Spinrad

Do you like to watch football on the box? We all like to watch football on the box. But it will never be the same again after you read here what we have been missing.

THE FOUNDING FATHER

I know you've got to start at the bottom in the television business, but producing sports shows is my idea of cruel and unusual punishment. Sometime in the dim past, I had the idea that I wanted to make films, and the way to get to make films seemed to be to run up enough producing and directing credits on television, and the way to do *that* was to take whatever came along, and what came along was an offer to do a series of sports specials on things like kendo, sumo wrestling, jousting, Thai boxing, in short, ritual violence. This was at the height (or the depth) of the antiviolence hysteria, when you couldn't so much as show the bad guy getting an on-camera rap in the mouth from the good guy on a moron western. The only way you could give the folks what they really wanted was in the All-American wholesome package of a sporting event. Knowing this up front – unlike the jerks who warm chairs as network executives – I had no trouble producing the kind of sports specials the network executives knew people wanted to see without quite knowing why, and thus I achieved the status of boy genius. Which, alas, ended up in my being offered a long-term contract as a producer in the sports department that was simply too rich for me to pass up, I mean I make no bones about being a crass materialist.

So try to imagine my feelings when Herb Dieter, the network sports programming director, calls me into his inner sanctum and gives me The Word. 'Ed,' he tells me, 'as you know, there's now only one major football league, and the opposition has us frozen out of the picture with long-term contracts with the NFL. As you also know, the major league football games are clobbering us in the Sunday afternoon ratings, which is prime time as far as sports programming is concerned. And as you know, a sports programming director who can't hold a decent piece of the Sunday afternoon audience is not long for this fancy office. And as you know, there is no sport on God's green earth that can compete with major league football. Therefore, it would appear that I have been presented with an insoluble problem.

'Therefore, since you are the official boy genius of the sports department, Ed, I've decided that you must be the solution to my problem. If I don't come up with something that will hold its own against pro football by the beginning of next season, my head will roll. Therefore, I've decided to give you the ball and let you run with it. Within ninety days, you will have come up with a solution or the fine print boys will be instructed to find a way for me to break your contract.'

I found it very hard to care one way or the other. On the one hand, I liked the bread I was knocking down, but on the other, the job was a real drag and it would probably do me good to get my ass fired. Of course the whole thing was unfair from my point of view, but who could fault Dieter's logic, he personally had nothing to lose by ordering his best creative talent to produce a miracle or be fired. Unless I came through, *he* would be fired, and then what would he care about gutting the sports department, it wouldn't be his baby anymore. It wasn't very nice, but it was the name of the game we were playing.

'You mean all I'm supposed to do is invent a better sport than football in ninety days, Herb, or do you mean something more impossible?' I couldn't decide whether I was trying to be funny or not.

But Dieter suddenly had a 20-watt bulb come on behind his eyes (about as bright as he could get). 'I do believe you've hit on it already, Ed,' he said. 'We can't get any pro football, so you're right, you've got to *invent* a sport that will outdraw pro football. Ninety days, Ed. And don't take it too hard; if you bomb out, we'll see each other at the unemployment office.'

So there I was, wherever *that* was. I could easily get Dieter to do for me what I didn't have the willpower to do for myself and get me out of the stinking sports department – all I had to do was *not* invent a game that would outdraw pro football. On the other hand, I liked living the way I did, and I didn't like the idea of losing *anything* because of failure.

So the next Sunday afternoon, I eased out the night before's chick, turned on the football game, smoked two joints of Acapulco Gold and consulted my muse. It was the ideal set of conditions for a creative mood: I was being challenged, but if I failed, I gained too, so I had no inhibitions on my creativity. I was stoned to the point where the whole situation was a game without serious consequences; I was hanging loose.

Watching two football teams pushing each other back and forth across my color television screen, it once again occurred to me how much football was a ritual sublimation of war. This seemed perfectly healthy. Lots of cultures are addicted to sports that are sublimations of the natural human urge to clobber people. Better the sublimation than the clobbering. People dig violence, whether anyone likes the truth or not, so it's a public service to keep it on the level of a spectator sport.

Hmmm . . . that was probably why pro football had replaced baseball as the National Pastime in a time when people, having had their noses well rubbed in the stupidity of war, needed a war substitute. How could you beat something that got the American armpit as close to the gut as that?

And then from the blue grass mountaintops of Mexico, the flash hit me: the only way to beat football was at its own game! Start with football itself, and convert it into something that was an even *closer* metaphor for war, something that could be called—

!!COMBAT FOOTBALL!!

Yeah, yeah, Combat Football, or better, COMBAT football. Two standard football teams, standard football field, standard football rules, except:

Take off all their pads and helmets and jerseys and make it a warm-weather game that they play in shorts and sneakers like boxing. More meaningful, more intimate violence. Violence is what sells football, so give 'em a bit more violence than football, and you'll draw a bit more than football. The more violent you can make it and get away with it, the better you'll draw.

Yeah . . . and you could get away with punching, after all boxers belt each other around and they still allow boxing on television; sports have too much All American Clean for the antiviolence freaks to attack, in fact, where their heads are at, they'd *dig* Combat Football. Okay. So in ordinary football, the defensive team tackles the ball carrier to bring him to his knees and stop the play. So in Combat, the defenders can slug the ball carrier, kick him, tackle him, why not, anything to bring him to his knees and stop the play. And to make things fair, the ball carrier can slug the defenders to get them out of his way. If the defense slugs an offensive player who doesn't have possession, it's ten yards and an automatic first down. If anyone but the ball carrier slugs a defender, it's ten yards and a loss of down.

Presto: Combat Football!

And the final touch was that it was a game that any beer-sodden moron who watched football could learn to understand in sixty seconds, and any lout who dug football would have to like Combat better.

The boy genius had done it again! It even made sense after I came down.

Farewell to the Giants

Jeez, I saw a thing on television last Sunday you wouldn't believe. You really oughta watch it next week, I don't care who the Jets or the Giants are playing. I turned on the TV to watch the Giants game and went to get a beer, and when I came back from the kitchen I had some guy yelling something about today's professional combat football game, and it's not the NFL announcer, and it's a team called the New York Sharks playing a team called the Chicago Thunderbolts, and they're playing in L.A. or Miami, I didn't catch which, but someplace with palm trees anyway, and all the players are bare-ass! Well, not really bare-ass, but all they've got on is sneakers and boxing shorts with numbers across the behind – blue for New York, green for Chicago. No helmets, no pads, no protectors, no jerseys, no nothing!

I check the set and sure enough I've got the wrong channel. But I figured I could turn on the Giants game anytime, what the hell, you can see the Giants all the time, but what in hell is *this*?

New York kicks off to Chicago. The Chicago kick-returner gets the ball on about the 10 – bad kick – and starts upfield. The first New York tackler reaches him and goes for him and the Chicago player just belts him in the mouth and runs by him! I mean, with the ref standing there watching it, and no flag thrown! Two more tacklers come at him on the 20. One dives at his legs, the other socks him in the gut. He trips and staggers out of the tackle, shoves another tackler away with a punch in the chest, but he's slowed up enough so that three or four New York players get to him at once. A couple of them grab his legs to stop his motion, and the others knock him down, at about the 25. Man, what's going on here?

I check my watch. By this time the Giants game has probably started, but New York and Chicago are lined up for the snap on the 25, so I figure what the hell, I gotta see some more of this thing, so at least I'll watch one series of downs.

On first down, the Chicago quarterback drops back and throws a long one way downfield to his flanker on maybe the New York 45; it looks good, there's only one player on the Chicago flanker, he beats this one man and catches it, and it's a touchdown, and the pass looks right on the button. Up goes the Chicago flanker, the ball touches his hands – and pow, right in the kisser! The New York defender belts him in the mouth and he drops the pass. Jeez, what a game!

Second and ten. The Chicago quarterback fades back, but it's a fake, he hands off to his fullback, a gorilla who looks like he weighs about two-fifty, and the Chicago line opens up a little hole at left tackle and the fullback hits it holding the ball with one hand and punching with the other. He belts out a tackler, takes a couple of shots in the gut, slugs a second tackler, and then someone has him around the ankles; he drags himself forward another half yard or so, and then he runs into a good solid punch and he's down on the 28 for a three-yard gain.

Man, I mean *action!* What a game! Makes the NFL football look like something for faggots! Third and seven, you gotta figure Chicago for the pass, right? Well on the snap, the Chicago quarterback just backs up a few steps and pitches a short one to his flanker at about the line of scrimmage. The blitz is on and everyone comes rushing in on the quarterback and before New York knows what's happening, the Chicago flanker is five yards downfield along the left sideline and picking up speed. Two New York tacklers angle out to stop him at maybe the Chicago 40, but he's got up momentum and one of the New York defenders runs right into his fist – I could hear the thud even on television – and falls back right into the other New York player, and the Chicago flanker is by them, the 40, the 45, he angles back toward the center of the field at mid-field, dancing away from one more tackle, then on maybe the New York 45 a real fast New York defensive back catches up to him from behind, tackles him waist-high, and the Chicago flanker's motion is stopped as two more tacklers come at him. But he squirms around inside the tackle and belts the tackler in the mouth with his free hand, knocks the New York back silly, breaks the tackle, and he's off again downfield with two guys chasing him – 40, 35, 30, 25, he's running away from them. Then from way over the right side of the field, I see the New York safety man running flat out across the field at the ball carrier, angling toward him so it looks like they'll crash like a couple of locomotives on about the 15, because the Chicago runner just doesn't see this guy. Ka-boom! The ball carrier running flat out runs right into the fist of the flat out safety at the 15 and he's knocked about ten feet one way and the football flys ten feet the other way, and the New York safety scoops it up on the 13 and starts upfield, 20, 25, 30, 35, and then slam, bang, whang, half the Chicago team is all over him, a couple of tackles, a few in the gut, a shot in the head, and he's down. First and ten for New York on their own 37. And that's just the first series of downs!

Well let me tell you, after that you know where they can stick the Giants game, right? This Combat Football, that's the real way to play the game, I mean it's football and boxing all together, with a little wrestling thrown in, it's a game with *balls*. I mean, the *whole game* was like that first series. You oughta take a look at it next week. Damn, if they played the thing in New York we could even go out to the game together. I'd sure be willing to spend a couple of bucks to see something like that.

Commissioner Gene Kuhn Address to the First Annual Owners' Meeting of the National Combat Football League

Gentlemen, I've been thinking about the future of our great sport. We're facing a double challenge to the future of Combat football, boys. First of all, the NFL is going over to Combat rules next season, and since you can't copyright a sport (and if you could the NFL would have us by the short hairs anyway) there's not a legal thing we can do about it. The only edge we'll have left is that they'll have to at least wear heavy uniforms because they play in regular cities up north. But they'll have the stars, and the stadiums, and the regular home town fans and fatter television deals.

Which brings me to our second problem, gentlemen, namely that the television network which created our great game is getting to be a pain in our sport's neck, meaning that they're shafting us in the crummy percentage of the television revenue they see fit to grant us.

So the great task facing our great National Pastime, boys, is to ace out the network by putting ourselves in a better bargaining position on the television rights while saving our million-dollar asses from the NFL competition, which we just cannot afford.

Fortunately, it just so happens your commissioner has been on the ball, and I've come up with a couple of new gimmicks that I am confident will insure the posterity and financial success of our great game while stiff-arming the NFL and the TV network nicely in the process.

Number one, we've got to improve our standing as a live spectator sport. We've got to start drawing big crowds on our own if we want some clout in negotiating with the network. Number two, we've got to give the customers something the NFL can't just copy from us next year and clobber us with.

There's no point in changing the rules again because the NFL can always keep up with us there. But one thing the NFL is locked into for keeps is the whole concept of having teams represent cities; they're committed to that for the next twenty years. We've only been in business four years and our teams never play in the damned cities they're named after because it's too cold to play bare-ass Combat in those cities during the football season, so it doesn't have to mean anything to us.

So we make two big moves. First, we change our season to spring and summer so we can play up north where the money is. Second, we throw out the whole dumb idea of teams representing cities; that's old-fashioned stuff. That's crap for the coyotes. Why not six teams with *national* followings? Imagine the clout that'll give us when we renegotiate the TV contract. We can have a flexible schedule so that we can put any game we want into any city in the country any time we think that city's hot and draw a capacity crowd in the biggest stadium in town.

How are we gonna do all this? Well look boys, we've got a six-team league, so instead of six cities, why not match up our teams with six national groups?

I've taken the time to draw up a hypothetical league lineup just to give you an example of the kind of thing I mean. Six teams: the Black Panthers, the Golden Supermen, the Psychedelic Stompers, the Caballeros, the Gay Bladers and the Hog Choppers. We do it all up the way they used to do with wrestling, you know, the Black Panthers are all spades with naturals, the Golden Supermen are blond astronaut types in red-white-and-blue bunting, the Psychedelic Stompers have long hair and groupies in miniskirts up to their navels and take rock bands to their games, the Caballeros dress like gauchos or something, whatever makes Latin types feel feisty, the Gay Bladers and Hog Choppers are mostly all-purpose villains – the Bladers are black-leather-and-chainmail faggots and the Hog Choppers we recruit from outlaw motorcycle gangs.

Now is that a *league*, gentlemen? Identification is the thing, boys. You gotta identify your teams with a large enough group of people to draw crowds, but why tie yourself to something local like a city? This way, we got a team for the spades, a team for the frustrated Middle Americans, a team for the hippies and kids, a team for the spics, a team for the faggots, and a team for the motorcycle nuts and violence freaks. And any American who can't identify with any of those teams is an odds-on bet to hate one or more of them enough to come out to the game to see them stomped. I mean, who wouldn't want to see the Hog Choppers and the Panthers go at each other under Combat rules?

Gentlemen, I tell you it's creative thinking like this that made our country great, and it's creative thinking like this that will make Combat football the greatest goldmine in professional sports.

Stay Tuned, Sportsfans. . . .

Good afternoon, Combat fans, and welcome to today's major league Combat football game between the Caballeros and the Psychedelic Stompers brought to you by the World Safety Razorblade Company, with the sharpest, strongest blade for your razor in the world.

It's 95 degrees on this clear New York day in July, and a beautiful day for a Combat football game, and the game here today promises to be a real smasher, as the Caballeros, only a game behind the league-leading Black Panthers take on the fast-rising, hard-punching Psychedelic Stompers and perhaps the best running back in the game today, Wolfman Ted. We've got a packed house here today, and the Stompers, who won the toss, are about to receive the kickoff from the Caballeros. . . .

And there it is, a low bullet into the end zone, taken there by Wolfman Ted. The Wolfman crosses the goal line, he's up to the 5, the 10, the 14, he brings down number 71 Pete Lopez with a right to the windpipe, crosses the 15, takes a glancing blow to the head from number 56 Diaz, is tackled on the 18 by Porfirio Rubio, number 94, knocks Rubio away with two quick rights to the head, crosses the 20, and takes two rapid blows to the midsection in succession from Beltran and number 30 Orduna, staggers and is tackled low from behind by the quick-recovering Rubio and slammed to the ground under a pile of Caballeros on the 24.

First and ten for the Stompers on their own 24. Stompers quarterback Ronny Seede brings his team to the line of scrimmage in a double flanker formation with Wolfman Ted wide to the right. A long count—

The snap, Seede fades back to—

A quick hand-off to the Wolfman charging diagonally across the action toward left tackle, and the Wolfman hits the line on a dead run, windmilling his right fist, belting his way through one, two, three Caballeros, getting two, three yards, then taking three quick ones to the ribcage from Rubio, and staggering right into number 41 Manuel Cardozo, who brings him down on about the 27 with a hard right cross.

Hold it! A flag on the play! Orduna number 30 of the Caballeros and Dickson number 83 of the Stompers are waling away at each other on the 26! Dickson takes two hard ones and goes down, but as Orduna kicks him in the ribs, number 72, Merling of the Stompers, grabs him from behind and now there are six or seven assistant referees breaking it up. . . .

Something going on in the stands at about the 50 too – a section of Stompers rooters mixing it up with the Caballero fans—

But now they've got things sorted out on the field, and it's

10 yards against the Caballeros for striking an ineligible player, nullified by a 10-yarder against the Stompers for illegal offensive striking. So now it's second and seven for the Stompers on their own 27—

It's quieted down a bit there above the 50-yard line, but there's another little fracas going in the far end zone and a few groups of people milling around in the aisles of the upper grandstand—

There's the snap, and Seede fades back quickly, dances around, looks downfield, and throws one intended for number 54, Al Viper, the left end at about the 40. Viper goes up for it, he's got it—

And takes a tremendous shot along the base of his neck from number 94 Porfirio Rubio! The ball is jarred loose. Rubio dives for it, he's got it, but he takes a hard right in the head from Viper, then a left. Porfirio drops the ball and goes at Viper with both fists! Viper knocks him sprawling and dives on top of the ball, burying it and bringing a whistle from the head referee as Rubio rains blows on his prone body. And here come the assistant referees to pull Porfirio off as half the Stompers come charging downfield toward the action—

They're at it again near the 50-yard line! About forty rows of fans going at each other. There goes a smoke bomb!

They've got Rubio away from Viper now, but three or four Stompers are trying to hold Wolfman Ted back and Ted has blood in his eye as he yells at number 41, Cardozo. Two burly assistant referees are holding Cardozo back. . . .

There go about a hundred and fifty special police up into the midfield stands. They've got their mace and prods out . . .

The head referee is calling an official's time out to get things organized, and we'll be back to live National Combat Football League action after this message. . . .

The Circus Is in Town

'We've got a serious police problem with Combat football,' Commissioner Minelli told me after the game between the Golden Supermen and the Psychedelic Stompers last Sunday in which the Supermen slaughtered the Stompers 42-14 and during which there were ten fatalities and 189 hospitalizations among the rabble in the stands.

'Every time there's a game, we have a riot, your honor,'

Minelli (who had risen through the ranks) said earnestly. 'I recommend that you should think seriously about banning Combat football. I really think you should.'

This city is hard enough to run without free advice from politically ambitious cops. 'Minelli,' I told him, 'you are dead wrong on both counts. First of all, not only has there *never* been a riot in New York during a Combat football game, but the best studies show that the incidence of violent crimes and social violence diminishes from a period of three days before a Combat game clear through to a period five days afterward, not only here, but in every major city in which a game is played.'

'But only this Sunday ten people were killed and nearly two hundred injured, including a dozen of my cops—'

'In the *stands*, you nitwit, not in the streets!' Really, the man was too much!

'I don't see the difference—'

'Ye gods, Minelli, can't you see that Combat football keeps a hell of a lot of violence off the streets? It keeps it in the stadium, where it belongs. The Romans understood that two thousand years ago! We can hardly stage gladiator sports in this day and age, so we have to settle for a civilized substitute.'

'But what goes on in there is murder. My cops are taking a beating. And we've got to assign two thousand cops to every game. It's costing the taxpayers a fortune, and you can bet . . . *someone* will be making an issue out of it in the next election.'

I do believe that the lout was actually trying to pressure me. Still, in his oafish way, he had put his finger on the one political disadvantage of Combat football: the cost of policing the games and keeping the fan clubs in the stands from tearing each other to pieces.

And then I had one of those little moments of blind inspiration when the pieces of a problem simply fall into shape as an obvious pattern of solution.

Why bother keeping them from tearing each other to pieces?

'I think I have the solution, Minelli,' I said. 'Would it satisfy your sudden sense of fiscal responsibility if you could take all but a couple of dozen cops off the Combat football games?'

Minelli looked at me blankly. 'Anything less than two thousand cops in there would be mincemeat by half time,' he said.

'So why send them in there?'

'Huh?'

'All we really need is enough cops to guard the gates, frisk the fans for weapons, seal up the stadium with the help of riot doors, and make sure no one gets out till things have simmered down inside.'

'But they'd tear each other to ribbons in there with no cops!'

'So let them. I intend to modify the conditions under which the city licenses Combat football so that anyone who buys a ticket legally waives his right to police protection. Let them fight all they want. Let them really work out their hatreds on each other until they're good and exhausted. Human beings have an incurable urge to commit violence on each other. We try to sublimate that urge out of existence, and we end up with irrational violence on the streets. The Romans had a better idea – give a rabble a socially harmless outlet for violence. We spend billions on welfare to keep things pacified with bread, and where has it gotten us? Isn't it about time we tried circuses?'

As American as Apple Pie

Let me tell it to you, brother, we've sure been waiting for the Golden Supermen to play the Panthers in *this* town again, after the way those blond mothers cheated us 17-10 the last time and wasted three hundred of the brothers! Yeah man, they had those stands packed with honkies trucked in from as far away as Buffalo – we just weren't ready, is why we took the loss.

But this time we planned ahead and got ourselves up for the game even before it was announced. Yeah, instead of waiting for them to announce the date of the next Panther-Supermen game in Chicago and then scrambling with the honkies for tickets, the Panther Fan Club made under the table deals with ticket brokers for blocks of tickets for whenever the next game would be, so that by the time today's game was announced, we controlled two-thirds of the seats in Daley Stadium and the honkies had to scrape and scrounge for what was left.

Yeah man, today we pay them back for that last game! We got two-thirds of the seats in the stadium and Eli Wood is back in action and we gonna just go out and *stomp* those mothers today!

* * *

Really, I'm personally quite cynical about Combat; most of us who go out to the Gay Bladers games are. After all, if you look at it straight on, Combat football is rather a grotty business. I mean, look at the sort of people who turn out at Supermen or Panthers or for God's sake *Caballero* games: the worst sort of proletarian apes. Aside from us, only the Hogs have any semblance of class, and the Hogs have beauty only because they're so incredibly up-front gross, I mean all that shiny metal and black leather!

And of course that's the only real reason to go to the Blader games: for the spectacle. To see it and to be part of it! To see semi-naked groups of men engaging in violence and to be violent yourself – and especially with those black leather and chain mail Hog Lovers!

Of course I'm aware of the cynical use the loathsome government makes of Combat. If there's nastiness between the blacks and P.R.s in New York, they have the league schedule a Panther-Caballero game and let them get it out on each other safely in the stadium. If there's college campus trouble in the Bay Area, it's a Stompers-Supermen game in Oakland. And us and the Hogs when just *anyone* anywhere needs to release general hostility. I'm not stupid, I know that Combat football is a tool of the Establishment. . . .

But lord, it's just so much bloody *fun*!

We gonna have some fun today! The Hogs is playing the Stompers and that's the wildest kind of Combat game there is! Those crazy freaks come to the game stoned out of their minds, and you know that at least Wolfman Ted is playing on something stronger than pot. There are twice as many chicks at Stomper games than with any other team the Hogs play because the Stomper chicks are the only chicks beside ours who aren't scared out of their boxes at the thought of being locked up in a stadium with twenty thousand hot-shot Hogger rape artists like us!

Yeah, we get good and stoned, and the Stomper fans get good and stoned, and the Hogs get stoned, and the Stompers get stoned, and then we all groove on beating the piss out of each other, *whoo*-whee! And when we win in the stands, we drag off the pussy and gang-bang it.

Oh yeah, Combat is just good clean dirty fun!

It makes you feel good to go out to a Supermen game, makes you feel like a real American is supposed to, like a man. All week you've got to take crap from the niggers and the spics and your goddamn crazy doped-up kids and hoods and bums and faggots in the streets, and you're not even supposed to think of them as niggers and spics and crazy doped-up kids and bums and hoods and faggots. But Sunday you can go out to the stadium and watch the Supermen give it to the Panthers, the Caballeros, the Stompers, the Hogs, or the Bladers and maybe kick the crap out of a few people whose faces you don't like yourself.

It's a good healthy way to spend a Sunday afternoon, out in the open air at a good game when the Supermen are hot and we've got the opposition in the stands outnumbered. Combat's a great thing to take your kid to too!

I don't know, all my friends go to the Caballero games, we go together and take a couple of six packs of beer apiece, and get *muy boracho* and just have some crazy fun, you know? Sometimes I come home a little cut up and my wife is all upset and tries to get me to promise not to go to the Combat games anymore. Sometimes I promise, just to keep her quiet, she can get on my nerves, but I never really mean it.

Hombre, you know how it is, women don't understand these things like men do. A man has got to go out with his friends and feel like a man sometimes. It's not too easy to find ways to feel *muy macho* in this country, *amigo.* The way it is for us here, you know. It's not as if we're hurting anyone we shouldn't hurt. Who goes out to the Caballero games but a lot of dirty gringos who want to pick on us? So it's a question of honor, in a way, for us to get as many *amigos* as we can out to the Caballero games and show those *cabrónes* that we can beat them any time, no matter how drunk we are. In fact, the drunker we are, the better it is, '¿ tu sabes?'

Baby, I don't know what it is, maybe it's just a chance to get it all out. It's a unique trip, that's all, there's no other way to get that particular high, that's why I go to Stompers games. Man, the games don't mean anything to me as games; games are like *games,* dig. But the whole Combat scene is its own reality.

You take some stuff – acid is a groovy high but you're liable to get wasted, lots of speed and some grass or hash is more recommended – when you go in, so that by the time the game starts you're really loaded. And then man, you just groove behind the violence. There aren't any cops to bring you down. What chicks are there are there because they dig it. The people you're enjoying beating up on are getting the same kicks beating up on you, so there's no guilt hang-up to get between you and the total experience of violence.

Like I say, it's a unique trip. A pure violence high without any hang-ups. It makes me feel good and purged and kind of together just to walk out of that stadium after a Combat football trip and know I survived; the danger is groovy too. Baby, if you can dig it, Combat can be a genuine mystical experience.

Hogs Win It All, 21-17, 1578(23)-989(14)!

Anaheim, October 8. It was a slam-bang finish to the National Combat Football League Pennant Race, the kind of game Combat fans dream about. The Golden Supermen and the Hog Choppers in a dead-even tie for first place playing each other in the last game of the season, winner take all, before nearly 60,000 fans. It was a beautiful sunny 90-degree Southern California day as the Hogs kicked off to the Supermen before a crowd that seemed evenly divided between Hog Lovers who had motorcycled in all week from all over California and Supermen Fans whose biggest bastion is here in Orange County.

The Supermen scored first blood midway through the first period when quarterback Bill Johnson tossed a little screen pass to his right end, Seth West, on the Hog 23, and West slugged his way through five Hog tacklers, one of whom sustained a mild concussion, to go in for the touchdown. Rudolf's conversion made it 7-0, and the Supermen Fans in the stands responded to the action on the field by making a major sortie into the Hog Lover section at midfield, taking out about 20 Hog Lovers, including a fatality.

The Hog fans responded almost immediately by launching an offensive of their own in the bleacher seats, but didn't do much better than hold their own. The Hogs and the Supermen pushed each other up and down the field for the rest of the period without a score, while the Supermen Fans seemed to be getting the better of the Hog Lovers, especially in the midfield sections of the grandstand, where at least 120 Hog Lovers were put out of action.

The Supermen scored a field goal early in the second period to make the score 10-0, but more significantly, the Hog Lovers seemed to be dogging it, contenting themselves with driving back continual Supermen Fan sorties, while launching almost no attacks of their own.

The Hogs finally pushed in over the goal line in the final minutes of the first half on a long pass from quarterback Spike Horrible to his flanker Greasy Ed Lee to make the score 10-7 as the half ended. But things were not nearly as close as the field score looked, as the Hog Lovers in the stands were really taking their lumps from the Supermen Fans who had bruised them to the extent of nearly 500 take outs including 5 fatalities, as against only about 300 casualties and 3 fatalities chalked up by the Hog fans.

During the half time intermission, the Hog Lovers could be seen marshaling themselves nervously, passing around beer, pot and pills, while the Supermen Fans confidently passed the time entertaining themselves with patriotic songs.

The Supermen scored again halfway through the third period, on a handoff from Johnson to his big fullback Tex McGhee on the Hog 41. McGhee slugged his way through the left side of the line with his patented windmill attack, and burst out into the Hog secondary swinging and kicking. There was no stopping the Texas Tornado, though half the Hog defense tried, and McGhee went 41 yards for the touchdown, leaving three Hogs unconscious and three more with minor injuries in his wake. The kick was good, and the Supermen seemed on their way to walking away with the championship, with the score 17-7, and the momentum, in the stands and on the field, going all their way.

But in the closing moments of the third period, Johnson threw a long one downfield intended for his left end, Dick Whitfield. Whitfield got his fingers on the football at the Hog 30, but Hardly Davidson, the Hog cornerback, was right on him, belted him in the head from behind as he touched the ball, and then managed to catch the football himself before either it or Whitfield had hit the ground. Davidson got back to midfield before three Supermen tacklers took him out of the rest of the game with a closed eye and a concussion.

All at once, as time ran out in the third period, the 10-point

Supermen lead didn't seem so big at all as the Hogs advanced to a first down on the Supermen 35 and the Hog Lovers in the stands beat back Supermen Fan attacks on several fronts, inflicting very heavy losses.

Spike Horrible threw a five-yarder to Greasy Ed Lee on the first play of the final period, then a long one into the end zone intended for his left end, Kid Filth, which the Kid dropped as Gordon Jones and John Lawrence slugged him from both sides as soon as he became fair game.

It looked like a sure pass play on third and five, but Horrible surprised everyone by fading back into a draw and handing the ball off to Loser Ludowicki, his fullback, who plowed around right end like a heavy tank, simply crushing and smashing through tacklers with his body and fists, picked up two key blocks on the 20 and 17, knocked Don Barnfield onto the casualty list with a tremendous haymaker on the 7, and went in for the score.

The Hog Lovers in the stands went Hog-wild. Even before the successful conversion by Knuckleface Bonner made it 17-14, they began blitzing the Supermen Fans on all fronts, letting out everything they had seemed to be holding back during the first three quarters. At least 100 Supermen Fans were taken out in the next three minutes, including two quick fatalities, while the Hog Lovers lost no more than a score of their number.

As the Hog Lovers continued to punish the Supermen Fans, the Hogs kicked off to the Supermen, and stopped them after two first downs, getting the ball back on their own 24. After marching to the Supermen 31 on a sustained and bloody ground drive, the Hogs lost the ball again when Greasy Ed Lee was rabbit-punched into a fumble.

But the Hog fans still sensed the inevitable and pressed their attacks during the next two Supermen series of downs, and began to push the Supermen Fans toward the bottom of the grandstand.

Buoyed by the success of their fans, the Hogs on the field recovered the ball on their own 29 with less than two minutes to play when Chain Mail Dixon belted Tex McGhee into a fumble and out of the game.

The Hogs crunched their way upfield yard by yard, punch by punch, against a suddenly shaky Supermen opposition, and all at once, the whole season came down to one play:

With the score 17-14 and 20 seconds left on the clock, time

enough for one or possibly two more plays, the Hogs had the ball third and four on the 18-yard line of the Golden Supermen.

Spike Horrible took the snap as the Hog Lovers in the stands launched a final all-out offensive against the Supermen Fans, who by now had been pushed to a last stand against the grandstand railings at fieldside. Horrible took about ten quick steps back as if to pass, and then suddenly ran head down fist flailing at the center of the Supermen line with the football tucked under his arm.

Suddenly Greasy Ed Lee and Loser Ludowicki raced ahead of their quarterback, hitting the line and staggering the tacklers a split second before Horrible arrived, throwing them just off balance enough for Horrible to punch his way through with three quick rights, two of them k.o. punches. Virtually the entire Hog team roared through the hole after him, body-blocking, and elbowing, and crushing tacklers to the ground. Horrible punched out three more tacklers as the Hog Lovers pushed the first contingent of fleeing Supermen Fans out onto the field, and went in for the game and championship-winning touchdown with two seconds left on the clock.

When the dust had cleared, not only had the Hog Choppers beaten the Golden Supermen 21-17, but the Hog Lovers had driven the Golden Supermen Fans from their favorite stadium, and had racked up a commanding advantage in the casualty statistics, 1,578 casualties and 23 fatalities inflicted, as against only 989 and 14.

It was a great day for the Hog Lovers and a great day in the history of our National Pastime.

The Voice of Sweet Reason

Go to a Combat football game? Really, do you think I want to risk being injured or possibly killed? Of course I realize that Combat is a practical social mechanism for preserving law and order, and to be frank, I find the spectacle rather stimulating. I watch Combat often, almost every Sunday.

On television, of course. After all, everyone who is anyone in this country knows very well that there are basically two kinds of people in the United States: people who go out to Combat games and people for whom Combat is strictly a television spectator sport.

113

The *Phoenix* races against
time and death toward . . .

THE ULTIMATE END

. . . to save the city from certain destruction
at the hands of a mad genius!

Dick Glass

*Dick Glass is a young man who works very hard in a library
to support his efforts to write and interpret the world today. I
think he is justified in his labors and it is a pleasure to print his
first story here.*

CHAPTER TWELVE: *Flaming Justice!*

The park. The sun-filled children's haven. The park. A man
had endured unspeakable agony to breathe those two words
before he died. The park. No poetry-reading professors on its
rolling green hills today. The park. This day the key to carnage. This day it would be touched by a Salamander whose
hand would engulf the entire city in flaming destruction. Dres-
den would be a mere spark in comparison!

The flame-red roadster carrying the *Phoenix* roared through
the cool, concrete canyons. The throaty throb of its mighty
engine struck the stony heights, shook the windows as if to
warn the innocent people inside, then fell screaming in the
vacuum left behind by its passage.

David Cawber laughed at the little people blurring past his
windshield. Poor puny, helpless fools! Let them give Rita the
credit for tipping off the police last night. Let them think Rita
van Beelan, crime-busting woman newscaster, helped to round
up the Salamander's horde before they could ransom the city
with their all-consuming fires. Let them believe it was the
girl's bravery that had led the police and National Guard to
the condemned theater-in-the-round.

The deluded, gullible children!

For all they knew the Salamander had been killed during

the raid. For all they knew the Salamander had been 'Fingers' John Horner, the shady bail-bondsman who had his thumb in many an illegal pie. For all they knew his right-hand man, Mitchell, would be pulled in momentarily along with the other four gunmen who had escaped last night.

The *Phoenix* knew better!

Mitchell had been *tipped* to the raid moments before the police burst through the doors. He and his kill-crazy men had edged toward the side of the stage. From the orchestra pit Mitchell had gunned down the man garbed in the Salamander's orange and yellow asbestos suit. It hadn't been a stray police bullet!

The *Phoenix* had followed with his gun drawn. He had been quick enough to escape the police net, but not quick enough to keep up with the slippery killers. It did not matter. The *Phoenix* knew the Salamander's secret!

The Salamander was alive! The *Phoenix* had learned the full truth only ten minutes before. A narrow smile flickered across Cawber's lips as he remembered the Crime Commission's telecast less than a half hour before.

David Cawber had stood in the shadows behind the bright lights watching Rita van Beelan give her testimony. Cawber was unimportant, he was only the playboy munitions tycoon who escorted the crusading Miss van Beelan. But as the *Phoenix* he knew that only a member of the Commission could have warned Mitchell of the raid so soon after Rita had called in the location of the Salamander's lair. One of the members of the august Crime Commission *was* the Salamander!

From behind their large, parabolic desk, the seven-member Crime Commission had focused on Rita van Beelan as the cameras had focused on them. When the beautiful, young newswoman had finished and had stepped down, the cameras had moved in for close-ups. As the cameras had leap-frogged left to right, tight on each trusted face, each member of the Commission had spoken his mind.

Harve Morgenstern had shifted his Neanderthal bulk and had promised, as Chief of Police, that Mitchell would be hunted down and rounded up within twenty-four hours.

Hurd Filurmann, the deceptively rotund Fire Chief, had stated that his department could now handle any threat to the city with the insane horde of pyromaniacs behind bars or in the morgue.

Lomas Misty, the suave, pencil-moustached District Attorney, had promised that the Salamander's legions would be dealt with speedily and fully under the law. The dapper D. A. had then shot a glance at Rita who was standing in the shadows next to Cawber. The young prosecuter knew the girl's heart belonged to the *Phoenix* whose justice was not only swifter and surer, but more final as well.

Commissioner Nassen had run his thin fingers through his silver mane. A look of fatherly concern had crossed his dignified face. He had said he was relieved that the current wave of pain and death was finally past. He had spoken of a time in the future, soon he prayed, when the emergency commission could be disbanded, for justice would then fill the streets of the city.

Ambitious Scott Bramley, the representative from the Governor's office, had disagreed with the Commissioner. He had not only wanted to continue with the Commission's activities, but he had also wanted to tie them closer to the State House.

Major General Richard O. Eastland, who had come in from Second Army Headquarters to oversee the military aspects of the campaign against the Salamander, had said he was personally glad to turn the matter back to the local National Guard and to get back to the real war.

Lieutenant Colonel James Danvers of the local National Guard had taken the opportunity to rescind the curfew put on the city by the military and to deactivate all but a clean-up company.

In the shadows opposite Rita and Cawber, Mace Hurdley, the quiet Commission stenographer, had taken down each word and had gathered together his notes as Commissioner Nassen returned the situation to its normal programming.

As the Klieg lights had cooled, Cawber had taken the package Rita had been carrying and had slipped off to a dark alcove. He had opened the package with swift fingers. He had changed his tie and shirt. He had slipped on his shoulder holster with its .357 Magnum contents and had tested its draw. He had drawn his fiery, beaked mask over his handsome features. He had donned the red-violet, wide-brimmed fedora and the long, matching cloak which drove fear into the hearts of the underworld.

It had been time for the *Phoenix* to pay a call on Commissioner Nassen!

Seconds later, the dark avenger had been poised on the ledge outside Nassen's office. The *Phoenix*'s keen mind had sensed something amiss at the thick drapes being drawn over the half-opened window. Magically, the *Phoenix*'s gun had appeared ready in his fist as he had heard . . .

'The city will be my pyre, Commissioner, but you will not see it! You know my destination so you must feel the touch of the *Salamander*! Mitchell!'

The purple phantom had burst through the window into the office just as a soul-searing scream had torn the air. Commissioner Nassen had been smothered in flame!

The gun had barked in the *Phoenix*'s fist, but the Salamander and Mitchell had already cleared the door as the slugs had slammed into the wall behind them.

The *Phoenix* had quickly torn down the thick drapes and had wrapped them around the Commissioner's flaming body. Heedless of his own danger, Cawber had put out the flames seconds later, but he had little hope that Nassen would live.

As Cawber had cradled his still smoldering head, the Commissioner reached up a charred hand to pull the *Phoenix*'s ear closer. Enough life had still clung to the great man's black, burned husk for him to have whispered two words.

'The park . . .'

With that, the once noble man had sighed and had turned his melted, sightless eyes toward the ceiling. He would feel no more pain.

Then the *Phoenix* had burned with righteous vengeance. Then the *Phoenix* had vowed that Commissioner Nassen had not died in vain!

Cawber could not remember scooping up the Commissioner's revolver from his desk. He could not remember running through the studio like a demon with his cloak flapping behind him. He could not remember how he had dodged the bullets of the police, who thought *he* had murdered Nassen, as he ran across the street and into the alley which held his powerful red roadster.

The *Phoenix* only knew that he had recognized the voice of

the Salamander when it had no hood to muffle it – the voice of Mace Hurdley! The *Phoenix* only knew that the city thought it was safe. He was the only living man who knew that the Salamander was going to destroy the city. Between the *Phoenix* and the madman who would make the city his funeral pyre would be Mitchell and his four trained killers.

The *Phoenix* stood alone against six crazed mass assassins! He was the city's only hope for salvation!

If only he wasn't too late!

Now Cawber drove his roadster with Nassen's revolver in his fist. Only after Nassen's gun had spoken with vengeance would the *Phoenix* draw his own .357 Magnum. It was only right. It was justice in her purest sense!

As the *Phoenix*'s roadster screamed around the last corner, David Cawber saw he faced certain death. Three of Mitchell's back-up men stood blocking the park entrance with automatic rifles!

They crouched and fired sending forth a deadly, leaden swarm. Tracers flickered about the careening roadster prophesying the fires to come. In the gathering dusk each flaming glob of death hungered for the life of the *Phoenix*!

The *Phoenix* laughed!

Their bursts went wild. They could not face this exterminating angel of justice. These cravens were no match for him. Only Mitchell or the Salamander himself could hope to slow the *Phoenix*!

As the minions of the Salamander tried to change clips, Nassen's gun barked three times. One man dropped with the back of his head a pulpy mess. One fell clutching his exploded intestines. The third man spun around on his shattered leg. Another shot made a bloody ruin of his chest.

The mighty red automobile shot past the oozing, cooling meat on into the darkening park. Two shots left from Nassen. One for Mitchell, one for his helper. The *Phoenix*'s own gun would take care of the Salamander. Where *were* they? Nassen's soul would soon find rest.

The Freedom Arch stood in the center of the huge park. It was the symbol of man's dignity and progress. The Freedom Arch – it could only be within its hallowed bowels that the

Salamander had secreted the fuse terminals for his lethal legacy. Cawber hated him for that.

Cawber hated him for the death of Nassen. Cawber hated the fiend for all the fear and pain and death which he had inflicted on countless, innocent people. The *Phoenix* would take care of the guilty madman!

The *Phoenix* would kill *all* such scum so that they would no longer pollute this great city. The *Phoenix* would shoot them so they would die slowly, painfully – yearning for that final darkness.

The gravel crunched beneath the wheels of the speeding red roadster as it all but flew across the stone bridge over the center of the placid, dumbell-shaped lake. There . . . through the serene trees . . . Cawber could see Freedom Arch.

The *Phoenix* would be in time!

He was almost to the last, gentle curve . . .

Cough! Cough!

Two spidery holes appeared in the windshield on the right side – .45 automatic fire! Cawber slunk down in his seat and spun the car to the right. Nassen's gun was eagerly ready in his steady grip.

The fool!

He had given away his position with the muzzle flashes. Nothing could save a slave of evil once the *Phoenix* knew his whereabouts! Cawber flicked on his mighty headlamps, pinning, blinding the culprit in their penetrating beam.

Blinking, the gunman shot for the headlights of the oncoming car. He missed.

Nassen's gun shouted to be heard. Once. Twice. Two shots placed close together in the groin and gut. The man fell. It wasn't Mitchell.

Brrrrrraap!

Long, leaden fingers burrowed along the left front fender searching for the wheel or the engine.

Cawber dropped Nassen's spent gun and swung hard to the left with both hands on the wheel.

There stood Mitchell in the diminishing distance in the deepening shadows under the Arch. He stood braced against the gray stone with a Thompson submachine gun.

Mitchell mouthed obscenities as he fired short bursts at the onrushing juggernaut of justice.

Dancing death ripped and tore and marched up the hood of the gleaming red roadster. Cawber ducked, throwing up his left arm to protect the flashing eyes burning in his mask-shadowed face.

The windshield disintegrated into a thousand sharp fragments which ripped at the protecting arm and embedded in it. Bullets whizzed by the *Phoenix*, angry at not finding his soft flesh. Blood spattered the face of the *Phoenix* as Cawber brought his arm down to grip the wheel once more.

The grip was nothing. The arm was useless.

The *Phoenix* gripped the wheel with his knees as he reached for his .357 Magnum. Another burst buzzed through the torn interior of the car. It shattered Cawber's right shoulder.

A grim smile formed on the *Phoenix*'s tight lips as he fought the pain. He pushed the accelerator to the floor and aimed the great roadster straight down Mitchell's blazing muzzle!

Mitchell saw what Cawber planned to do and fired for the car's engine. His slugs began taking their toll on the great machine. The gunman stepped away from the age-grayed stone with his finger on the trigger.

He could not stop the dying car!

Recognition, then fear, filled the assassin's insane eyes. He tried to sidestep. Too late.

The grill struck Mitchell, bouncing him back against the wall. Cawber nudged his door open. A scream escaped from Mitchell's lips. His tommy gun chattered, stitching holes in the bottom of the arch overhead. The shells chipped out stone flakes, which drifted down like gray snow. Cawber tried to keep clear. Not soon enough.

The car struck the wall full force. Mitchell's upper torso and head merged with stone and metal. The barrel of his weapon was crushed. The breach exploded.

The car crumpled and turned over, catching Cawber just above the knees. The *Phoenix* could feel his bones being crushed from the knees down beneath the great weight of the dead metal. The car accordioned in around the motor, dragging Cawber with it. The *Phoenix* struck his face against the stone wall just as the car came to a rest. All was silence.

The drifting stone flakes hit the pavement.

Cawber was broken but not beaten. The *Phoenix* was shattered but he did not surrender. He could feel the blood oozing down his broken face and dripping out of his torn and shattered arms. He could feel nothing from the waist down.

He fought the shock and pain and dizziness from loss of blood, which threatened to drag him down into darkness. Had he failed?

No! He could not! Not so close!

The *Phoenix* started to lift himself up. Pain racked his body. His shattered right shoulder refused to move. His left arm was powerless. Cawber all but blacked out as he painfully shook the blood from his eyes. The night air caressed his face.

The *Phoenix* had been unmasked! How long had he been out?

Cawber stared up at the madman clad in the orange and yellow asbestos exoskeleton of the Salamander who towered above him.

'Ah, Cawber, you're awake. How nice of you. I wanted *so* much to share my triumph with someone and you *have* taken everyone else away. Can you *see* it? Can you see my triumph?

'No, I guess you can't down there all twisted and broken. Too bad. Really too bad.

'I can see *you*, you know. Forgive me for not unmasking myself, however. I must stay in uniform if I am to enjoy my triumph as long as possible. Shall I describe it to you?

'Of course I shall!

'It's a *masterpiece*! I've really outdone myself! I've outdone those Indian rajahs who had their *whole households* burned with them. *I* have a whole *city*! Nero had nothing on me. He wasn't even in town when Rome burned! I *personally* conceived and executed *my* pyre! Brilliant, don't you think?

'The flames won't reach here for an hour yet. I've been very precise and *systematic*, you see. The bombs are timed to go off from the outskirts of the city inward. They're *all* trapped! All *mine*! Like a fisherman I will gather in my tightening net of flame drawing hundreds of thousands to me! They will die like squirming, gasping fish, come to die in my homage.

'Gasping for air!

'In another few minutes the fire storms will start! The fire storms will push them before the great winds while sucking the air from their scorched lungs. The storms will fan the fires to even *higher* greatness!'

The Salamander bent closer. 'I will let you stay alive for

that. Imagine the heat *coursing* across your bared nerve endings – the air leaving your lungs! Perhaps you'll still be alive to feel all your *hair* being singed off? Delightful, *nicht wahr*?

'I trust your single-minded determination will keep you alive until the flames reach the edge of the park here in the heart of the city. That will be my cue to set off your gas tank. After all, phoenixes are *supposed* to rise on such occasions, hmmmm?

'Well, it'll be goodbye to *you*, Phoenix! *I* will rise from *your* pile of ashes! You see, *Salamanders* are impervious to flame!

'Excuse me now if I leave your field of vision. I must go fasten myself in the base of the Arch so I don't blow away. You present no problem, your body is so much useless meat. I'll be out of your reach at any rate. You can think all the *bad thoughts* about me you want!'

The Salamander threw back his head and laughed insanely. When he stopped he looked down again. Cawber could almost see the smile beneath the asbestos hood.

'I *do* hope your narrow mind is capable of visualizing what's going on out there. It would all be worth it then.'

The fiend stood up and turned his back. 'Well, so long! If you believe in anything besides your own ego – like an after life I'll see you there!' he tossed back contemptuously over his shoulder.

The Salamander fastened himself to the base of the Arch. He stood totally lost in the hellish scene his incendiary bombs were painting.

The *Phoenix* winced in pain. He winced at the nightmare visions swirling in his tortured brain.

Explosion and fire enveloped the city!

Carnage confetti blew out of the sides of the crumbling buildings!

Masonry and metal fell smoldering through the erotic, leaping flames to shower the gibbering mobs with pain and death!

Now the menace of the howling fire storm screamed through the streets! The winds blew debris and fanned the flames with hurricane force. Fiery flowers blossomed and blew away sucking the oxygen from the mouths of staggering, charred women and children!

Cars bounced down the panic-filled streets to crash and

tangle into each other. Blood boiled on the pavements. Everything was crushed under the flaming boulders of collapsing concrete.

The Salamander stood chained to the Arch like Odysseus tied to the mast against the Siren's call. His head was thrown back as he laughed and cried to the gods in the ecstasy of his insanity!

The *Phoenix* blinked through the blood that masked his broken face. A snarl rose in his throat. Purpose rose in his heart. Even with his legs crushed to pulp and splinters, his left arm shredded, his right arm shattered, the *Phoenix* could not allow this madman to go unpunished!

Painfully fighting back the darkness, which threatened to swallow him, the *Phoenix* bent over. He pushed back his coat with his broken nose. He pulled his .357 Magnum from its shoulder holster with his remaining teeth. Slipping his long, nimble tongue past the sawed off trigger guard, he took aim at the fiend responsible for the death of an entire city.

The eyes of the *Phoenix* flamed with vengeance as his tongue tip pressed the quick trigger. As the gun battered the roof of his already bloodied mouth, the *Phoenix* spat leaden justice!

Three large, blood-red flowers blossomed in the middle of the Salamander's orange and yellow back. Three blood-red stains oozed down his back as he slumped lifeless against the chains fastening him to the Arch.

David Cawber dropped his gun and laughed.

The *Phoenix* had won again!

And, as the light of the nearing flames grew more intense in the night sky, he found that final darkness.

PITY
THE POOR OUTDATED
MAN

Philip Shofner

There must be some connection between the arts. Painters write, writers dance, dancers paint. Philip Shofner is a young actor who is also a stage manager at the Old Globe theater in San Diego. And now an author. This is his first published story.

A small herd of unicorns frolicked in the green and flowered meadow, their silvery horns sparkling in the afternoon sun. With unbelievable agility they romped and grazed and leaped back and forth over one another. Their musical whinnies rose teasingly to the pegasus gliding shyly over the field, begging him to come down and join the fun. The pegasus circled indecisively, torn between his bashful nature and the urge to play, and gazed longingly at the unicorn festivity.

Come down, cajoled the unicorns, but the pegasus, hearing the cries of his brothers, flew off to join them in a game of hide-and seek in the clouds. The unicorns whinnied in disappointment, but they understood that a pegasus feels secure only with his own kind, and their disappointment didn't last.

Somewhere in the woods a dragon dreamed of battle and pillage, of looting and treasure, of captive maidens, ruined villages and avenging knights on strong white chargers. The thought of avenging knights made the dragon uneasy, for he was a peaceable sort of lizard in spite of his curious racial memories, and he snorted in his sleep, sending a dark puff of smoke high in the air.

Miss Emily and her class of first-graders, watching the unicorns from the edge of the field, heard the dragon's snort. It was like the sound of a distant blast furnace; the children shivered with delicious chills. 'Look, Miss Emily,' said one small voice, 'the dragon's breath.'

Miss Emily looked across the meadow and saw the puff of smoke hanging lazily just above the treetops. She smiled and patted the tiny blonde girl. 'Don't be frightened, love, for the dragon is asleep and is only dreaming.'

'Dragons always sleep in the daytime, don't they, Miss Emily?' said a dark-haired boy, proud of his knowledge of draconic habits.

'Most of the time, James, most of the time. Sometimes they like to wake up early and walk around in the sun.'

'Ooooooh,' said the class, in unison. They cast fearful glances at the puff of smoke, certain that it would develop immense jaws and gobble them up.

Miss Emily laughed. 'Watch the unicorns, my darlings,' she said. 'They don't fear the dragon. If there were the slightest danger the unicorns would run off very fast; then we would know to run very fast, too.'

'The dragons here are good dragons, aren't they, Miss Emily?' asked the small dragon expert.

'Yes, James, these are gentle dragons, vegetarian dragons, good-natured dragons. They wouldn't even hurt an insect.'

Almost as if he'd heard, the dragon shifted uneasily in his sleep. Deep inside, down in his heart of hearts and his soul of souls, the dragon was just the least bit ashamed of his gentility. He nursed a secret desire to be like his wilder brethren, those lizards of the Blackwood, chomping and flaming and striking terror into the hearts of men. But he was a pretty sharp old dragon, too, fat and comfortable, and he knew he wouldn't like the life in the hunting preserves, being chased by men with spears and guns. So he gave a steamy little sigh and went back to his dreams.

'It's time to leave, children,' said Miss Emily, and was gratified by the groans of her young charges. 'Don't be sad, my loves; we'll come back again. I have a surprise for you.'

The children naturally clamored to know what it was, but Miss Emily only smiled a wait-and-see smile, so they finally settled for one last wistful look at the happy dance of the unicorns. Miss Emily, too, felt the tug of the unicorns, and it was poignant, because Miss Emily was no longer a child, and the game was lost forever. That was a sad thing about growing up. One had to make way for the younger children.

And the children, ah, that was the surprise. Tomorrow Miss Emily would bring them back to this meadow and let them run out onto the soft grass to join the one-horned horses in their gambols. And she would sit, as she had before, in the shade at the edge of the woods, with perhaps a tear running slowly down one cheek, and merely watch the fun.

They had turned to leave when there was a commotion among the nearby trees, and the class turned to watch, straining through the underbrush to see the cause of the noise. A beautiful young woman, naked and voluptuously proportioned, burst laughing from cover and ran lightly into the meadow. Miss Emily was slightly embarrassed; the children not at all. An achingly handsome youth, equally naked, leaped joyfully after her. His upper torso was bronzed and muscular, but his legs were bent and furred, ending finally in the cloven hooves of a goat. A prodigious erection sprouted from his loins. The two proceeded to play a dizzy game of tag in the field, oblivious to the children and their teacher, until the small giggles and soft whispers made them stop and look.

The satyr's golden eyes widened as they focused on Miss Emily; his ears twitched and he smiled a knowing smile, an inviting smile. Miss Emily felt her eyelids grow warm and heavy; the heat spread to her face, then coursed down through her body to settle and blaze in her midriff. An answering smile touched her lips.

The beautiful nymph, aware of this, wrapped her arms around the satyr from behind, breathed gently in his ear. One hand brushed lightly across the golden hair on his chest; the other dropped to gently stroke the proud phallus. Instantly the satyr turned and grabbed, but the nymph was off, bounding for the trees on the far side of the meadow. The satyr laughed, glanced once more at Miss Emily, and gave chase. They disappeared into the woods.

Miss Emily sighed. 'Will he catch her, Miss Emily?' asked the blonde girl.

'Eventually, yes,' she replied softly, picturing it in her mind. 'What will he do with her?'

'He will make her very happy,' said Miss Emily. Then, abruptly: 'Come along, darlings, that's all for today.'

They started back along the trail, each lost in private thoughts of wonderful things. *I may not be able to join the unicorns*, Miss Emily mused, *but I don't have to just sit and watch*. The field trip, for today at least, was over.

The nymph allowed herself to be caught by a sylvan pool, and she cried with delight as her satyr made his thrust. They gasped and panted, moaned and shouted, rolled and giggled among the rushes until the final overwhelming crash of delicious pleasure. Then they lay together, trading caresses, whispering of this and that, in the quiet afterglow.

A mermaid, her upper body propped on a rock at the side of the pool, her twin tails swishing lazily through the water, turned from the display of passion to the young man sitting cross-legged beside her. 'If,' she said, 'love rules in this place, as they say it does, then surely those two are among the highest nobility.'

The young man seemed disinterested. He carried on the conversation, it seemed, not so much because he wanted to, but because it was simply easier than remaining silent. 'Why do you say that?' He shook his head. 'Everything else here is supposedly motivated by the same emotion. Why should they be different?'

The mermaid's long auburn hair streamed back from her head to float on the water. She moved one hand sensuously over her breasts, smiling at the young man. 'Because, you see, they live for nothing *but* love. They revel in it; it is endlessly fascinating to them. And their love is unrestricted. Watch the pegasus as it soars through the sky. The poor beast longs to approach other animals, but it is too timorous to mingle with any but its own kind. And so it remains an ornament to be admired at a distance.

'And the unicorns, ah, they have an odd sort of morality. They belong to the innocent. Thus, only the young and virginal can ride them. However, you may have noticed that the nymph and the satyr are also allowed to approach the herd. Have you ever wondered why?'

'Not really,' yawned the young man. He felt like getting up and walking away; however, although he wasn't particularly happy where he was, he wouldn't have been any better off anywhere else.

'They, too, are totally innocent. They feel no shame, no guilt, no inhibitions, and that is the source of their innocence.'

The young man yawned again, and made a noncommittal noise.

The mermaid gave him a solemn look. 'William,' she asked, 'do you love me?'

'No.'

'Do you want to make love to me?' asked the mermaid.

'No.'

'No?' The mermaid was surprised. 'Have you never wondered what it's like to float in the water, washed in ecstasy, my twin tails wrapped around your body, and you deep in my mythological recesses? It is, I assure you, an unequaled experience.'

William shrugged. 'It would be too much trouble.'

'I'm very strong. I could hold you in my arms, bear you up. Your head would never get wet.'

'Thanks all the same.'

'I could seduce you,' said the mermaid. 'You attract me. I could sing my siren song and draw you to me.' She began to hum.

'There's no point to it,' said William. 'I'm not in the mood. You don't interest me.'

'Why, how cruel,' exclaimed a new female voice. 'How can you be so selfish?'

William looked up and saw the nymph and the satyr, arms linked, playing the audience for the scene.

'You can give her something she wants,' said the satyr. 'It would be so easy for you, so enjoyable. You can give and receive unbounded joy all at the same time. Surely you are not so disinterested as all that?'

'To tell you the truth, I'm pretty damn bored by this whole thing.' The siren song had begun by this time, and William was obviously moved by the sound. Stubbornly he shook off the effects. He stood up, intending to leave, but the satyr raised his pipes and added his music to the mermaid's song. William stood rigid as the music swept over him, then his eyes took on a happy gleam, his mouth smiled as he fought against the compelling sound. Strangely, he looked younger, more energetic. . . .

And happier.

The music faltered, and the satyr lowered his pipes. The mermaid slid sadly back into the water and slowly off. William took a deep breath and cheerfully exhaled it. Then, this small victory enjoyed, he lost the feeling.

The satyr took a few steps forward, watching William curiously. 'You *are* a strange one.'

'Am I?'

'Well, one rarely sees a case of boredom like yours.'

'Why not?'

'There's too much to see and do,' said the satyr. 'Worlds of experience to gather.'

'Safe, secure, and predigested.'

There was a pause, and then the satyr smiled. 'Why do you want to fight, William? There's nothing really to fight against.'

William smiled back at the satyr, rather cynically. 'Yes,' he said, touching a stud on his belt, 'I know.' And with a whoosh he sailed up over the trees toward the city.

There was a man in the city who did a peculiar thing. Each evening, at sundown, he would go out on his terrace to watch the homing flight of the pegasi. He would raise his eyes to the heavens as the winged horses galloped through the sky in silent formation, bound for their nests cradled in the lofty peaks of the Sierra-Nevadas, and he would feel, as always, the burning ache of unrequited love, the sharp pain of wanting the unattainable.

This man was childlike in his obsession. He wanted nothing but to fly with pegasus, race through the clouds as one of them and play their games far above the land. Perfection, for him, rested with these shy chargers of the sky. And he knew that he could never realize his dream.

For once he had tried.

He had, and not too long before, flown up to the nesting grounds and hidden until the roosts were deserted. Seizing his chance, he flashed in and stole a newborn foal, a tiny little animal whose wings were still too feeble to lift him. And he'd returned to his apartment with his prize, determined to raise it without the timidity of its brethren.

The infant pegasus had shortly died of loneliness.

So now the man merely stood and watched, and dreamed, as the herd soared out of reach, untouchable. Remembering, he wept, sinking to his knees on the terrace, pouring out his grief for what could never be. And when the spasm had passed he walked slowly inside, secure in the knowledge that, if nothing else, he was at least a genuine misfit. It didn't provide much comfort.

The diminishing light of the setting sun activates a photo-electric switch and then, in the dusk, little doors pop open in the grass, in hillsides, beneath trees and shrubs. The time has come for the elves to emerge from their stainless steel burrows and roam the Park.

The elves are the whimsical gardeners of a world: lawn mowers, tree pruners, leaf rakers, hedge trimmers, and plant doctors. They scurry on their appointed rounds, thousands upon thousands of them, bustling tirelessly on their individual tasks, maintaining the beauty of the countryside.

The night belongs to the dragons as well, those beasties gentle enough to be allowed out of the Blackwood. They assist the elves by trimming away excess foliage.

The dragon near the lake woke from his dreams of battle and lumbered from his cave, blinking sleepily at the illumination that brightened the sky above the nearest city. A mighty yawn stretched his jaws, and a trickle of flame escaped. He began browsing for his dinner.

Small patches of cold light zipped here and there to all sides of his scaly body; the dragon lashed his tail in greeting, for this was the firefly-glow of the elves as they went about their duties. Tiny hands waved in return, and a few of the miniature androids deposited armfuls of grass and leaves in front of the dragon's head. The dragon gratefully chewed them down, for he was fat and just a bit slothful; he disliked clumping up and down the forest in search of tender vegetation. The elves, for their part, knew logically that the best way to get rid of the trimmed and cut plants was by feeding the lizards. No waste, no mess, everything useful.

The dragon, in a contemplative mood, began to enjoy his dinner.

A rabbit appeared in front of him.

The rabbit had been hopping along, engrossed in his rabbity thoughts, so he was less alert than he might have been. The sight of the dragon froze him in his tracks; for an instant he stood transfixed, nose quivering pinkly in surprise and shock.

And in that instant the dragon, without thinking, roasted the rabbit with one short, hot whisper.

Then, shifting uneasily from one massive foot to another, he stared in bewilderment at the smoking carcass, somewhat irritated at the reflex that had taken control of him. *Now why did I do that?* he wondered. The thought briefly struck him that he could get in trouble for this breach of manners, but dragons don't have a very large attention span, and this thought was driven out by a sneaking sort of pride in his act. It made him feel . . . well . . . fearsome. And, with the thrill of sin coursing in his veins, he reached down his great head and daintily munched the rabbit, savoring with great pleasure the long-forgotten taste of roast meat.

After that he continued to forage for salad, feeling just a little guilty about the incident. Still, he felt, what was the loss of one rabbit, more or less? What could it hurt, if I don't do it again? After all, one gets a bit tired of nothing but vegetables eventually. Maybe I'll eat another one someday, in twenty or thirty years, just to keep in practice.

It gave him something to think about as he ate.

'Do you know what mythology means?' Miss Emily asked the class. They were strolling along the path that led to the meadow of the unicorns.

'Mythology is old stories,' piped up James, the dragon expert.

'Fairy stories,' said a tiny dark beauty.

'Very good, darlings,' said Miss Emily in delight. 'Myths are legends, stories that are mostly untrue.'

The class looked puzzled. 'But unicorns come from legends,' said a boy, 'and mermaids, and dragons, and pegasuses, and . . .'

'But those things are real. They're not myths.'

Miss Emily smiled. 'They used to be, my loves. You see we have a magical sort of world, and quite a lot of it didn't exist at one time.'

'Why, Miss Emily?'

'Well, when God made the world He made it in a certain way, a way that appealed to Him. But men had their own ideas about the way things should be, about things that were beautiful, or awe-inspiring, and they made up stories about those things. It must have saddened them, knowing deep down that the stories weren't true.' She put her hands on the shoulders of the two children closest to her. 'Finally we humans reached the point where we could do something about it; we could more or less tailor the world to our own specifications. And that's what happened. Out of the rough material God gave us we fashioned a work of art. So now all of these things are real, more or less.'

'They're not all real?'

'Not all.' Miss Emily was about to give an example when

she was interrupted by a frenzied ululation, which suddenly erupted in a nearby tree. The class jumped, then followed Miss Emily's pointing finger to a bird whose brightly colored wings frantically beat the air.

'What is it?' the children whispered.

'A phoenix. Watch.'

The bird began to shimmer, its bright colors wavering and running together. Tiny plumes of smoke rose delicately from its agitated body. And then the orange flames sprang out here and there, growing and spreading and joining until at last the bird was totally hidden by the bright crackling fire. Strangely, the tree was not harmed. The pyre rose gloriously and then died down, leaving nothing but ash in its wake.

Some of the children were crying.

'Don't weep, loves,' said Miss Emily. 'Just watch.'

As tiny hands rubbed wetness from pink cheeks the ash in the tree began to move, stirring fitfully as if disturbed by some slight breeze. Stronger, it pulled together and piled itself up. Then, with an abrupt blaze of light that hurt the eye the ash swirled, reformed and stood revealed as that same phoenix that had just been incinerated. The bird cooed happily.

The children laughed and clapped their hands. And, although she had expected it, Miss Emily also felt a surge of joy. 'The phoenix,' she explained, 'is not exactly alive, nor is it exactly dead. It is a compromise between the natural and the artificial, and we have to be satisfied with it.'

A fearful voice spoke up. 'Unicorns are real, aren't they, Miss Emily?'

'Oh yes, darling, unicorns, pegasi, dragons, mermaids, satyrs – they're all very much alive. But some of the more exotic creatures are artificial. The chimera, for instance, or the cockatrice. They'd be dangerous if they were real.'

'Some dragons are dangerous.'

'Yes, but they are under control. They are allowed to be wild so that hunters can hunt them.'

Little James got a faraway look in his eye. 'I will hunt them,' he said. 'When I am older I will go to the Blackwood and fight the biggest dragon I can find. And I'll use a spear, too. I won't use a gun.'

Miss Emily tenderly patted his head. 'And you'll get a fine trophy, my darling warrior. But you must promise to be careful, James, for the dragons of Blackwood Preserve are strong and fierce.'

'They won't hurt me.'

'Of course they won't,' smiled Miss Emily.

An attractive elderly couple strolled by, going the other way, and exchanged smiles and waves with the group of children. 'Have you been to the meadow at the end of the path?' asked Miss Emily.

'We've just come from there,' said the gentleman.

'Did you see the unicorns?'

The woman nodded. 'We saw them. They're in a fine humor this morning.'

'How marvelous!'

'Yes,' said the woman as they walked on, 'yes, it is.'

The children laughed in delight when they reached the meadow and again saw the game of the one-horned horses. the sun gleamed from the silvery spikes, sending brilliant shafts of light flashing off everywhere; the whinnies were bell-like in the soft clean air. Miss Emily was struck by the sweet melancholic knowledge that the game, for her, was closed.

'Today, my little loves,' she breathed, tears sparkling in eyes held spellbound by the cavorting animals, 'you can go out and play with them.'

There were ecstatic shouts, and small forms danced with excitement. 'Quiet, children, you must be quiet. Unicorns are skittish and easily frightened, so you must not make them nervous.'

'Won't they run from us, Miss Emily?'

'They will be happy to have you join them,' she answered, 'if you show them that you love them. Now run along and enjoy yourselves, for all too soon will come the day when you can only stand and watch them.'

The children, in a babble of laughter and talk, skipped out to join the herd. All, that is, but James. He held back, aching to go with the rest, but unwilling to leave Miss Emily alone. 'Won't you come too, Miss Emily?'

'I can't, darling, I can't. When I was as young as you I danced with the unicorns, but now that I'm older they would run away from me.'

'Are you sad?'

'A little, maybe. But you see, James, the games of the unicorns are for the children alone. You are the ones who enjoy them the most. And when you get older you'll be content to observe them for their beauty, leaving them for the younger ones to play with.'

'That will make me cry.'

'Perhaps a bit, at first. But by then you'll be eager to become a brave dragon hunter, and it won't bother you quite so much.'

'That's right, isn't it?' His face lit up with joy. 'The dragons will be waiting, won't they?'

'Yes, James, my darling; you do understand. There are so many, many things for you to see and do when you're older. The unicorns are here for you now. So go and have a good time.'

He gave a wave and ran off, bolting like an arrow from the bow across the grass to join the others. And Miss Emily put her hands to her lips and smiled a tiny smile, suddenly realizing that everything she told him was true.

The satyr had never known true unhappiness. But then, why should he? He was the living, breathing symbol of love – physical, sexual love, true, but of all the loves possible, perhaps that is the deepest, the most honest. It may be that it has the shortest existence, lasting at times no longer than a heartbeat, but it is no less real for all of that, and in that moment, oh, what fires can burn! In the space of a glimpse it is passion unchained, the lifeblood of the satyr. And whether anything comes of it, whether it changes into love of a different sort or ends as suddenly as it came is of no importance. It is enough that it happened.

He'd seen unhappiness; he'd wandered around the fringes. There were people, even now, who just couldn't seem to relax and enjoy themselves, who just couldn't. . . . But why submerge your own particular self in the self-imposed misery of others? The satyr tried to ease sadness where he found it, but he was wise in the ways of emotion, and he knew that true healing must come from within. The most he could hope for was to point the way.

The satyr had once been human, and, if he so desired, could be again, but the thought never even entered his mind. Why be merely human when one could be a satyr, beloved by everything and adoring everything, feeling the heady liquor of life filling your body? The satyr possessed so much ecstatic rapture that at times he had to let it overflow, spill out and wash everything around him.

This was such a time. He sat, naked as always, on a grassy knoll a few hundred feet from the mermaid pool, elbows resting on lifted knees, his pipes filling the air with their hypnotic melody. Chipmunks and squirrels, rabbits, cats, foxes, dogs, sheep and deer surrounded him quietly and listened. Birds, envious and admiring, sat on their branches and themselves swayed to the rhythm. Grass and flowers leaned toward him, bathing in his sun-bright music.

Miss Emily approached and sat beside him, face flushed, eyes downcast, her clothes hot and suddenly uncomfortable against her skin.

The satyr ended his song, kissed Miss Emily with lips like satin, and smiled at her radiant smile. 'I heard your music,' she said softly.

'Yes. I know.'

'Did you play it for me?'

'Yes,' he answered, with another kiss. 'And for me. For anyone willing to listen.'

Her eyes wandered down his body, lingered briefly on his sudden erection, and then moved shyly away. 'Your song touches everyone.'

'Not everyone. Some people can't listen.'

'How sad.'

'They are getting fewer.'

'And I love you,' he laughed. He kissed her again, and stroked her breast.

'Do you really? Do you really love me?'

'Of course,' he said. 'I love without reservation; I love everyone. But right here and right now – at this particular moment in this particular place – I love you most of all.'

She reached out a hand and touched his face. Her other hand ran along the seam of her garment; it opened and slid smoothly from her shoulders. She shook out her hair and stretched luxuriously, reveling in the sun as it covered her with light. The satyr began his caresses, and the warmth inside her threatened to shame the heat of the day.

'I fear I shan't be faithful,' she said, her breath panting out in that most natural way.

'Nor shall I,' said he, 'but I shall still love you. Remember that, and we shall be true to the meaning, if not the fact.'

'I vow,' she said as she pulled him close, 'I vow my faith in you.'

'We have each other for the moment,' he whispered, and entered her, 'and for the moment, nothing is more important.'

When Miss Emily woke up, the first thing she saw was William leaning against a nearby tree. She reached hastily for her shift, but, remembering the song of the satyr, let her arm relax. 'Hello,' she said.

William watched her for a moment. Then: 'Are you content?' he asked. 'Do you enjoy life?'

Her face registered surprise. 'Yes. Yes to both questions.'

'All the time? You don't get bored occasionally? Angry? Dissatisfied?'

'With so much to experience? How could I?'

William frowned, and kicked at some leaves. 'Yesterday,' he said at last, pointing in the direction of the pool, 'I sat over there for a long time. I was almost seduced by a mermaid, but I fought against it. Even your satyr failed to influence me.'

'But why? Why fight? It would have been very nice.'

William slid to a sitting position, still leaning against the tree. 'Well, there was no point, you see. When it was over it wouldn't have mattered at all. Better not to happen.'

'How can you say that? The act, the action, is important in itself. You would have had that moment.'

'The moment? That's worthless. I can always find something to amuse me for the moment, and always I wonder what I'll be doing the next moment.'

Miss Emily looked at him with great sympathy. 'You must be very unhappy.'

He shrugged. 'No, I don't think so. I am merely indifferent.'

'I can't believe that your life could be so empty.'

William grinned and looked at the ground, shaking his head. 'The only difference between my life and yours is that I admit the emptiness. It's small comfort, but it's all I have.'

Miss Emily started to speak, hesitated, then got to her feet. She picked her shift off the ground and slipped it over her head. 'Why is life empty?' she asked at last.

'Because it's meaningless. It's static. There is nothing important enough to fight for.'

'There is no need to fight. The battles have all been won.'

'And life,' said William quietly, 'has no purpose anymore.'

Miss Emily was truly shocked. 'What do you mean?'

'Man's greatest reason for existence has always been the struggle against his misery. Hunger, tyranny, ignorance, squalor, danger – these are the things that gave Man his soul and his destiny. Without them, we are less than men. Without them, we merely drift through the boredom of our lives until finally death puts an end to the mockery. And after it's over there has been no sense to it; the fact that we lived at all makes no difference one way or another.'

'I'm sorry,' said Miss Emily.

'The pattern of our existence has been locked into an unending circle,' William continued, almost to himself. 'In that circle, there is no glory; there can be no aspirations. The time of change is ended, and the lotus eaters surround me. I am useless; there are no worlds for me to save.'

The lump in Miss Emily's throat was a knot of pain. The tears washing her cheeks blurred William's image. 'I am so terribly sorry,' she whispered.

William stood. 'Your pity is misdirected,' he said. 'I realize what we are, and therein lies hope. Cry for those who live in darkness.' He watched her a moment longer, then turned and walked away.

And Miss Emily, powerless to help him, stood sobbing on the grassy hillside.

The dragon drowsed on a rock in front of his cave, the afternoon sun sending a glow of honeyed warmth spreading through his veins. Not really asleep, but definitely not awake, he was content to bask in the heat, letting his mythological dreams carry toward dusk and dinnertime.

The sound of doom blasted the still air, a sound like thunder in rage, crashing and booming so loudly that even the trees seemed to cringe before it. The dragon jumped and froze, shocked wide awake, every muscle tense and on edge. He smelled a burning smell, not unlike the familiar odor of one of his wild, rampaging brethren. But how could a beast of the Wildwood manage to wander into this tame and peaceful place? Curious, the dragon lumbered to his feet as another explosion ripped the afternoon. He looked around, unsure of the direction.

Close by, the field of the unicorns dissolved into chaos. The roar, the horrible flash of light, the huge chunks of earth torn out of the ground transformed the meadow into a picture of hell. And the unicorns, having never experienced anything like this before, stampeded in terror, maddened by a force they couldn't understand. Some fell, shredded apart, others lay torn and bleeding, crying their pain, their grief and their confusion.

At the edge of the meadow stood William, a third grenade in his hand, set to throw. His arm cocked back, his eyes strained through the dust, searching for the fleeing herd.

Something moved at the corner of his eye.

He whirled, ready to throw, then checked the move. Off to the side, near the woods, stood Miss Emily, surrounded by the children. They huddled against her, weeping. Miss Emily stood tall, as if unaware that she should fear this man and what he carried. Her face had such sorrow, such pity; it was a barrier between them, and William turned and fled.

And the satyr waited for him by the side of the trail. William couldn't use his grenade — the explosion would get both of them. So he hurled it far off the side, relishing the sound and the fury. Bits of dirt and shrubbery rained down on them.

'Stay out of my way,' he screamed.

The satyr, beautiful and grim, raised one hand. 'Hail, William,' he said, 'the new Messiah.'

'Don't laugh at me!'

'I can't laugh at you, William. I worship you. You are saving us from our stagnation. You are helping us out of the abyss of our happiness.'

'It has to be done!'

'Not for our sake, William. Please, don't do it for us.'

William reached in the bag at his side and grabbed another salvation. 'The struggle must resume. The battle must be won.' He hurled the words over his shoulder as he plunged through the trees.

'You're too late, William,' called the satyr. 'You're much too late.'

The last explosion was in this direction. The dragon walked carefully through the tall grass, skirting the trees in his path. And then a human rose up in front of him, a human throwing a rock, a human who made the ground shake and the dirt bite. The dragon's hide was lacerated by the explosion; his feet flew out from under him.

And William saw the dragon rise, towering high above him, nostrils smoking, bellowing a roar that matched the thunder of the grenades. And, with visions of glory and carnage dancing through his brain, the dragon let loose a mighty ribbon of flame that crackled over the man and consumed him. The dragon also consumed William.

And then, the madness gone, the dragon whimpered at the thought of what he had done. He had killed a human. And what's worse, he had eaten him, just as if he still lived in the Blackwood. For this sin, he *would* live in the Blackwood, banished forever from his peaceful, contented, lazy existence.

He'd be found out. The rangers would come for him and paralyze him; they would put him in one of their great machines and throw him to the mercy of the wilderness. He would live out his life as a target for the hunters, condemned to the violent legends he dreamed about.

The other dragons would hurt him, because he had no practice in the business of survival. Everything would be a danger.

The dragon cried his panic and stormed through the brush in a wild attempt to reach the safety of his cave, cool, damp and secure near the pool of the mermaids. Blindly he waddled, crushing plants underfoot and knocking aside the smaller trees.

And inside his cave, when he reached it, he curled up and shivered in an agony of fear and guilt. His wounds hurt also, sending steel bolts of pain through his body. He would have vomited the man if he could, vomited the experience, but dragons don't do that sort of thing. So he waited, and ached and tried not to think of his punishment.

The industrious elves came out of their burrows early this evening and set to work repairing the damage wrought by William's grenades. They tenderly removed the bodies of the dead unicorns and took them away to use as fertilizer, continuing the cycle that had been started so long ago. The rest of the herd, blessed by short memories, soon forgot why they had run and settled down to rest for the night.

Miss Emily and the children were not so blessed, but the teacher knew that, although the children had seen death, senseless, brutal and ugly, the love around them would reassure them, help them retain their innocence. They would understand, perhaps better than anyone else, just how precious their world really was.

As for the satyr, well, he had followed William, and so witnessed the outcome of his meeting with the dragon. And as the dragon lay terrorized in his cave the satyr sat cross-legged on the ground outside it, raised his pipes and sent a gentle melody in to lull the huge lizard with tranquil harmonies. And as he played, the tension left the dragon's form, the panic slipped away, the memories vanished. He calmed, relaxed and slept.

And still the satyr played, filling the dragon's dreams with loving tunes, giving him visions of soft flowers and running brooks, bright baubles and laughing children.

The knights in armor were gone.

THE
EXHIBITION

Scott Edelstein

Is there a future to the arts and do artists have a future? Not a very nice one in an overpopulated world, Scott Edelstein tells us, not a nice one at all.

His name, according to his identagram (No. 5551070023), is Wilson Francis Howell Markham. There are eleven other Wilson Francis Howell Markhams also alive, none of whom knows he exists. He knows none of them.

His profession, according to his identagram, is pnt: imp. An impressionist painter. One of 8,997,020 living impressionist painters.

His economic classification, according to his identagram, is DOLE. Meaning he is still on the Allowance; meaning he is an unknown. Meaning he is a failure. Meaning his apartment walls are adorned by his own work only.

He is a tall, lanky, tired young man with slightly slumped shoulders and lines reaching down from his nose to his mouth. With thin, straight, long yellow hair and a soft, urgent voice, with sad features and a sagging walk. With long, slender fingers that move quickly and smoothly and deliberately.

He has been a painter for ten years and has painted one hundred and five oils. Before he became a painter, he went to Art School and graduated with honors. Before that he received an M.A. and a Ph.D. from Michigan College, and before that he received a B.A. from Southern University. Before that he attended Academy and before that Basic Ed.

At this moment, Wilson Francis Howell Markham lies slumped in his armchair, asleep and exhausted, his fingers wrapped around a No. 3 paintbrush. In front of him is his easel, and on it his one hundred and fifth painting, just finished. A piece of W.F.H. Markham (which is how he signs his paintings) on canvas, and another line added to his aging face.

When he awakens, he must call Art Center, division nine, and say to them, 'I, number five five five one oh seven oh oh two three, have finished my hundred-and-fifth painting. It is called "Reluctant Sunset." ' And the computer will say, in return, 'Thank you for reporting. We will file this information, and we wish you the best of luck in your career.' And the circuit will disconnect and the computer will flipflop first this way, then that, and it will file the painting between 'Reluctant Soldiers' by No. 4113908891 and 'The Reluctant Women' by No. 4189767720, and also under No. 55510700230105, and again as painting No. 1908055944. And W.F.H. Markham will go out of his apartment and will try to sell his painting to famous artists to hang on their walls. Then perhaps he will go back to his apartment and eat, or perhaps he will stand in line to visit the park, or perhaps he will try to find someone to copulate with. Perhaps he will cry. Artists do cry.

Man in the City

It is early afternoon, and W.F.H. Markham awakens dizzily. He is covered with the sticky, odorous sweat of artistic labor, and he does not feel well rested. He exhales loudly and stands, rubbing his eyes. He looks at his one-hundred-and-fifth painting, which has taken over a month to finish. He smiles inwardly, proud and satisfied with his creation.

This, he thinks, is his greatest work. And he feels, inside, that this will be the painting that will sell, that will make him Recognized. He feels excitement on top of accomplishment. Perhaps, perhaps . . .

He calls Art Center, division nine, and tells them of his painting. The computer thanks him and wishes him the best of luck in his career.

He calls Jerome J.N. Nathan. Nathan's secretarial machine answers. He makes an appointment for three o'clock that afternoon, Jerome J.N. Nathan can give him fifteen minutes, he is told. He thanks the secretary and hangs up.

He can feel it, growing stronger – an inner stirring, a combination of yearning and joy. 'Reluctant Sunset' is his masterpiece, the final product of a life of study and work. It is all that is his life, all that is his environment, all that is his mind and soul. All that is good, all that is real.

He removes his clothing, goes to the cleanser in the corner of the room, stands under it and turns it on. He feels the dirt and moisture being sucked from his skin.

Today. Today is a beginning.

From across the room, he stares at his hundred-and-fifth painting, and smiles.

On his way to Nathan's home, Markham passes the open-space art gallery for his subcomplex. Several of his paintings are on exhibit at this gallery and are available for purchase and reproduction by Recognized artists. None of his paintings has yet been bought.

Markham checks his chronometer, finds that he has a few spare minutes. He sits cross-legged on the grass near the small display of his work and watches the passersby peruse his paintings.

A well-dressed middle-aged man, probably a Recognized artist, glances briefly at Markham's paintings, walks past. Another Recognized man examines the exhibit more carefully, gazing at each individual painting for several moments before moving on to the next. At the last painting he grimaces and turns away. Markham thinks he hears the man sigh. He grasps his most recent painting more tightly.

A young woman passes by next. She is tall and striking, and Markham thinks that she had probably been the model for many paintings by Recognized artists. She looks briefly at the first painting on display, then turns, her hair bouncing against her shoulders, then walks past Markham's other paintings, disinterested.

Markham feels a brief twinge of failure. Then, clutching his newly finished work, he rises and continues to Nathan's residence. His hopes remain with him.

Pilgrimage to Canterbury

'Hellow, Wilson,' Nathan says pleasantly, looking up from his easel and putting his brush down on the table beside him. 'You've brought something for me to look at?'

Markham smiles a ridiculous smile. Jerome Jeremiah Nevil Nathan is an abstract artist, one of 12,525,611 abstract artists. One of the most famous. He is, in fact, one of the ten or twelve best-known artists in the Middle Atlantic Complex. And he is noted for his willingness to look at the work of young, struggling, unknown artists. He is always encouraging, and many artists who have sold paintings to him have rapidly achieved Recognition, and then success.

When Markham brought Nathan his one-hundred-and fourth painting, Nathan smiled and said, 'This isn't bad, you know, this isn't bad.' He nodded, twice. 'You may make it yet.' And he smiled again and very politely showed Markham to the door. No sale.

But that was two months ago, and that painting (or so Markham thinks now) was vastly inferior to the one which he now holds proudly in his slightly trembling hands.

'Yes,' Markham says softly, removing the painting from its protective covering and holding it out for Nathan to take. 'My latest. My best, too, I think.'

Nathan, smiling, removes his own work-in-progress from his easel, places it gently on the table. He takes Markham's painting and puts it on the easel. He stands back, rubs his chin and examines it.

Anxious, as always, Markham looks around the large studio. Paintings cover the walls – not paintings of Nathan's own, but those of other artists, other famous artists. And a few little-knowns. Markham imagines his own work hanging beside the work of such famous men and women. He looks back at Nathan, who, still smiling, continues to peruse the painting.

Again, the feeling, the tremulous feeling of expectation.

'Interesting,' Nathan says politely, looking away from the painting. 'Your sense of perspective gets better and better, Wilson.'

Markham nods slightly in what he hopes is a humble gesture.

Nathan raises an eyebrow, sees Markham's eager expression. 'You're getting there,' he says.

W.F.H. Markham, young, hopeful artist, waits impatiently for the verdict.

'But you're still learning,' Nathan concludes. 'Your work is still a little gaudy. You've got to learn to tone your colors down; you just can't seem to keep your painting in control. Sorry, but no.'

Visit of the Queen of Sheba to King Solomon

Wilson Francis Howell Markham sits quietly, tiredly in his armchair, his sense of accomplishment replaced by a growing sense of failure. Every artist he has tried so far – Nathan, Mathwin, Simonson, Fletcher – has smiled sweetly at him and told him that he didn't want his painting. There are three more artists he can and will try – tomorrow – but he no longer hopes so strongly for success. *I'll admit it to myself*, he thinks with a heavy sigh. *I'm a failure.*

Wait a minute. You go through this every time you get a painting rejected.

But I never worked so hard on a painting before; I don't know if I can do any better. If my best isn't good enough . . .

A knock on his door.

Sighing again, fighting back what he realizes with slight surprise are real tears, he shuffles to the door and pushes the *admit* button.

Sharon Linda something, a slightly spaced-out writer of what Markham considers overwritten, emotional garbage. She stands in the doorway, smiling and fidgeting. She likes him and comes down often from her apartment two stories above for a visit. They have made love two or three times, never to Markham's real satisfaction.

'Wilson,' she says before he can utter a mandatory greeting. 'Do you remember my book *Bonds of Fellowship?*'

Markham nods. 'What about it?'

Her smile becomes a huge, almost imbecilic grin. 'I sold it to Claude Jameison for five hundred dollars. I'm Recognized now.'

He forces a smile onto his face, knowing she expects one. 'That's wonderful,' he says, with false happiness. His own aching need for achievement grows suddenly stronger; *she* has been Recognized, why cannot he be?

Still grinning, she looks directly into his eyes. 'I'm so happy. I've always wanted this to happen . . . Wilson, I think I'm going to cry.' She steps toward him, and Markham sees that her eyes are indeed wet. However, he feels no emotion toward her; she has cried in his presence before, never for sufficient reason.

She puts her palms on his sides and presses lightly. Tears are now forming in the corners of her eyes. Markham realizes that he is expected to reach out and hold her in his arms, but he makes no movement.

Sharon is not put off by his lack of emotion. She circles her arms about him and rests her head on his chest, sniffing.

He feels disgust − not even hatred for her, only disgust and misery. He pushes her away. 'Get out,' he says, almost pleading himself.

Finally, she senses that something is wrong with him. 'Wilson,' she says, rubbing her eyes, 'what's the matter?'

Again, 'Get out.'

Puzzled but uncaring, she says, 'I'll call you tomorrow,

when you feel better. Take care of yourself, Wilson.' This she says with a hint of mock concern, as if she doubts his sanity. She blows him a kiss, sniffs one last time and hurries out the door.

The Artist in His Studio

The pit in his stomach has grown deeper and deeper.

He stands before the last door; he has seen two of the remaining three artists who might have bought his work. Both said no with wide grins on their faces. He is beginning to dislike faces that smile.

Hesitantly, with the perverse rising hope of the man who knows that he has just one chance to avoid being doomed to failure, he knocks.

The door slides open almost immediately. A long, bony, surly face stares down at him.

'Mr. Carstenson?' Markham says, suppressing the quiver in his voice. 'I called earlier.'

A frown. 'You're Markham, is that right? Markham.'

'Wilson Markham. I've just completed a painting that I'd like to show you, if you have the time.' He has learned through past experience in dealing with Carstenson to be humble and polite no matter how obnoxious the man might become.

Carstenson grunts. 'Come in.'

Markham does.

Inside, paintings cover the walls. More are stacked on tables and chairs. Still more rest on easels, uncompleted.

'Well?' the older artist says, extending his arms and hands. 'Do you want to show me what you've done or not? I really don't have time to watch you stare at my walls. I have my own paintings to work on, as you can see.'

Markham hands him his painting.

Carstenson examines the painting closely, frowning deeply. He hands it back to Markham and has him hold it up while he steps back to look at it from a distance. He continues to frown.

Holding the painting tightly, Markham experiences the fantasy of the condemned man. He imagines the frown on Carstenson's face suddenly turning into a smile, while the man walks cockily over, pats him on the back and says, 'Markham, I want to buy this.'

'Markham.' Loudly and with a tinge of annoyance. Carstenson has finished examining the painting, is now sitting on the edge of a chair, his rump and lower back brushing against a stack of framed paintings and prints.

Painful, worried anticipation. Tense hope.

'Markham, sometimes you really bother me. Do you seriously expect me to buy something like this? You've shown me some of your other stuff, and at least some of it wasn't too bad. But this one is nothing but a piece of shit, and if you can't realize that, then you probably never knew what you were doing in the first place.'

Markham looks into the older artist's eyes, amazed and hurt. Carstenson glares back for a moment; then his mouth twitches slightly as he sees the unstifled emotion on Markham's face. 'Look, don't cry,' he says. 'Do you think I'm telling you this for my own benefit?' His glare grows colder. 'Face up to it, Markham, you're just not an artist. Not a painter, anyway. All your work is way too subdued, too confined. If you want to be Recognized, you're going to have to try some other field.'

Markham, stunned, simply stares helplessly, silently, into the other man's face.

Not at all deeply moved, Carstenson stares back. 'Listen, Markham, I'm only trying to keep you from beating your head against a wall for the rest of your life. I know talent when I see it; I've bought dozens of paintings from new artists in the past couple of years, and most of those artists have been doing very well. But those people were *painters*. You just aren't; it's as simple as that.'

Mechanically, Markham blinks his eyes, turns, walks to the door. Carstenson says nothing.

Without looking back – looking back is too terrifying now, nearly as terrifying as looking forward – he opens the door and shuffles out. He clutches the painting tightly. His hands feel empty, but his burden is ten years heavy.

Still Life

Slowly he realizes that he is back in his apartment, in the armchair, staring at his easel. On the easel is 'Reluctant Sunset.' He tries to remember how long he has been sitting, finds no answer, gives up. He considers getting up and eating something, rejects the idea. He feels no desire for food.

Sex. He thinks of Sharon and shivers in disgust. *Recog-*

nized. She is no longer merely the loud, tacky girl upstairs who wants his body.

He sighs deeply and shivers again. He rubs his hands back and forth on the chair.

He is more than tired. Empty. Emptied.

He stands up wearily and rubs his forehead. He picks up a brush and fingers it absentmindedly. Tonight, he will begin a new painting. He must. Each time, after returning with an unsold painting, he forces himself to begin anew. Next time, next time . . .

You're just not an artist.

He will begin again. He must. He must. He must.

Wracked by pain and failure, he falls back into the chair. The paintbrush falls from his trembling fingers. He lifts his hands to his face and begins to cry.

The Adoration of the Shepherds

Below, the crowd babbles excitedly.

He waits patiently for the audience to grow larger.

He smiles, coldly.

It is quite a crowd: two thousand, perhaps three thousand people. He has called up Police Center, division four-A, several hours before, and notified it of his intentions, and it in turn has done a good job of spreading the word around to the general public.

The huge bouquet of faces stares up at him, anxious, expectant. Waiting.

He has waited long enough.

At his first movement, a tremendous shiver shoots through him. *Is this the solution?* he thinks, for the twentieth time. *Can't I keep trying, and someday, maybe, I'll make it?*

And then, again, he hears the words: *You're just not an artist.*

No.

Am I just trying to spite the world? Am I getting back at society for not making me a success? Who am I trying to revenge: who am I mad at? Nathan? Carstenson? Sharon? Myself?

Five stories below, the crowd begins clapping furiously.

'*It's too late now*', he thinks, partly in fear, partly with relief. He *must* go through with it now.

He smiles again. Feeling alone and empty but somewhat excited, he waves down at the crowd.

The throngs cheer for him.

He begins.

Buckets of paint and several brushes of various sizes rest beside him on the rooftop. He picks up a large brush and dips it into the bright blue paint.

As the thousands gaze up at him, he paints his face blue.

Again the crowd cheers for him.

He tosses the brush off the roof. Hundreds of hands reach greedily to grab it. The noise of the crowd increases as someone catches it.

He begins to take off his clothes. He removes his shirt, tosses this, too, to the crowd. And he paints his chest a fiery red.

Next, he removes his pants and undershorts, paints his left leg green, his right leg orange and his genitals a deep purple. For some reason, which he himself cannot grasp, he feels compelled to fold his pants and underwear in a small pile next to the paints.

Finally, he picks up a can of black, pours its contents over one arm, then the other.

Dripping, he holds his arms up for silence. The crowd, faces turned upward like young birds seeking food, becomes quiet. Silently, the policemen push the crowd back to give him room.

With a mad flourish, he lifts the can of turpentine and splashes the fluid all over his body.

He walks to the very edge of the roof, looks down. He is not afraid, nor regretful, nor unhappy.

I wonder if people will appreciate my paintings after I die, he thinks. *So many artists were scorned during their lifetimes – and when they died, their work became famous.*

He picks up the matches, takes one and strikes it. He watches it flare for a moment, then looks down at the crowd one final time.

And again, he smiles. And ignites himself. And hurls himself off the edge of the rooftop.

The crowd utters a great gasp as the body bursts into flames and begins to fall.

'My God, it's beautiful,' an onlooker murmurs.

'Yeah,' her companion answers. 'But is it art?'

149

SKETCHES AMONG
THE RUINS OF
MY MIND

Philip José Farmer

I like Phil Farmer. His scowling, hawk faced, midwest exterior is a fake and he is one of the nicest people you might want to meet. And he is a writer of note. In 1952 his story 'The Lovers' introduced the concept of sex to science fiction, a concept that had great popularity elsewhere but had previously been prominent by its absence from this whiter-than-white area of literary enterprise. He not only writes well but he writes about original concepts, something very hard to do among the well picked-over bones of SF ideas. Now he takes a familiar idea, loss of memory, and shows that we have never considered all of the chilling possibilities that it might involve.

I

June 1, 1980

It is now 11:00 P.M., and I am afraid to go to bed. I am not alone. The whole world is afraid of sleep.

This morning I got up at 6:30 A.M., as I do every Wednesday. While I shaved and showered, I considered the case of the state of Illinois against Joseph Lankers, accused of murder. It was beginning to stink as if it were a three-day-old fish. My star witness would undoubtedly be charged with perjury.

I dressed, went downstairs, and kissed Carole good morning. She poured me a cup of coffee and said, 'The paper's late.'

That put me in a bad temper. I need both coffee and the morning newspaper to get me started.

Twice during breakfast, I left the table to look outside. Neither paper nor newsboy had appeared.

At seven, Carole went upstairs to wake up Mike and Tom, aged ten and eight respectively. Saturdays and Sundays they rise early even though I'd like them to stay in bed so their horsing around won't wake me. School days they have to be dragged out.

The third time I looked out of the door, Joe Gale, the

paperboy, was next door. My paper lay on the stoop.

I felt disorientated, as if I'd walked into the wrong courtroom or the judge had given my client, a shoplifter, a life sentence. I was out of phase with the world. This couldn't be Sunday. So what was the Sunday issue, bright in its covering of the colored comic section, doing there? Today was Wednesday.

I stepped out to pick it up and saw old Mrs. Douglas, my neighbor to the left. She was looking at the front page of her paper as if she could not believe it.

The world rearranged itself into the correct lines of polarization. My thin panic dwindled into nothing. I thought, the *Star* has really goofed this time. That's what comes from depending so much on a computer to put it together. One little short circuit, and Wednesday's paper comes out in Sunday's format.

The *Star*'s night shift must have decided to let it go through; it was too late for them to rectify the error.

I said, 'Good morning, Mrs. Douglas! Tell me, what day is it?'

'The twenty-eighth of May,' she said. 'I think . . .'

I walked out into the yard and shouted after Joe. Reluctantly, he wheeled his bike around.

'What is this?' I said, shaking the paper at him. 'Did the *Star* screw up?'

'I don't know, Mr. Franham,' he said. 'None of us knows, honest to God.'

By 'us' he must have meant the other boys he met in the morning at the paper drop.

'We all thought it was Wednesday. That's why I'm late. We couldn't understand what was happening, so we talked a long time and then Bill Ambers called the office. Gates, he's the circulation manager, was just as bongo as we was.'

'Were,' I said.

'What?' he said.

'We *were*, not *was*, just as bongo, whatever that means,' I said.

'For God's sake, Mr. Franham, who cares!' he said.

'Some of us still do,' I said. 'All right, what did Gates say?'

'He was upset as hell,' Joe said. 'He said heads were gonna roll. The night staff had fallen asleep for a couple of hours, and some joker had diddled up the computers, or . . .'

'That's all it is?' I said. I felt relieved.

When I went inside, I got out the papers for the last four days from the cycler. I sat down on the sofa and scanned them.

I didn't remember reading them. I didn't remember the past four days at all!

Wednesday's headline was: MYSTERIOUS OBJECT ORBITS EARTH.

I did remember Tuesday's articles, which stated that the big round object was heading for a point between the Earth and the moon. It had been detected three weeks ago when it was passing through the so-called asteroid belt. It was at that time traveling approximately 57,000 kilometers per hour, relative to the sun. Then it had slowed down, had changed course several times, and it became obvious that, unless it changed course again, it was going to come near Earth.

By the time it was eleven million miles away, the radars had defined its size and shape, though not its material composition. It was perfectly spherical and exactly half a kilometer in diameter. It did not reflect much light. Since it had altered its path so often, it had to be artificial. Strange hands, or strange somethings, had built it.

I remembered the panic and the many wild articles in the papers and magazines and the TV specials made overnight to discuss its implications.

It had failed to make any response whatever to the radio and laser signals sent from Earth. Many scientists said that it probably contained no living passengers. It had to be of interstellar origin. The sentient beings of some planet circling some star had sent it out equipped with automatic equipment of some sort. No being could live long enough to travel between the stars. It would take over four years to get from the nearest star to Earth even if the object could travel at the speed of light, and that was impossible. Even one-sixteenth the speed of light seemed incredible because of the vast energy requirements. No, this thing had been launched with only electromechanical devices as passengers, had attained its top speed, turned off its power, and coasted until it came within the outer reaches of our solar system.

According to the experts, it must be unable to land on Earth because of its size and weight. It was probably just a surveying vessel, and after it had taken some photographs and made some radar/laser sweeps, it would proceed to wherever it was supposed to go, probably back to an orbit around its home planet.

2

Last Wednesday night, the president had told us that we had nothing to fear. And he'd tried to end on an optimistic note. At least, that's what Wednesday's paper said. The beings who had sent The Ball must be more advanced than we, and they must have many good things to give us. And we might be able to make beneficial contributions to them. Like what? I thought.

Some photographs of The Ball, taken from one of the manned orbiting laboratories, were on the second page. It looked just like a giant black billiard ball. One TV comic had suggested that the other side might bear a big white 8. I may have thought that this was funny last Wednesday, but I didn't think so now. It seemed highly probable to me that The Ball was connected with the four-days' loss of memory. How, I had no idea.

I turned on the 7:30 news channels, but they weren't much help except in telling us that the same thing had happened to everybody all over the world. Even those in the deepest diamond mines or submarines had been affected. The president was in conference, but he'd be making a statement over the networks sometime today. Meantime, it was known that no radiation of any sort had been detected emanating from The Ball. There was no evidence whatsoever that the object had caused the loss of memory. Or, as the jargon-crazy casters were already calling it, 'memloss.'

I'm a lawyer, and I like to think logically, not only about what has happened but what might happen. So I extrapolated on the basis of what little evidence, or data, there was.

On the first of June, a Sunday, we woke up with all memory of May 31 back through May 28 completely gone. We had thought that yesterday was the twenty-seventh and that this morning was that of the twenty-eighth.

If The Ball had caused this, why had it only taken four days of our memory? I didn't know. Nobody knew. But perhaps The Ball, its devices, that is, were limited in scope. Perhaps they couldn't strip off any more than four days of memory at a time from everybody on Earth.

Postulate that this is the case. Then, what if the same thing happens tomorrow? We'll wake up tomorrow, June 2, with all memory of yesterday, June 1, and three more days of May, the twenty-seventh through the twenty-fifth, gone. Eight days in one solid stretch.

And if this ghastly thing should occur the following day, June 3, we'll lose another four days. All memory of June 2 will have disappeared. With it will go the memory of three more days, from May twenty-fourth through the twenty-second. Twelve days in all from June 2 backward!

And the next day? June 3 lost, too, along with May 21 through May 19. Sixteen days of a total blank. And the next day? And the next?

No, it's too hideous, and too fantastic, to think about.

While we were watching TV, Carole and the boys besieged me with questions. She was frantic. The boys seemed to be enjoying the mystery. They'd awakened expecting to go to school, and now they were having a holiday.

To all their questions, I said, 'I don't know. Nobody knows.'

I wasn't going to frighten them with my extrapolations. Besides, I didn't believe them myself.

'You'd better call up your office and tell them you can't come in today,' Carole said, 'Surely Judge Payne'll call off the session today.'

'Carole, it's Sunday, not Wednesday, remember?' I said.

She cried for a minute. After she'd wiped away the tears, she said, 'That's just it! I *don't* remember! My God, what's happening?'

The newscasters also reported that the White House was flooded with telegrams and phone calls demanding that rockets with H-bomb warheads be launched against The Ball. The specials, which came on after the news, were devoted to The Ball. These had various authorities, scientists, military men, ministers, and a few science-fiction authors. None of them radiated confidence, but they were all temperate in their approach to the problem. I suppose they had been picked for their level-headedness. The networks had screened out the hotheads and the crackpots. They didn't want to be generating any more hysteria.

But Anel Robertson, a fundamentalist faith healer with a powerful radio/TV station of his own, had already declared that The Ball was a judgment of God on a sinful planet. It was

The Destroying Angel. I knew that because Mrs. Douglas, no fanatic but certainly a zealot, had phoned me and told me to dial him in. Robertson had been speaking for an hour, she said, and he was going to talk all day.

She sounded frightened, and yet, beneath the fear, was a note of joy. Obviously, she didn't think that she was going to be among the goats when the last days arrived. She'd be right in there with the whitest of the sheep. My curiosity finally overcame my repugnance for Robertson. I dialed the correct number but got nothing except a pattern. Later today, I found out his station had been shut down for some infraction of FCC regulations. At least, that was the explanation given on the news, but I suspected that the government regarded him as a hysteria monger.

At eleven, Carole reminded me that it was Sunday and that if we didn't hurry, we'd miss church.

The Forrest Hill Presbyterian has a good attendance, but its huge parking lot has always been adequate. This morning, we had to park two blocks up the street and walk to church. Every seat was filled. We had to stand in the anteroom near the front door. The crowd stank of fear. Their faces were pale and set; their eyes, big. The air conditioning labored unsuccessfully to carry away the heat and humidity of the packed and sweating bodies. The choir was loud but quavering; their 'Rock of Ages' was crumbling.

Dr. Boynton would have prepared his sermon on Saturday afternoon, as he always did. But today he spoke impromptu. Perhaps, he said, this loss of memory *had* been caused by The Ball. Perhaps there were living beings in it who had taken four days away from us, not as a hostile move but merely to demonstrate their immense powers. There was no reason to anticipate that we would suffer another loss of memory. These beings merely wanted to show us that we were hopelessly inferior in science and that we could not launch a successful attack against them.

'What the hell's he doing?' I thought. 'Is he trying to scare us to death?'

Boynton hastened then to say that beings with such powers, of such obvious advancement, would not, could not, be hostile. They would be on too high an ethical plane for such evil things as war, unless they were attacked, of course. They would regard us as beings who had not yet progressed to their level but had the potentiality, the God-given potentiality, to be brought up to a high level. He was sure that, when they made contact with us, they would tell us that all was for the best.

They would tell us that we must, like it or not, become true Christians. At least, we must all, Buddhists, Moslems and so forth, become Christian in spirit, whatever our religion or lack thereof. They would teach us how to live as brothers and sisters, how to be happy, how to truly love. Assuredly, God had sent The Ball, since nothing happened without His knowledge and consent. He had sent these beings, whoever they were, not as Destroying Angels but as Sharers of Peace, Love and Prosperity.

That last, with the big P, seemed to settle down most of the congregation. Boynton had not forgotten that most of his flock were of the big-business and professional classes. Nor had he forgotten that, inscribed on the arch above the church entrance was, THEY SHALL PROSPER WHO LOVE THEE.

3

We poured out into a bright warm June afternoon. I looked up into the sky but could see no Ball, of course. The news media had said that, despite its great distance from Earth, it was circling Earth every sixty-five minutes. It wasn't in a free fall orbit. It was applying continuous power to keep it on its path, although there were no detectable emanations of energy from it.

The memory loss had occurred all over the world between 1:00 A.M. and 2:00 A.M. Central Standard Time. Those who were not already asleep fell asleep for a minimum of an hour. This had, of course, caused hundreds of thousands of accidents. Planes not on automatic pilot had crashed, trains had collided or been derailed, ships had sunk, and more than two hundred thousand had been killed or seriously injured. At least a million vehicle drivers and passengers had been injured. The ambulance and hospital services had found it impossible to handle the situation. The fact that their personnel had been asleep for at least an hour and that it had taken them some time to recover from their confusion on awakening had aggravated the situation considerably. Many had died who might have lived if immediate service had been available.

There were many fires, too, the largest of which were still raging in Tokyo, Athens, Naples, Harlem, and Baltimore.

I thought, Would beings on a high ethical plane have put us to sleep knowing that so many people would be killed and badly hurt?

One curious item was about two rangers who had been thinning a herd of elephants in Kenya. While sleeping, they had been trampled to death. Whatever it is that's causing this, it's very specific. Only human beings are affected.

The optimism, which Boynton had given us in the church, melted in the sun. Many must have been thinking, as I was, that if Boynton's words were prophetic, we were helpless. Whatever the things in the The Ball, whether living or mechanical, decided to do for us, or to us, we were no longer masters of our own fate. Some of them must have been thinking about what the technologically superior whites had done to various aboriginal cultures. All in the name of progress and God.

But this would be, must be, different, I thought. Boynton must be right. Surely such an advanced people would not be as we were. Even we are not what we were in the bad old days. We have learned.

But then an advanced technology does not necessarily accompany an advanced ethics.

'Or whatever,' I murmured.

'What did you say, dear?' Carole said.

I said, 'Nothing,' and shook her hand off my arm. She had clung to it tightly all through the service, as if *I* were the rock of the ages. I walked over to Judge Payne, who's sixty years old but looked this morning as if he were eighty. The many broken veins on his face were red, but underneath them was a grayishness.

I said hello and then asked him if things would be normal tomorrow. He didn't seem to know what I was getting at, so I said, 'The trial will start on time tomorrow?'

'Oh, yes, the trial,' he said. 'Of course, Mark.'

He laughed whinnyingly and said, 'Provided that we all haven't forgotten today when we wake up tomorrow.'

That seemed incredible, and I told him so.

'It's not law school that makes good lawyers,' he said, 'It's experience. And experience tells us that the same damned thing, with some trifling variations, occurs over and over, day after day. So what makes you think this evil thing won't happen again? And if it does, how're you going to learn from it when you can't remember it?'

I had no logical argument, and he didn't want to talk any

157

more. He grabbed his wife by the arm, and they waded through the crowd as if they thought they were going to step in a sinkhole and drown in a sea of bodies.

This evening, I decided to record on tape what's happened today. Now I lay me down to sleep, I pray the Lord my memory to keep, if I forget while I sleep . . .

Most of the rest of today, I've spent before the TV. Carole wasted hours trying to get through the lines to her friends for phone conversations. Three-fourths of the time, she got a busy signal. There were bulletins on the TV asking people not to use the phone except for emergencies, but she paid no attention to it until about eight o'clock. A TV bulletin, for the sixth time in an hour, asked that the lines be kept open. About twenty fires had broken out over the town, and the firemen couldn't be informed of them because of the tie-up. Calls to hospitals had been similarly blocked.

I told Carole to knock it off, and we quarreled. Our suppressed hysteria broke loose, and the boys retreated upstairs to their room behind a closed door. Eventually, Carole started crying and threw herself into my arms, and then I cried. We kissed and made up. The boys came down looking as if we had failed them, which we had. For them, it was no longer a fun-adventure from some science-fiction story.

Mike said, 'Dad, could you help me go over my arithmetic lessons?'

I didn't feel like it, but I wanted to make it up to him for that savage scene. I said sure and then, when I saw what he had to do, I said. 'But all this? What's the matter with your teacher? I never saw so much . . .'

I stopped. Of course, he had forgotten all he'd learned in the last three days of school. He had to do his lessons all over again.

This took us until eleven, though we might have gone faster if I hadn't insisted on watching the news every half-hour for at least ten minutes. A full thirty minutes were used listening to the president, who came on at 9 : 30. He had nothing to add to what the newsmen had said except that, within thirty days, The Ball would be completely dealt with – one way or another. If it didn't make some response to our signals within two days, then we would send up a four-man expedition, which would explore The Ball.

If it can get inside, I thought.

If, however, The Ball should commit any more hostile acts, then the United States would immediately launch, in conjunction with other nations, rockets armed with H-bombs.

Meanwhile, would we all join the president in an inter-denominational prayer?

We certainly would.

At eleven, we put the kids to bed. Tom went to sleep before we were out of the room. But about half an hour later, as I passed their door, I heard a low voice from the TV. I didn't say anything to Mike, even if he did have to go to school next day.

At twelve, I made the first part of this tape.

But here it is, one minute to one o'clock in the morning. If the same thing happens tonight as happened yesterday, then the nightside hemisphere will be affected first. People in the time zone which bisects the South and North Atlantic oceans and covers the eastern half of Greenland, will fall asleep. Just in case it does happen again, all airplanes have been grounded. Right now, the TV is showing the bridge and the salon of the trans-Atlantic liner *Pax*. It's five o'clock there, but the salon is crowded. The passengers are wearing party hats and confetti, and balloons are floating everywhere. I don't know what they could be celebrating. The captain said a little while ago that the ship's on automatic, but he doesn't expect a repetition of last night. The interviewer said that the governments of the dayside nations have not been successful keeping people home. We've been getting shots from everywhere, the sirens are wailing all over the world, but, except for the totalitarian nations, the streets of the daytime world are filled with cars. The damned fools just didn't believe it would happen again.

Back to the bridge and the salon of the ship. My God! They *are* falling asleep!

The announcers are repeating warnings. Everybody lie down so they won't get hurt by falling. Make sure all home appliances, which might cause fires, are turned off. And so on and so on.

I'm sitting in a chair with a tilted back. Carole is on the sofa.

Now I'm on the sofa. Carole just said she wanted to be holding on to me when this horrible thing comes.

The announcers are getting hysterical. In a few minutes, New York will be hit. The eastern half of South America is under. The central section is going under.

4

True date: June 2, 1980. Subjective date: May 25, 1980

My God! How many times have I said, 'My God!' in the last two days?

I awoke on the sofa beside Carole and Mike. The clock indicated three in the morning. Chris Turner was on the TV. I didn't know what he was talking about. All I could understand was that he was trying to reassure his viewers that everything was all right and that everything would be explained shortly.

What was I doing on the sofa? I'd gone to bed about eleven the night of May 24, a Saturday. Carole and I had had a little quarrel because I'd spent all day working on the Lankers case, and she said that I'd promised to take her to see *Nova Express*. And so I had — if I finished work before eight, which I obviously had not done. So what were we doing on the sofa, where had Mike come from, and what did Turner mean by saying that today was June 2?

The tape recorder was on the table near me, but it didn't occur to me to turn it on.

I shook Carole awake, and we confusedly asked each other what had happened. Finally, Turner's insistent voice got our attention, and he explained the situation for about the fifth time so far. Later, he said that an alarm clock placed by his ear had awakened him at two-thirty.

Carole made some coffee, and we drank four cups apiece. We talked wildly, with occasional breaks to listen to Turner, before we became half-convinced that we had indeed lost all memory of the last eight days. Mike slept on through it, and finally I carried him up to his bed. His TV was still on. Nate Frobisher, Mike's favorite spieler, was talking hysterically. I turned him off and went back downstairs. I figured out later that Mike had gotten scared and come downstairs to sit with us.

Dawn found us rereading the papers from May 24 through June 1. It was like getting news from Mars. Carole took a tranquilizer to quiet herself down, but I preferred Wild Turkey. After she'd seen me down six ounces, Carole said I should lay off the bourbon. I wouldn't be fit to go to work. I told her that if she thought anybody'd be working today, she was out of her mind.

At seven, I went out to pick up the paper. It wasn't there.

At a quarter to eight, Joe delivered it. I tried to talk to him, but he wouldn't stop. All he said, as he pedaled away, was, 'It ain't Saturday!'

I went back in. The entire front page was devoted to The Ball and this morning's events up to four o'clock. Part of the paper had been set up before one o'clock. According to a notice at the bottom of the page, the staff had awakened about three. It took then an hour to straighten themselves out, and then they'd gotten together the latest news and made up the front page and some of section C. They'd have never made it when they did if it wasn't for the computer, which printed justified lines from voice input.

Despite what I'd said earlier, I decided to go to work. First, I had to straighten the boys out. At ten, they went off to school. It seemed to me that it was useless for them to do so. But they were eager to talk with their classmates about this situation. To tell the truth, I wanted to get down to the office and the courthouse for the same reason. I wanted to talk this over with my colleagues. Staying home all day with Carole seemed a waste of time. We just kept saying the same thing over and over again.

Carole didn't want me to leave. She was too frightened to stay home by herself. Both our parents are dead, but she does have a sister who lives in Hannah, a small town nearby. I told her it'd do her good to get out of the house. And I just had to get to the courthouse. I couldn't find out what was happening there because the phone lines were tied up.

When I went outside to get into my car, Carole ran down after me. Her long blonde hair was straggling; she had big bags under her eyes; she looked like a witch.

'Mark! Mark!' she said.

I took my finger off the starter button and said, 'What is it?'

'I know you'll think I'm crazy, Mark,' she said. 'But I'm about to fall apart!'

'Who isn't?' I said.

'Mark,' she said, 'what if I go out to my sister's and then forget how to get back? What if I forgot *you*?'

'This thing only happens at night,' I said.

'So far!' she screamed. 'So far!'

'Honey,' I said, 'I'll be home early. I promise. If you don't want to go, stay here. Go over and talk to Mrs. Knight. I see her looking out her window. She'll talk your leg off all day.'

I didn't tell her to visit any of her close friends, because she didn't have any. Her best friend had died of cancer last year, and two others with whom she was familiar had moved away.

'If you do go to your sister's,' I said, 'make a note on a map reminding you where you live and stick it on top of the dashboard, where you can see it.'

'You son of a bitch,' she said. 'It isn't funny!'

'I'm not being funny,' I said. 'I got a feeling . . .'

'What about?' she said.

'Well, we'll be making notes to ourselves soon. If this keeps up,' I said.

I thought I was kidding then. Thinking about it later today I see that that is the only way to get orientated in the morning. Well, not the only way, but it'll have to be the way to get started when you wake up. Put a note where you can't overlook it, and it'll tell you to turn on a recording, which will, in turn, summarize the situation. Then you turn on the TV and get some more information.

I might as well have stayed home. Only half of the courthouse personnel showed up, and they were hopelessly inefficient. Judge Payne wasn't there and never will be. He'd had a fatal stroke at six that morning while listening to the TV. Walter Barbindale, my partner, said that the judge probably would have had a stroke sometime in the near future, anyway. But this situation must certainly have hastened it.

'The stock market's about hit bottom,' he said. 'One more day of this, and we'll have another worldwide depression. Nineteen twenty-nine won't hold a candle to it. And I can't even get through to my broker to tell him to sell everything.'

'If everybody sells, then the market *will* crash,' I said.

'Are you hanging onto your stocks?' he said.

'I've been too busy to even think about it,' I said. 'You might say I forgot.'

'That isn't funny,' he said.

'That's what my wife said,' I answered. 'But I'm not trying to be funny, though God knows I could use a good laugh. Well, what're we going to do about Lankers?'

'I went over some of the records,' he said. 'We haven't got a chance. I tell you, it was a shock finding out, for the second time, mind you, though I don't remember the first, that our star witness is in jail on a perjury charge.'

Since all was chaos in the courthouse, it wasn't much use trying to find out who the judge would be for the new trial for Lankers. To tell the truth, I didn't much care. There were far more important things to worry about than the fate of an undoubtedly guilty murderer.

I went to Grover's Rover Bar, which is a block from the courthouse. As an aside, for my reference or for whoever might be listening to this someday, why am I telling myself things I know perfectly well, like the location of Grover's? Maybe it's because I think I might forget them some day.

Grover's, at least, I remembered well, as I should, since I'd been going there ever since it was built, five years ago. The air was thick with tobacco and pot smoke and the odors of pot, beer and booze. And noisy. Everybody was talking fast and loud, which is to be expected in a place filled with members of the legal profession. I bellied up to the bar and bought the D.A. a shot of Wild Turkey. We talked about what we'd done that morning, and then he told me he had to release two burglars that day. They'd been caught and jailed two days before. The arresting officers had, of course, filed their reports. But that wasn't going to be enough when the trial came up. Neither the burglars nor the victims and the officers remembered a thing about the case.

'Also,' the D.A. said, 'at two-ten this morning, the police got a call from the Black Shadow Tavern on Washington Street. They didn't get there until three-thirty because they were too disorientated to do anything for an hour or more. When they did get to the tavern, they found a dead man. He'd been beaten badly and then stabbed in the stomach. Nobody remembered anything, of course. But from what we could piece together, the dead man must've gotten into a drunken brawl with a person or persons unknown shortly before 1:00 A.M. Thirty people must've witnessed the murder. So we have a murderer or murderers walking the streets today who don't even remember the killing or anything leading up to it.'

'They might know they're guilty if they'd been planning it for a long time,' I said.

He grinned and said, 'But he, or they, won't be telling anybody. No one except the corpse had blood on him nor did anybody have bruised knuckles. Two were arrested for carrying saps, but so what? They'll be out soon, and nobody, but nobody, can prove they used the saps. The knife was still half-sticking in the deceased's belly, and his efforts to pull it out destroyed any fingerprints.'

5

We talked and drank a lot, and suddenly it was 6:00 P.M. I was in no condition to drive and had sense enough to know it. I tried calling Carole to come down and get me, but I couldn't get through. At 6:30 and 7:00, I tried again without success. I decided to take a taxi. But after another drink, I tried again and this time got through.

'Where've you been?' she said. 'I called your office, but nobody answered. I was thinking about calling the police.'

'As if they haven't got enough to do,' I said. 'When did *you* get home?'

'You're slurring,' she said coldly.

I repeated the question.

'Two hours ago,' she said.

'The lines were tied up,' I said. 'I tried.'

'You knew how scared I was, and you didn't even care,' she said.

'Can I help it if the D.A. insisted on conducting business at the Rover?' I said. 'Besides, I was trying to forget.'

'Forget what?' she said.

'Whatever it was I forgot,' I said.

'You ass!' she screamed. 'Take a taxi!'

The phone clicked off.

She didn't make a scene when I got home. She'd decided to play it cool because of the kids, I suppose. She was drinking gin and tonic when I entered, and she said, in a level voice, '*You*'ll have some coffee. And after a while you can listen to the tape you made yesterday. It's interesting, but spooky.'

'What tape?' I said.

'Mike was fooling around with it,' she said. 'And he found out you'd recorded what happened yesterday.'

'That kid!' I said. 'He's always snooping around. I told him to leave my stuff alone. Can't a man have any privacy around here?'

'Well, don't say anything to him,' she said. 'He's upset as it is. Anyway, it's a good thing he did turn it on. Otherwise, you'd have forgotten all about it. I think you should make a daily record.'

164

'So you think it'll happen again?' I said.

She burst into tears. After a moment, I put my arms around her. I felt like crying, too. But she pushed me away, saying, 'You stink of rotten whiskey!'

'That's because it's mostly bar whiskey,' I said. 'I can't afford Wild Turkey at three dollars a shot.'

I drank four cups of black coffee and munched on some shrimp dip. As an aside, I can't really afford that, either, since I only make forty-five thousand dollars a year.

When we went to bed, we went to bed. Afterward, Carole said, 'I'm sorry, darling, but my heart wasn't really in it.'

'That wasn't all,' I said.

'You've got a dirty mind,' she said. 'What I meant was I couldn't stop thinking, even while we were doing it, that it wasn't any good doing it. We won't remember it tomorrow, I thought.'

'How many do we really remember?' I said. 'Sufficient unto the day is the, uh, good thereof.'

'It's a good thing you didn't try to fulfil your childhood dream of becoming a preacher,' she said. 'You're a born shyster. You'd have made a lousy minister.'

'Look,' I said, 'I remember the especially good ones. And I'll never forget our honeymoon. But we need sleep. We haven't had any to speak of for twenty-four hours. Let's hit the hay and forget everything until tomorrow. In which case . . .'

She stared at me and then said, 'Poor dear, no wonder you're so belligerently flippant! It's a defense against fear!'

I slammed my fist into my palm and shouted, 'I know! I know! For God's sake, how long is this going on?'

I went into the bathroom. The face in the mirror looked as if it were trying to flirt with me. The left eye wouldn't stop winking.

When I returned to the bedroom, Carole reminded me that I'd not made today's recording. I didn't want to do it because I was so tired. But the possibility of losing another day's memory spurred me. No, not another day, I thought. If this occurs tomorrow, I'll lose another four days. Tomorrow and the three preceding May 25. I'll wake up June 3 and think it's the morning of the twenty-second.

I'm making this downstairs in my study. I wouldn't want Carole to hear some of my comments.

Until tomorrow then. It's not tomorrow but yesterday that

won't come. I'll make a note to myself and stick it in a corner of the case which holds my glasses.

6

True date: June 3, 1980

I woke up thinking that today was my birthday, May 22. I rolled over, saw the piece of paper half-stuck from my glasses case, put on my glasses and read the note.

It didn't enlighten me. I didn't remember writing the note. And why should I go downstairs and turn on the recorder? But I did so.

As I listened to the machine, my heart thudded as if it were a judge's gavel. My voice kept fading in and out. Was I going to faint?

And so half of today was wasted trying to regain twelve days in my mind. I didn't go to the office, and the kids went to school late. And what about the kids in school on the dayside of Earth? If they sleep during their geometry class, say, then they have to go through that class again on the same day. And that shoves the schedule forward, or is it backward, for that day. And then there's the time workers will lose on their jobs. They have to make it up, which means they get out an hour later. Only it takes more than an hour to recover from the confusion and get orientated. What a mess it has been! What a mess it'll be if this keeps on!

At eleven, Carole and I were straightened out enough to go to the supermarket. It was Tuesday, but Carole wanted me to be with her, so I tried to phone in and tell my secretary I'd be absent. The lines were tied up, and I doubt that she was at work. So I said to hell with it.

Our supermarket usually opens at eight. Not today. We had to stand in a long line, which kept getting longer. The doors opened at twelve. The manager, clerks and boys had had just as much trouble as we did unconfusing themselves, of course. Some didn't show at all. And some of the trucks which were to bring fresh stores never appeared.

By the time Carole and I got inside, those ahead of us had cleaned out half the supplies. They had the same idea we had. Load up now so there wouldn't be any standing in line so many times. The fresh milk was all gone, and the powdered milk shelf had one box left. I started for it but some teen-ager beat

166

me to it. I felt like hitting him, but I didn't, of course.

The prices for everything were being upped by a fourth even as we shopped. Some of the stuff was being marked upward once more while we stood in line at the checkout counter. From the time we entered the line until we pushed out three overflowing carts, four hours had passed.

While Carole put away the groceries, I drove to another supermarket. The line there was a block long; it would be emptied and closed up before I ever got to its doors.

The next two supermarkets and a corner grocery store were just as hopeless. And the three liquor stores I went to were no better. The fourth only had about thirty men in line, so I tried that. When I got inside, all the beer was gone, which didn't bother me any, but the only hard stuff left was a fifth of rotgut. I drank it when I went to college because I couldn't afford anything better. I put the terrible stuff and a half-gallon of cheap muscatel on the counter. Anything was better than nothing, even though the prices had been doubled.

I started to make out the check, but the clerk said, 'Sorry, sir. Cash only.'

'What?' I said.

'Haven't you heard, sir?' he said. 'The banks were closed at 2 : 00 P.M. today.'

'The banks are closed?' I said. I sounded stupid even to myself.

'Yes, sir,' he said. 'By the federal government. It's only temporary, sir, at least, that's what the TV said. They'll be reopened after the stock market mess is cleared up.'

'But . . .' I said.

'It's destructed,' he said.

'Destroyed,' I said automatically. 'You mean, it's another Black Friday?'

'It's Tuesday today,' he said.

'You're to young to know the reference,' I said. And too uneducated, too, I thought.

'The president is going to set up a rationing system,' he said. 'For The Interim. And price controls, too. Turner said so on TV an hour ago. The president is going to lay it all out at six tonight.'

When I came home, I found Carole in front of the TV. She was pale and wide-eyed.

'There's going to be another depression!' she said. 'Oh,

Mark, what are we going to do?'

'I don't know,' I said. 'I'm not the president, you know.' And I slumped down onto the sofa. I had lost my flippancy.

Neither of us, having been born in 1945, knew what a Depression, with a big capital D, was; that is, we hadn't experienced it personally. But we'd heard our parents, who were kids when it happened, talk about it. Carole's parents had gotten along, though they didn't live well, but my father used to tell me about days when he had nothing but stale bread and turnips to eat and was happy to get them.

The president's TV speech was mostly about the depression, which he claimed would be temporary. At the end of half an hour of optimistic talk, he revealed why he thought the situation wouldn't last. The federal government wasn't going to wait for the sentients in The Ball – if there were any there – to communicate with us. Obviously, The Ball was hostile. So the survey expedition had been canceled. Tomorrow, the USA, the USSR, France, West Germany, Israel, India, Japan and China would send up an armada of rockets tipped with H-bombs. The orbits and the order of battle were determined this morning by computers; one after the other, the missiles would zero in until The Ball was completely destroyed. It would be over-kill with a vengeance.

'That ought to bring up the stock market!' I said.

And so, after I've finished recording, to bed. Tomorrow, we'll follow our instructions on the notes, relisten to the tapes, reread certain sections of the newspapers and await the news on the TV. To hell with going to the courthouse; nobody's going to be there anyway.

Oh, yes. With all this confusion and excitement, everybody, myself included, forgot that today was my birthday. Wait a minute! It's *not* my birthday!

True date: June 5, 1980. Subjective date: May 16, 1980

I woke up mad at Carole because of our argument the previous day. Not that of June 4, of course, but our brawl of May 15. We'd been at a party given by the Burlingtons, where I met a beautiful young artist, Roberta Gardner. Carole thought I way paying too much attention to her because she looked like Myrna. Maybe I was. On the other hand, I really was interested in her paintings. It seemed to me that she had a genuine talent. When we got home, Carole tore into me, accused me of still being in love with Myrna. My protests did no good whatsoever.

Finally, I told her we might as well get a divorce if she couldn't forgive and forget. She ran crying out of the room and slept on the sofa downstairs.

I don't remember what reconciled us, of course, but we must have worked it out, otherwise we wouldn't still be married.

Anyway, I woke up determined to see a divorce lawyer today. I was sick about what Mike and Tom would have to go through. But it would be better for them to be spared our terrible quarrels. I can remember my reactions when I was an adolescent and overheard my parents fighting. It was a relief, though a sad one, when they separated.

Thinking this, I reached for my glasses. And I found the note. And so another voyage into confusion, disbelief and horror.

Now that the panic has eased off somewhat, May 18 is back in the saddle – somewhat. Carole and I are, in a sense, still in that day, and things are a bit cool.

It's 1:00 P.M. now. We just watched the first rockets take off. Ten of them, one after the other.

It's 1:35 P.M. Via satellite, we watched the Japanese missiles.

We just heard that the Chinese and Russian rockets are being launched. When the other nations send theirs up, there will be thirty-seven in all.

No news at 12:30 A.M., June 5. In this case, no news must be bad news. But what could have happened? The newscasters won't say; they just talk around the subject.

7

True date: June 6, 1980. Subjective date: May 13, 1980

My records say that this morning was just like the other four. Hell.

One o'clock. The president, looking like a sad old man, though he's only forty-four, reported the catastrophe. All thirty-seven rockets were blown up by their own H-bombs about three thousand miles from The Ball. We saw some photographs of them taken from the orbiting labs. They weren't very impressive. No mushroom clouds, of course, and not even much light.

The Ball has weapons we can't hope to match. And if it can activate our H-bombs out in space, it should be able to do the same to those on Earth's surface. My God! It could wipe out all life if it wished to do so!

Near the end of the speech, the president did throw out a line of hope. With a weak smile – he was trying desperately to give us his big vote-winning one – he said that all was not lost by any means. A new plan, called Project Toro, was being drawn up even as he spoke.

Toro was Spanish for bull, I thought, but I didn't say so. Carole and the kids wouldn't have thought it funny, and I didn't think it was so funny myself. Anyway, I thought, maybe it's a Japanese word meaning *victory* or *destruction* or something like that.

Toro, as it turned out, was the name of a small irregularly shaped asteroid about 2.413 kilometers long and 1.609 kilometers wide. Its peculiar orbit had been calculated in 1972 by an L. Danielsson of the Swedish Royal Institute of Technology and a W. H. Ip of the University of California at San Diego. Toro, the president said, was bound into a resonant orbit with the Earth. Each time Toro came near the Earth – 'near' was sometimes 12.6 million miles – it got exactly enough energy or 'kick' from the Earth to push it on around so that it would come back for another near passage.

But the orbit was unstable, which meant that both Earth and Venus take turns controling the asteroid. For a few centuries, Earth governs Toro; then Venus takes over. Earth has controled Toro since A.D. 1580. Venus will take over in 2200. Earth grabs it again in 2350; Venus gets it back in 2800.

I was wondering what all this stuff about this celestial Ping-pong game was about. Then the president said that it was possible to land rockets on Toro. In fact, the plan called for many shuttles to land there carrying parts of huge rocket motors, which would be assembled on Toro.

When the motors were erected on massive and deep stands, power would be applied to nudge Toro out of its orbit. This would require many trips by many rockets with cargoes of fuel and spare parts for the motors. The motors would burn out a number of times. Eventually, though, the asteroid would be placed in an orbit that would end in a direct collision with The Ball. Toro's millions of tons of hard rock and nickel-steel would destroy The Ball utterly, would turn it into pure energy.

'Yes,' I said aloud, 'but what's to keep The Ball from just changing its orbit? Its sensors will detect the asteroid; it'll change course; Toro will go on by it, like a train on a track.'

This was the next point of the president's speech. The failure of the attack had revealed at least one item of information, or, rather, verified it. The radiation of the H-bombs had blocked off, disrupted, all control and observation of the rockets by radar and laser. In their final approach, the rockets had gone in blind, as it were, unable to be regulated from Earth. But if the bombs did this to our sensors, they must be doing the same to The Ball's.

So, just before Toro's course is altered to send it into its final path, H-bombs will be set off all around The Ball. In effect, it will be enclosed in a sphere of radiation. It will have no sensor capabilities. Nor will The Ball *believe* that it will have to alter its orbit to dodge Toro. It will have calculated that Toro's orbit won't endanger it. After the radiation fills the space around it, it won't be able to *see* that Toro is being given a final series of nudges to push it into a collision course.

The project is going to require immense amounts of materials and manpower. The USA can't handle it alone; Toro is going to be a completely international job. What one nation can't provide, the other will.

The president ended with a few words about how Project Toro, plus the situation of memory loss, is going to bring about a radical revision of the economic setup. He's going to announce the outlines of the new structure – not just policy but structure – two days from now. It'll be designed, so he says, to restore prosperity and, not incidentally, rid society of many problems plaguing it since the industrial revolution.

'Yes, but how long will Project Toro take?' I said. 'Oh, Lord, how long?'

Six years, the president said, as if he'd heard me. Perhaps longer.

Six years!

I didn't tell Carole what I could see coming. But she's no dummy. She could figure out some of the things that were bound to happen in six years, and none of them were good.

I never felt so hopeless in my life, and neither did she. But we do have each other, and so we clung tightly for a while. May 18 isn't forgotten, but it seems so unimportant. Mike and Tom cried, I suppose because they knew that this exhibition of love meant something terrible for all of us. Poor kids! They get upset by our hatreds and then become even more upset by our love.

When we realized what we were doing to them, we tried to be jolly. But we couldn't get them to smile.

True date: middle of 1981. Subjective date: middle of 1977

I'm writing this, since I couldn't get any new tapes today. The shortage is only temporary, I'm told. I could erase some of the old ones and use them, but it'd be like losing a vital part of myself. And God knows I've lost enough.

Old Mrs. Douglas next door is dead. Killed herself, according to my note on the calendar, April 2 of this year. I never would have thought she'd do it. She was such a strong fundamentalist, and these believe as strongly as the Roman Catholics that suicide is well-nigh unforgivable. I suspect that the double shock of her husband's death caused her to take her own life. April 2 of 1976 was the day he died. She had to be hospitalized because of shock and grief for two weeks after his death. Carole and I had her over to dinner a few times after she came home, and all she could talk about was her dead husband. So I presume that, as she traveled backward to the day of his death, the grief became daily more unbearable. She couldn't face the arrival of the day he died.

Hers is not the only empty house on the block. Jack Bridger killed his wife and his three kids and his mother-in-law and himself last month – according to my records. Nobody knows why, but I suspect that he couldn't stand seeing his three-year-old girl become no more than an idiot. She'd retrogressed to the day of her birth and perhaps beyond. She'd lost her language abilities and could no longer feed herself. Strangely, she could still walk, and her intelligence potential was high. She had the brain of a three-year-old, fully developed, but lacking all postbirth experience. It would have been better if she hadn't been able to walk. Confined to a cradle, she would at least not have had to be watched every minute.

Little Ann's fate is going to be Tom's. He talks like a five-year-old now. And Mike's fate . . . my fate . . . Carole's . . . God! We'll end up like Ann! I can't stand thinking about it.

Poor Carole. She has the toughest job. I'm away part of the day, but she has to take care of what are, in effect, a five-year-old and an eight-year-old, getting younger every day. There is no relief for her, since they're always home. All educational institutions, except for certain research laboratories, are closed.

The president says we're going to convert ninety percent of all industries to cybernation. In fact, anything that can be cybernated will be. They have to be. Almost everything, from the mines to the loading equipment to the railroads and trucks and the unloading equipment and the arrangement and dispersal of the final goods at central distribution points.

Are six years enough to do this?

And who's going to pay for this? Never mind, he says. Money is on its way out. The president is a goddamned radical. He's taking advantage of this situation to put over his own ideas, which he sure as hell never revealed during his campaign for election. Sometimes I wonder who put The Ball up there. But that idea is sheer paranoia. At least, this gigantic WPA project is giving work to those who are able to work. The rest are on, or going to be on, a minimum guaranteed income, and I mean minimum. But the president says that, in time, everybody will have all he needs, and more, in the way of food, housing, schooling, clothing, etc. *He* says! What if Project Toro doesn't work? And what if it does work? Are we then going to return to the old economy? Of course not! It'll be impossible to abandon everything we've worked on; the new establishment will see to that.

I tried to find out where Myrna lived. I'm making this record in my office, so Carole isn't going to get hold of it. I love her – Myrna, I mean – passionately. I hired her two weeks ago and fell headlong, burningly, in love with her. All this was in 1977, of course, but today, inside of *me, is* 1977.

Carole doesn't know about this, of course. According to the letters and notes from Myrna, which I should have destroyed but, thank God, never had the heart to do, Carole didn't find out about Myrna until two years later. At least, that's what this letter from Myrna says. She was away visiting her sister then and wrote to me in answer to my letter. A good thing, too, otherwise I wouldn't know what went on then.

My reason tells me to forget about Myrna. And so I will.

I've traveled backward in our affair, from our final bitter parting, to this state, when I was most in love with her. I know this because I've just reread the records of our relationship. It began deteriorating about six months before we split up, but I don't feel those emotions now, of course. And in two weeks I won't feel anything for her. If I don't refer to the records, I won't even know she ever existed.

This thought is intolerable. I have to find her, but I've had no success at all so far. In fourteen days, no, five, since every day ahead takes three more of the past, I'll have no drive to locate her. Because I won't know what I'm missing.

I don't hate Carole. I love her, but with a cool much-married love. Myrna makes me feel like a boy again. I burn exquisitely.

But where is Myrna?

True date: October 30, 1981

I ran into Brackwell Lee, the old mystery story writer today. Like most writers who haven't gone to work for the government propaganda office, he's in a bad way financially. He's surviving on his GMI, but for him there are no more first editions of rare books, new sports cars, Western Reserve or young girls. I stood him three shots of the rotgut which is the only whiskey now served at Grover's and listened to the funny stories he told to pay me for the drinks. But I also had to listen to his tales of woe.

Nobody buys fiction or, in fact, any long works of any kind anymore. Even if you're a speed reader and go through a whole novel in one day, you have to start all over again the next time you pick it up. TV writing, except for the propaganda shows, is no alternative. The same old shows are shown every day and enjoyed just as much as yesterday or last year. According to my records, I've seen the hilarious pilot movie of the 'Soap Opera Blues' series fifty times.

When old Lee talked about how he had been dropped by the young girls, he got obnoxiously weepy. I told him that that didn't say much for him or the girls either. But if he didn't want to be hurt, why didn't he erase those records that noted his rejections?

He didn't want to do that, though he could give me no logical reason why he shouldn't.

'Listen,' I said with a sudden drunken inspiration, 'why don't you erase the old records and make some new ones? How you laid this and that beautiful young thing. Describe your conquests in detail. You'll think you're the greatest Casanova that ever lived.'

'But that wouldn't be true!' he said.

'You, a writer of lies, say that?' I said. 'Anyway, you

174

wouldn't know that they weren't the truth.'

'Yeah,' he said, 'but if I get all charged up and come bar-reling down here to pick up some tail, I'll be rejected and so'll be right back where I was.'

'Leave a stern note to yourself to listen to them only late at night, say, an hour before The Ball puts all to sleep. That way, you won't ever get hurt.'

George Palmer wandered in then. I asked him how things were doing.

'I'm up to here handling cases for kids who can't get drivers' licenses,' he said. 'It's true you can teach anybody how to drive in a day, but the lessons are forgotten the next day. Anyway, it's experience that makes a good driver, and . . . need I explain more? The kids have to have cars, so they drive them regardless. Hence, as you no doubt have forgotten, the traffic accidents and violations are going up and up.'

'Is that right?' I said.

'Yeah. There aren't too many in the mornings, since most people don't go to work until noon. However, the new transit system should take care of that when we get it, sometime in 1984 or 5.'

'What new transit system?' I said.

'It's been in the papers,' he said. 'I reread some of last week's this morning. The city of Los Angeles is equipped with a model system now, and it's working so well it's going to be extended throughout Los Angeles County. Eventually, every city of any size in the country'll have it. Nobody'll have to walk more than four blocks to get to a line. It'll cut air pollu-tion by half and the traffic load by two-thirds. Of course, it'll be compulsory; you'll have to show cause to drive a car. And I hate to think about the mess *that*'s going to be, the paper-work, the pile-up in the courts and so forth. But after the way the government handled the L. A. riot, the rest of the country should get in line.'

'How will the rest of the country know how the government handled it unless they're told?' I said.

'They'll be told. Every day,' he said.

'Eventually, there won't be enough time in the day for the news channels to tell us all we'll need to know,' I said. 'And even if there were enough time, we'd have to spend all day watching TV. So who's going to get the work done?'

'Each person will have to develop his own viewing specialty,' he said. 'They'll just have to watch the news that concerns them and ignore the rest.'

'And how can they do that if they won't know what concerns them until they've run through everything?' I said. 'Day after day.'

'I'll buy a drink,' he said. 'Liquor's good for one thing. It makes you forget what you're afraid not to forget.'

8

True date: late 1982. Subjective date: late 1974

She came into my office, and I knew at once that she was going to be more than just another client. I'd been suffering all day from the 'mirror syndrome,' but the sight of her stabilized me. I forgot the thirty-seven-year-old face my twenty-nine-year-old mind had seen in the bathroom that morning. She is a beautiful woman, only twenty-seven. I had trouble at first listening to her story; all I wanted to do was to look at her. I finally understood that she wanted me to get her husband out of jail on a murder rap. It seemed he'd been in since 1976 (real time). She wanted me to get the case reopened, to use the new plea of rehabilitation by retrogression.

I was supposed to know that, but I had to take a quick look through my resumé before I could tell her what chance she had. Under RBR was the definition of the term and a notation that a number of people had been released because of it. The main idea behind it is that criminals are not the same people they were before they became criminals, if they have lost all memory of the crime. They've traveled backward to goodness, you might say. Of course, RBR doesn't apply to hardened criminals or to someone who'd planned a crime a long time before it was actually committed.

I asked her why she would want to help a man who had killed his mistress in a fit of rage when he'd found her cheating on him?

'I love him,' she said.

And I love you, I thought.

She gave me some documents from the big rec bag she carried. I looked through them and said, 'But you divorced him in 1977?'

'Yes, he's really my ex-husband,' she said. 'But I think of him now as my husband.'

No need to ask her why.

'I'll study the case,' I said. 'You make a note to see me to-morrow. Meantime, how about a drink at the Rover bar so we can discuss our strategy?'

That's how it all started – again.

It wasn't until a week later, when I was going over some old recs, that I discovered it was *again*. It made no difference. I love her. I also love Carole, rather, *a* Carole. The one who married me six years ago, that is, six years ago in my memory.

But there is the other Carole, the one existing today, the poor miserable wretch who can't get out of the house until I come home. And I can't come home until late evening because I can't get started to work until about twelve noon. It's true that I could come home earlier than I do if it weren't for Myrna. I try. No use. I have to see Myrna.

I tell myself I'm a bastard, which I am, because Carole and the children need me very much. Tom is ten and acts as if he's two. Mike is a four-year-old in a twelve-year-old body. I come home from Myrna to bedlam every day, according to my records, and every day must be like today.

That I feel both guilt and shame doesn't help. I become enraged; I try to suppress my anger, which is born out of my desperation and helplessness and guilt and shame. But it comes boiling out, and then bedlam becomes hell.

I tell myself that Carole and the kids need a tower of strength now. One who can be calm and reassuring and, above all, loving. One who can handle the thousand tedious and aggravating problems that infest every household in this world of diminishing memory. In short, a hero. Because the real heroes, and heroines, are those who deal heroically with the everyday cares of life, though God knows they've been multiplied enormously. It's not the guy who kills a dragon once in his lifetime and then retires that's a hero. It's the guy who kills cockroaches and rats every day, day after day, and doesn't rest on his laurels until he's an old man, if then.

What am I talking about? Maybe I could handle the problems if it weren't for this memory loss. I can't adjust because I can't ever get used to it. My whole being, body and mind, must get the same high-voltage jolt every morning.

The insurance companies have canceled all policies for anybody under twelve. The government's contemplated taking over these policies but has decided against it. It will, however,

pay for the burials, since this service is necessary. I don't really
think that many children are being 'accidentally' killed because
of the insurance money. Most fatalities are obviously just
results of neglect or parents going berserk.

I'm getting away from Myrna, trying to, anyway, because I
wish to forget my guilt. I love her, but if I didn't see her tomorrow, I'd forget her. But I *will* see her tomorrow. My notes
will make sure of that. And each day is, for me, love at first
sight. It's a wonderful feeling, and I wish it could go on forever.

If I just had the guts to destroy all reference to her tonight.
But I won't. The thought of losing her makes me panic.

9

True date: middle of 1984. Subjective date: middle of 1968

I was surprised that I woke up so early.

Yesterday, Carole and I had been married at noon. We'd
driven up to this classy motel near Lake Geneva. We'd spent
most of our time in bed after we got there, naturally, though
we did get up for dinner and champagne. We finally fell asleep
about four in the morning. That was why I hadn't expected
to wake up at dawn. I reached over to touch Carole, wondering if she would be too sleepy. But she wasn't there.

She's gone to the bathroom, I thought. I'll catch her on the
way back.

Then I sat up, my heart beating as if it had suddenly discovered it was alive. The edges of the room got fuzzy, and
then the fuzziness raced in toward me.

The dawn light was filtered by the blinds, but I had seen that
the furniture was not familiar. I'd never been in this place
before.

I sprang out of bed and did not, of course, notice the note
sticking out of my glass case. Why should I? I didn't wear
glasses then.

Bellowing, 'Carole!' I ran down a long and utterly strange
hall and past the bathroom door, which was open, and into
the room at the other end of the hall. Inside it, I stopped. This
was a kids' bedroom: bunks, pennants, slogans, photographs
of two young boys, posters and blowups of faces I'd never
seen, except one of Laurel and Hardy, some science fiction
and Tolkien and Tarzan books, some school texts, and a large
flat piece of equipment hanging on the wall. I would not have

178

known that it was a TV set if its controls had not made its purpose obvious.

The bunks had not been slept in. The first rays of the sun fell on thick dust on a table.

I ran back down the hall, looked into the bathroom again, though I knew no one was there, saw dirty towels, underwear and socks heaped in a corner, and ran back to my bedroom. The blinds did not let enough light in, so I looked for a light switch on the wall. There wasn't any, though there was a small round plate of brass where the switch should have been. I touched it, and the ceiling lights came on.

Carole's side of the bed had not been slept in.

The mirror over the bureau caught me, drew me and held me. Who was this haggard old man staring out from my twenty-three-year-old self? I had gray hair, big bags under my eyes, thickening and sagging features, and a long scar on my right cheek.

After a while, still dazed and trembling, I picked up a book from the bureau and looked at it. At this close distance, I could just barely make out the title, and, when I opened it, the print was a blur.

I put the book down, *Be Your Own Handyman Around Your House*, and proceeded to go through the house from attic to basement. Several times, I whimpered, 'Carole! Carole!' Finding no one, I left the house and walked to the house next door and beat on its door. No one answered; no lights came on inside.

I ran to the next house and tried to wake up the people in it. But there weren't any.

A woman in a house across the street shouted at me. I ran to her, babbling. She was about fifty years old and also hysterical. A moment later, a man her age appeared behind her. Neither listened to me; they kept asking me questions, the same questions I was asking them. Then I saw a black and white police car of a model unknown to me come around the corner half a block away. I ran toward it, then stopped. The car was so silent that I knew even in my panic that it was electrically powered. The two cops wore strange uniforms, charcoal gray with white helmets topped by red panaches. Their aluminum badges were in the shape of a spread eagle.

I found out later that the police throughout the country had been federalized. These two were on the night shift and so had

had enough time to get orientated. Even so, one had such a case of shakes that the other told him to get back into the car and take it easy for a while.

After he got us calmed down, he asked us why we hadn't listened to our tapes.

'What tapes?' we said.

'Where's your bedroom?' he said to the couple.

They led him to it, and he turned on a machine on the bed-side table.

'Good morning,' a voice said. I recognized it as the husband's. 'Don't panic. Stay in bed and listen to me. Listen to everything I say.'

The rest was a resumé, by no means short, of the main events since the first day of memory loss. It ended by directing the two to a notebook that would tell them personal things they needed to know, such as where their jobs were, how they could get to them, where their area central distributing stores were, how to use their I.D. cards and so on.

The policeman said, 'You have the rec set to turn on at 6:30, but you woke up before then. Happens a lot.'

I went back, reluctantly, to the house I'd fled. It was mine, but I felt as if I were a stranger. I ran off my own recs twice. Then I put my glasses on and started to put together my life. The daily rerun of 'Narrative of an Old-Young Man Ship-wrecked on the Shoals of Time.'

I didn't go any place today. Why should I? I had no job. Who needs a lawyer who isn't through law school yet? I did have, I found out, an application in for a position on the police force. The police force was getting bigger and bigger but at the same time was having a large turnover. My recs said that I was to appear at the City Hall for an interview tomorrow.

If I feel tomorrow as I do today, and I will, I probably won't be able to make myself go to the interview. I'm too grief-stricken to do anything but sit and stare or, now and then, get up and pace back and forth, like a sick leopard in a cage made by Time. Even the tranquilizers haven't helped me much.

I have lost my bride the day after we were married. And I love Carole deeply. We were going to live a long happy life and have two children. We would raise them in a house filled with love.

But the recs say that the oldest boy escaped from the house and was killed by a car and Carole, in a fit of anguish and despair, killed the youngest boy and then herself.

They're buried in Springdale Cemetery.

I can't feel a retroactive grief for those strangers called Mike and Tom.

But Carole, lovely laughing Carole, lives in my mind.

Oh, God, why don't I just erase all my recs? Then I'd not have to suffer remorse for all I've done or failed to do. I wouldn't know what a bastard I'd been.

Why don't I do it? Take the past and shed its heartbreaks and its guilts as a snake sheds its skin. Or as the legislature cancels old laws. Press a button, fill the wastebasket, and you're clean and easy again, innocent again. That's the logical thing to do, and I'm a lawyer, dedicated to logic.

Why not? Why not?

But I can't. Maybe I like to suffer. I've liked to inflict suffering, and according to what I understand, those who like to inflict, unconsciously hope to be inflicted upon.

No, that can't be it. At least, not all of it. My main reason for hanging on to the recs is that I don't want to lose my identity. A major part of me, a unique person, is not in the neurons of my mind, where it belongs, but in an electromechanical device or in tracings of lead or ink on paper. The protein, the flesh for which I owe, can't hang on to *me*.

I'm becoming less and less, dwindling away, like the wicked witch on whom Dorothy poured water. I'll become a puddle, a wailing voice of hopeless despair, and then . . . nothing.

God, haven't I suffered enough! I said I owe for the flesh and I'm down in Your books. Why do I have to struggle each day against becoming a dumb brute, a thing without memory? Why not rid myself of the struggle? Press the button, fill the wastebasket, discharge my grief in a chaos of magnetic lines and pulped paper?

Sufficient unto the day is the evil thereof.

I didn't realize, Lord, what that really meant.

10

I will marry Carole in three days. No, I would have. No, I did.

I remember reading a collection of Krazy Kat comic strips

when I was twenty-one. One was captioned: COMA REIGNS. Coconing County was in the doldrums, comatose. Nobody, Krazy Kat, Ignatz Mouse, Officer Pupp, nobody had the energy to do anything. Mouse was too lazy even to think about hurling his brickbat. Strange how that sticks in my mind. Strange to think that it won't be long before it becomes forever unstuck.

Coma reigns today over the world.

Except for Project Toro, the TV says. And that is behind schedule. But the Earth, Ignatz Mouse, will not allow itself to forget that it must hurl the brickbat, the asteroid. But where Ignatz expressed his love, in a queer perverted fashion, by banging Kat in the back of the head with his brick, the world is expressing its hatred, and its desperation, by throwing Toro at The Ball.

I did manage today to go downtown to my appointment. I did it only to keep from going mad with grief. I was late, but Chief Moberly seemed to expect that I would be. Almost everybody is, he said. One reason for my tardiness was that I got lost. This residential area was nothing in 1968 but a forest out past the edge of town. I don't have a car, and the house is in the middle of the area, which has many winding streets. I do have a map of the area, which I forgot about. I kept going eastward and finally came to a main thoroughfare. This was Route 98, over which I've traveled many times since I was a child. But the road itself, and the houses along it, were strange. The private airport which should have been across the road was gone, replaced by a number of large industrial buildings.

A big sign near a roofed bench told me to wait there for the RTS bus. One would be along every ten minutes, the sign stated.

I waited an hour. The bus, when it came, was not the fully automated vehicle promised by the sign. It held a sleepy-looking driver and ten nervous passengers. The driver didn't ask me for money, so I didn't offer any. I sat down and watched him with an occasional look out of the window. He didn't have a steering wheel. When he wanted the bus to slow down or stop he pushed a lever forward. To speed it up, he pulled back on the lever. The bus was apparently following a single aluminum rail in the middle of the right-hand lane. My recs told me later that the automatic pilot and door-opening equipment had never been delivered and probably wouldn't be for some years – if ever. The grand plan of cybernating everything possible had failed. There aren't enough people who can provide the know-how or the man-hours. In fact, everything is going to hell.

The police chief, Adam Moberly, is fifty years old and looks as if he's sixty-five. He talked to me for about fifteen minutes and then had me put through a short physical and intelligence test. Three hours after I had walked into the station, I was sworn in. He suggested that I room with two other officers, one of whom was a sixty-year-old veteran, in the hotel across the street from the station. If I had company, I'd get over the morning disorientation more quickly. Besides, the policemen who lived in the central area of the city got preferential treatment in many things, including the rationed supplies.

I refused to move. I couldn't claim that my house was a home to me, but I feel that it's a link to the past, I mean the future, no, I mean the past. Leaving it would be cutting out one more part of me.

True date: late 1984. Subjective date: early 1967

My mother died today. That is, as far as I'm concerned, she did. The days ahead of me are going to be full of anxiety and grief. She took a long time to die. She found out she had cancer two weeks after my father died. So I'll be voyaging backward in sorrow through my mother and then through my father, who was also sick for a long time.

Thank God I won't have to go through every day of that, though. Only a third of them. And these are the last words I'm going to record about their illnesses.

But how can I not record them unless I make a recording reminding me not to do so?

I found out from my recs how I'd gotten this big scar on my face. Myrna's ex-husband slashed me before I laid him out with a big ashtray. He was shipped off this time to a hospital for the criminally insane where he died a few months later in the fire that burned every prisoner in his building. I haven't the faintest idea what happened to Myrna after that. Apparently I decided not to record it.

I feel dead tired tonight, and, according to my recs, every night. It's no wonder, if every day is like today. Fires, murders, suicides, accidents and insane people. Babies up to fourteen years old abandoned. And a police department which is ninety percent composed, in effect, of raw rookies. The victims are taken to hospitals where the nurses are only half-trained, if that, and the doctors are mostly old geezers hauled out of retirement.

I'm going to bed soon even if it's only nine o'clock. I'm so exhausted that even Jayne Mansfield couldn't keep me awake. And I dread tomorrow. Besides the usual reasons for loathing it, I have one which I can hardly stand thinking about.

Tomorrow my memory will have slid past the day I met Carole. I won't remember her at all.

Why do I cry because I'll be relieved of a great sorrow?

II

True date: 1986. Subjective date: 1962

I'm nuts about Jean, and I'm way down because I can't find her. According to my recs, she went to Canada in 1965. Why? We surely didn't fall in and then out of love? Our love would never die. Her parents must've moved to Canada. And so here we both are in 1962, in effect. Halfway in 1962, anyway. Amphibians of time. Is she thinking about me now? Is she unable to think about me, about anything, because she's dead or crazy? Tomorrow I'll start the official wheels grinding. The Canadian government should be able to find her through the International Information Computer Network, according to the recs. Meanwhile, I burn, though with a low flame. I'm so goddamn tired.

Even Marilyn Monroe couldn't get a rise out of me tonight. But Jean. Yeah, Jean. I see her as seventeen years old, tall, slim but full-busted, with creamy white skin and a high forehead and huge blue eyes and glossy black hair and the most kissable lips ever. And broadcasting sex waves so thick you can see them, like heat waves. Wow!

And so tired old Wow goes to bed.

February 6, 1987

While I was watching TV to get orientated this morning, a news flash interrupted the program. The president of the United States had died of a heart attack a few minutes before.

'My God!' I said. 'Old Eisenhower is dead!'

But the picture of the president certainly wasn't that of Eisenhower. And the name was one I never heard, of course.

I can't feel bad for a guy I never knew.

I got to thinking about him, though. Was he as confused every morning as I was? Imagine a guy waking up, thinking he's a senator in Washington and then he finds he's the president? At least, he knows something about running the country. But it's no wonder the old pump conked out. The TV says we've had five prexies, mostly real old guys, in the last seven years. One was shot; one dived out of the White House window onto his head; two had heart attacks; one went crazy and almost caused a war, as if we didn't have grief enough, for crying out loud.

Even after the orientation, I really didn't get it. I guess I'm too dumb for anything to percolate through my dome.

A policeman called and told me I'd better get my ass down to work. I said I didn't feel up to it, besides, why would I want to be a cop? He said that if I didn't show, I might go to jail. So I showed.

True date: late 1988. Subjective date: 1956

Here I am, eleven years old, going on ten.

In one way, that is. The other way, here I am forty-three and going on about sixty. At least, that's what my face looks like to me. Sixty.

This place is just like a prison except some of us get treated like trusties. According to the work chart, I leave through the big iron gates every day at twelve noon with a demolition crew. We tore down five partly burned houses today. The gang chief, old Rogers, says it's just WPA work, whatever that is. Anyway, one of the guys I work with kept looking more and more familiar. Suddenly, I felt like I was going to pass out. I put down my sledgehammer and walked over to him, and I said, 'Aren't you Stinky Davis?'

He looked funny and then he said, 'Jesus! You're Gabby! Gabby Franham!'

I didn't like him using the Lord's name in vain, but I guess he can be excused.

Nothing would've tasted good the way I felt, but the sandwiches we got for breakfast, lunch and supper tasted like they had a dash of oil in them. Engine oil, I mean. The head honcho, he's eighty if he's a day, says his recs tell him they're derived from petroleum. The oil is converted into a kind of protein and then flavoring and stuff is added. Oil-burgers, they call them.

Tonight, before lights-out, we watched the prez give a

185

speech. He said that, within a month, Project Toro will be finished. One way or the other. And all this memory loss should stop. I can't quite get it even if I was briefed this morning. Men on the moon, unmanned ships on Venus and Mars, all since I was eleven years old. And The Black Ball, the thing from outer space. And now we're pushing asteroids around. Talk about your science fiction!

12

September 4, 1988
Today's the day.

Actually, the big collision'll be tomorrow, ten minutes before 1:00 A.M. . . . but I think of it as today. Toro, going 150,000 miles an hour, will run head-on into The Ball. Maybe.

Here I am again, Mark Franham, recording just in case The Ball does dodge out of the way and I have to depend on my recs. It's 7:0 P.M. and after that raunchy supper of oil-burgers, potato soup and canned carrots, fifty of us gathered around set No. 8. There's a couple of scientists talking now, discussing theories about just what The Ball is and why it's been taking our memories away from us. Old Doctor Charles Presley – any relation to Elvis? – thinks The Ball is some sort of unmanned survey ship. When it finds a planet inhabited by sentient life, sentient means intelligent, it takes specimens. Specimens of the mind, that is. It unpeels people's minds four days' worth at a time, because that's all it's capable of. But it can do it to billions of specimens. It's like it was reading our minds but destroying the mind at the same time. Presley said it was like some sort of Heisenberg principle of the mind. The Ball can't observe our memories closely without disturbing them.

This Ball, Presley says, takes our memories and stores them. And when it's through with us, sucked us dry, it'll take off for another planet circling some far-off star. Someday, it'll return to its home planet, and the scientists there will study the recordings of our minds.

The other scientist, Dr. Marbles – he's still got his, ha! ha! – asked why any species advanced enough to be able to do this could be so callous? Surely, the extees must know what great damage they're doing to us. Wouldn't they be too ethical for this?

186

Doc Presley says maybe they think of us as animals, they are so far above us. Doc Marbles says that could be. But it could also be that whoever built The Ball have different brains than we do. Their mind-reading ray, or whatever it is, when used on themselves doesn't disturb the memory patterns. But we're different. The extees don't know this, of course. Not now, anyway. When The Ball goes home, and the extees read our minds, they'll be shocked at what they've done to us. But it'll be too late then.

Presley and Marbles got into an argument about how the extees would be able to interpret their recordings. How could they translate our languages when they have no references – I mean, referents? How're they going to translate *chair* and *recs* and *rock and roll* and *yucky* and so on when they don't have anybody to tell them their meanings. Marbles said they wouldn't have just words; they'd have mental images to associate with the words. And so on. Some of the stuff they spouted I didn't understand at all.

I do know one thing, though, and I'm sure those bigdomes do, too. But they wouldn't be allowed to say it over TV because we'd be even more gloomy and hopeless-feeling. That is, what if right now the computers in The Ball are translating our languages, reading our minds, as they're recorded? Then they know all about Project Toro. They'll be ready for the asteroid, destroy it if they have the weapons to do it, or, if they haven't, they'll just move The Ball into a different orbit.

I'm not going to say anything to the other guys about this. Why make them feel worse?

It's ten o'clock now. According to regulations posted up all over the place, it's time to go to bed. But nobody is. Not tonight. You don't sleep when the End of the World may be coming up.

I wish my Mom and Dad were here. I cried this morning when I found they weren't in this dump, and I asked the chief where they were. He said they were working in a city nearby, but they'd be visiting me soon. I think he lied.

Stinky saw me crying, but he didn't say anything. Why should he? I'll bet he's shed a few when he thought nobody was looking, too.

Twelve o'clock. Midnight. Less than an hour to go. Then, the big smash! Or, I hate to think about it, the big flop. We won't be able to see it directly because the skies are cloudy over most of North America. But we've got a system worked out so we can see it on TV. If there's a gigantic flash when the Toro and The Ball collide, that is.

What if there isn't? Then we'll soon be just like those grownup kids, some of them twenty years old, that they keep locked up in the big buildings in the northwest corner of this place. Saying nothing but Da Da or Ma Ma, drooling, filling their diapers. If they got diapers, because old Rogers says he heard, today, of course, they don't wear nothing. The nurses come in once a day and hose them and the place down. The nurses don't have time to change and wash diapers and give personal baths. They got enough to do just spoon-feeding them.

Three and a half more hours to go, and I'll be just like them. Unless, before then, I flip, and they put me in that building old Rogers calls the puzzle factory. They're all completely out of their skulls, he says, and even if memloss stops tonight, they won't change any.

Old Rogers says there's fifty million less people in the United States than there were in 1980, according to the recs. And a good thing, too, he says, because it's all we can do to feed what we got.

Come on, Toro! You're our last chance!

If Toro doesn't make it, I'll kill myself! I will! I'm not going to let myself become an idiot. Anyway, by the time I do become one, there won't be enough food to go around for those that do have their minds. I'll be starving to death. I'd rather get it over with now than go through that.

God'll forgive me.

God, You know I want to be a minister of the gospel when I grow up and that I want to help people. I'll marry a good woman, and we'll have children that'll be brought up right. And we'll thank You every day for the good things of life and battle the bad things.

Love, that's what I got, Lord. Love for You and love for Your people. So don't make me hate You. Guide Toro right into The Ball, and get us started on the right path again.

I wish Mom and Dad were here.

Twelve-thirty. In twenty minutes, we'll know.

The TV says the H-bombs are still going off all around The Ball.

The TV says the people on the East Coast are falling asleep. The rays, or whatever The Ball uses, aren't being affected by the H-bomb radiation. But that doesn't mean that its sensors aren't. I pray to God that they are cut off.

Ten minutes to go. Toro's got twenty-five thousand miles to go. Our sensors can't tell whether or not The Ball's still on its original orbit. I hope it is; I hope it is! If it's changed its path, then we're through! Done! Finished! Wiped out!

Five minutes to go; twelve thousand five hundred miles to go.

I can see in my mind's eyes The Ball, almost a mile in diameter, hurtling on its orbit, blind as a bat, I hope and pray, the bombs, the last of the five thousand bombs, flashing, and Toro, a mile and a half long, a mile wide, millions of tons of rock and nickel-steel, charging toward its destined spot.

If it *is* destined.

But space *is* big, and even The Ball and Toro are small compared to all that emptiness out there. What if the mathematics of the scientists is just a little off, or the rocket motors on Toro aren't working just like they're supposed to, and Toro just tears on by The Ball? It's got to meet The Ball at the exact time and place, it's just *got* to!

I wish the radars and lasers could see what's going on.

Maybe it's better they can't. If we knew that The Ball had changed course . . . but this way we still got hope.

If Toro misses, I'll kill myself, I swear it.

Two minutes to go. One hundred and twenty seconds. The big room is silent except for kids like me praying or talking quietly into our recs or praying and talking and sobbing.

The TV says the bombs have quit exploding. No more flashes until Toro hits The Ball – if it does. Oh, God, let it hit, let it hit!

The unmanned satellites are going to open their camera lenses at the exact second of impact and take a quick shot. The cameras are encased in lead, the shutters are lead, and the equipment is special, mostly mechanical, not electrical, almost like a human eyeball. If the cameras see the big flash, they'll send an electrical impulse through circuits, also encased in lead, to a mechanism that'll shoot a big thin-shelled ball out. This is crammed with flashpowder, the same stuff photographers use, and mixed with oxygen pellets so the powder will ignite. There's to be three of the biggest flashes you ever saw. Three. Three for Victory.

If Toro misses, then only one flashball'll be set off.

Oh, Lord, don't let it happen!

Planes with automatic pilots'll be cruising above the clouds, and their equipment will see the flashes and transmit them to the ground TV equipment.

One minute to go.

Come on, God!

Don't let it happen, please don't let it happen, that some place way out there, some thousands of years from now, some weird-looking character reads this and finds out to his horror what his people have done to us. Will he feel bad about it? Lot of good that'll do. You, out there, I hate you! God, how I hate you!

Our Father which art in Heaven, fifteen seconds, Hallowed be Thy name, ten seconds, Thy will be done, five seconds, Thy will be done, but if it's thumbs down, God, why? Why? What did I ever do to You?

The screen's blank! Oh, my God, the screen's blank! What happened? Transmission trouble? Or they're afraid to tell us the truth?

It's on! It's on!

YAAAAAAY!

13

July 4, A.D. 2002

I may erase this. If I have any sense, I will. If I had any sense, I wouldn't make it in the first place.

Independence Day, and we're still under an iron rule. But old Dick the Dictator insists that when there's no longer a need for strict control, the Constitution will be restored, and we'll be a democracy again. He's ninety-five years old and can't last much longer. The vice-president is only eighty, but he's as tough an octogenarian as ever lived. And he's even more of a totalitarian than Dick. And when have men ever voluntarily relinquished power?

I'm one of the elite, so I don't have it so bad. Just being fifty-seven years old makes me a candidate for that class. In addition, I have my Ph.D. in education and I'm a part-time minister. I don't know why I say part-time, since there aren't any full-time ministers outside of the executives of the North American Council of Churches. The People can't afford full-time divines. Everybody has to work at least ten hours a day. But I'm better off than many. I've been eating fresh beef and pork for three years now. I have a nice house I don't have to share with another family. The house isn't the one my recs say

I once owned. The People took it over to pay for back taxes. It did me no good to protest that property taxes had been canceled during The Interim. That, say the People, ended when The Ball was destroyed.

But how could I pay taxes on it when I was only eleven years old, in effect?

I went out this afternoon, it being a holiday, with Leona to Springdale. We put flowers on her parents' and sisters' graves, none of whom she remembers, and on my parents' and Carole's and the children's graves, whom I know only through the recs. I prayed for the forgiveness of Carole and the boys.

Near Carole's grave was Stinky Davis's. Poor fellow, he went berserk the night The Ball was destroyed and had to be put in a padded cell. Still mad, he died five years later.

I sometimes wonder why I didn't go mad, too. The daily shocks and jars of memloss should have made everyone fall apart. But a certain number of us were very tough, tougher than we deserved. Even so, the day-to-day attack by alarm syndrome did its damage. I'm sure that years of life were cut off the hardiest of us. We're the shattered generation. And this is bad for the younger ones, who'll have no older people to lead them in the next ten years or so.

Or is it such a bad thing?

At least, those who were in their early twenties or younger when The Ball was smashed are coming along fine. Leona herself was twenty then. She became one of my students in high school. She's thirty-five physically but only fifteen in what the kids call 'intage' or internal age. But since education goes faster for adults, and all those humanities courses have been eliminated, she graduated from high school last June. She still wants to be a doctor of medicine, and God knows we need M.D.'s. She'll be forty-two before she gets her degree. We're planning on having two children, the maximum allowed, and it's going to be tough raising them while she's in school. But God will see us through.

As we were leaving the cemetery, Margie Oleander, a very pretty girl of twenty-five, approached us. She asked me if she could speak privately to me. Leona didn't like that, but I told her that Margie probably wanted to talk to me about her grades in my geometry class.

Margie did talk somewhat about her troubles with her lessons. But then she began to ask some questions about the political system. Yes, I'd better erase this, and if it weren't for old habits, I'd not be doing this now.

After a few minutes, I became uneasy. She sounded as if she were trying to get me to show some resentment about the current situation.

Is she an agent provocateur or was she testing me for potential membership in the underground?

Whatever she was doing, she was in dangerous waters. So was I. I told her to ask her political philosophy teacher for answers. She said she'd read the textbook, which is provided by the government. I muttered something about, 'Render unto Caesar what is Caesar's,' and walked away.

But she came after me and asked if I could talk to her in my office tomorrow. I hesitated and then said I would.

I wonder if I would have agreed if she weren't so beautiful?

When we got home, Leona made a scene. She accused me of chasing after the younger girls because she was too old to stimulate me. I told her that I was no senile King David, which she should be well aware of, and she said she's listened to my recs and she knew what kind of man I was. I told her I'd learned from my mistakes. I've gone over the recs of the missing years many times.

'Yes,' she said, 'you know about them intellectually. But you don't *feel* them!'

Which is true.

I'm outside now and looking up into the night. Up there, out there, loose atoms and molecules float around, cold and alone, debris of the memory records of The Ball, atoms and molecules of what were once incredibly complex patterns, the memories of thirty-two years of the lives of four and a half billion human beings. Forever lost, except in the mind of One.

Oh, Lord, I started all over again as an eleven-year-old. Don't let me make the same mistakes again.

You've given us tomorrow again, but we've very little past to guide us.

Tomorrow I'll be very cool and very professional with Margie. Not too much, of course, since there should be a certain warmth between teacher and pupil.

If only she did not remind me of . . . whom?

But that's impossible. I can remember nothing from The Interim. Absolutely nothing.

But what if there are different kinds of memory?